IN
SPITE
OF
LIONS

IN SPITE OF LIONS

SCARLETTE PIKE

SWEETWATER
BOOKS

An imprint of Cedar Fort, Inc.
Springville, Utah

This is a work of fiction. The characters, names, incidents, places, and dialogue are products of the author's imagination and are not to be construed as real. The opinions and views expressed herein belong solely to the author and do not necessarily represent the opinions or views of Cedar Fort, Inc. Permission for the use of sources, graphics, and photos is also solely the responsibility of the author.

ISBN 13: 978-1-4621-2051-2

Published by Sweetwater Books, an imprint of Cedar Fort, Inc., 2373 W. 700 S., Springville, UT 84663
Distributed by Cedar Fort, Inc., www.cedarfort.com

LIBRARY OF CONGRESS CATALOGING-IN-PUBLICATION DATA

Names: Pike, Scarlette, 1987- author.
Title: In spite of lions / Scarlette Pike.
Description: Springville, Utah : Sweetwater Books An Imprint of Cedar Fort, Inc., [2017]
Identifiers: LCCN 2017039113 (print) | LCCN 2017042150 (ebook) | ISBN 9781462128068 (epub and Moby) | ISBN 9781462120512 ([perfect] : alk. paper)
Subjects: LCSH: Man-woman relationships--Fiction. | Africa, Southern, setting. | GSAFD: Regency fiction. | LCGFT: Novels. | Historical fiction. | Romance fiction.
Classification: LCC PS3616.I424 (ebook) | LCC PS3616.I424 I5 2017 (print) | DDC 813/.6--dc23
LC record available at https://lccn.loc.gov/2017039113

Cover design by Priscilla Chaves and Katie Payne
Cover design © 2017 by Cedar Fort, Inc.
Edited by Erin Tanner and Erica Myers
Typeset by Erica Myers

Printed in the United States of America

10 9 8 7 6 5 4 3 2 1

Printed on acid-free paper

To David and Mary Livingstone.
Here's to your eternal shade.

Chapter 1

ANNA

There is a subtle comfort in not knowing the place your foot will fall. I could not worry about my next step, because I could not change it. My faith had been buoyed out of darkening obscurity by a voice as sweet as the rush of a river. Time alone could not have awakened it, and my efforts alone, as vengeful or as angry as I acted, could never have so invigorated myself. Yet a voice of hope awakened the beast with agitated fervor and it roared now, pulling me forward into the vague and friendless unknown. And I was not afraid to follow.

As I peered from the window of a hired chaise out into the teeming London street, I felt calm and collected. I was surrounded by sweltering uncertainty and crushing heat that the rush of my fan could not lessen. I had no indication of where I would sleep, who should help me, or how I could reach a new home. I had made no plans and knew little to nothing of how to fend for myself. I had never spent a single night away from my mother's house. Yet faith, when used in proper context, dismisses such anxieties with an iron hand. Carts and horses pushed along the street, trying, I believe, to make as much noise as they were capable of. Vendors cried out from their seats on the ground and little boys and girls ran down the center of the road. Through the mayhem, though, I could discern the Thames rushing by, singing her methodical and lovely song. I was a quiet island in the midst of chaos. I realized now I had always been so.

Having reached my destination, the driver let down the steps and I attempted to remove myself from the steaming coach. My exit would be as humiliating as my entry had been. Many layers of skirts made the heat unbearable and escaping small carriages nearly impossible. My skirts were accustomed to a much larger chaise. The driver stood stationary at his post, unsure of how he was to assist me. Occasionally his hand would twitch and move toward me, but then his confidence would falter and his eyes would wander in uneasy embarrassment. My entire upper half was leaning outside of the vehicle while my lower half was being held back by swarms of petticoats, skirts, and other useless fabric. Finally extricating myself with a firm shove, I stepped onto the dirty London street and my skirts were, in an instant, ruined by the mud, left by last night's typical England shower. The driver's eyes widened, anticipating a lady of quality losing her temper at the sight of a ruined hem. These petty concerns did not worry me, but I did adjust my hair in an awkward attempt at some dignity.

"Please wait here," I asked the driver, a little breathless. He bowed deeply, although there was no need.

I stepped into a small, well-kept office of the London Missionary Society. The afternoon sun lit up the space nicely. The walls were decorated with several hundred books and pieces of literature, half of which I recognized. The rest were mysterious to me and I longed to crack open the old spines. There was enough decorum left in me to not rifle through personal belongings, but to direct my attention to the large balding man sitting behind the minuscule desk, which dominated the space. He looked up at my approach and smiled widely. I could easily imagine him with little grandchildren, reading to them on his knee and romping with them through fields creating scenarios with pure imagination.

"Good afternoon, Miss. How may I serve you?" he asked kindly.

"You may place me on your next departing ship, no matter the size," I said calmly. My words gave him pause, then he chuckled nervously.

"And where is your escort?" he bluntly questioned.

"I have no need of one," I said. I hated myself for following the etiquette from my polite society. I would be bound by them no longer.

"But, Miss," he began, "my next ship is destined for—"

"I have no need to know the heading, thank you." I held up a hand to shield me from the news. "Please allow me passage on it, is all I require."

He hesitated, his eyebrows coming together to commune on this dilemma.

"I cannot, in good conscience, let you board a ship, to which you do not know the destination and without an escort." He seemed slightly amused, but still his eyebrows would not separate.

"Then you will deprive this business of surplus, sir," I cautioned.

He simply stared in silence, allowing me to continue.

"I am prepared to offer you five thousand pounds for my passage," I said. His mouth dropped open. I paused. "You sail your ships around the world, and thus are in need of money. To further your work in this world, unfortunately, money is sometimes required." Suddenly I remembered another request. "Oh, and I would like to become a missionary, if you would be so kind as to tell me how to become one. The idea of being a missionary has had great appeal to me since I was a small girl."

There was a long, silent moment as, I'm sure, he considered how many ships could sail around the world with such a sum. He would certainly be praised by his supervisors, even if the girl became destitute or if she incurred damages. He considered a moment, consulting the papers at his desk, shaking his head, then turned to my cold, determined face. He peered up at me through thick brows.

"The next ship does contain a small family that I am sure would be your happy companions on such a long voyage," he said slowly and purposefully, as if trying to root out my story with his words. "The ship will leave tomorrow morning with the tide. And it will return after only a few days of berth. So you may return to England within the year."

"No return trip will be needed." I smiled, laying down the promised money on his desk. His eyes grew wide as they took in the crisp pounds. I suppose he was not expecting to be paid in full, nor so quickly. But I had no need of monetary gain any longer. Frankly, it felt good to be rid of such an evil, tiresome burden.

He took a moment to compose himself.

"I suppose you may be considered a missionary," he said hesitantly. He shook his head again. "Allow me to introduce myself," he finally said, standing. "I am Mr. Bartholomew. And you are?"

He reached out to take my hand in a delicate gesture. I grasped his and shook with fervor, as I had seen my father do. "Anna," I said simply. He stared with his mouth parted in confusion. First names were not part of a conventional introduction.

"What is your first name?" I asked. He hesitated.

"James?" he said, as if unsure.

"Pleasure," I said with a smile. I then turned and walked out to the street to find an inn to spend the night. James gaped after me.

"What a vulgar girl!" he quietly told his desk.

These words, not meant for my ears, produced a broad smile from my lips.

My steps were determined. I was ready and excited to serve a God I had never sought out, but who had sought me out most earnestly. With a single familiar voice I had been convinced that not only had God been watching my clumsy footsteps, but had been waiting for the perfect moment to set me free of my constraints.

I had no real fear of being discovered. There were no clues to follow for my rescue, or abduction rather. Faith had made me confident. Even if I was found, it mattered not. I was doing as I was told. I did not worry that I would stumble into someone I knew or who knew my family. Would you worry about paltry details when an angelic voice had given you instructions?

I asked my hired driver to relocate to the nearest inn. Any place where I might rest would do, no matter the quality. He was bewildered from the beginning when he had picked up a young, single girl, walking alone, and she had demanded to be taken into town. Perhaps now he had decided not to be surprised by any request I asked of him. He knew of a modest two-story inn located half a mile from the dock with an old, but clean, face. If it took on human characteristics, I imagine it would look a great deal like the old gentleman, James, who I had just encountered. I could hear the bustle and commotion of a large group inside, but I was not deterred. I paid my driver handsomely, instructed him to be ready the following morning at dawn, and marched forward.

The ceiling of the inn was high, revealing that, at least in the main entrance, the two stories were combined into one grand dining room. Strong, stalwart beams held the place together. To my right was the main dining hall and to my left the innkeeper and several of his helpmates stood in readiness. As I entered the foyer of the establishment, a hush fell over the crowd. I observed that there was not a single lady present, only men. The situation was so drastically against convention that I could barely contain a smile. All the men held in the dining hall were enjoying their dinner. Every eye was fixed on me as I bustled into the room. But I was not afraid of men. I was not afraid of any living soul, save one.

The innkeeper approached me.

"Good evenin', Miss. An' how can I help ye?"

"I am in need of a simple bedroom for the night. Pray direct me to it. You may supply my supper in there as well," I said as I tugged off my kid gloves.

"Begging yer pardon, Miss. I have naught but gentleman 'ere this evenin'." The innkeeper spoke to me cautiously, as if I were the most slow-witted female he had ever encountered. "Unless your husband be escortin' ye, I don't think it'll be none too proper for ye—"

"There is no husband and there is no need for your squabbles, sir," I said firmly. "Please direct me to a room and see that my luggage is brought up."

"Yes, ma'am. I'll be preparing a room also for yer maid," he suggested hopefully.

"Pray do not make any more assumptions," I said, exasperated. "There is no maid. Direct me to my room with no further interruptions." As I said this, I handed him a large purse filled with coins and he bowed and rushed ahead obediently.

I followed him through the dining hall as the men continued to stare. I made steady eye contact with several of them and they looked away gruffly. The innkeeper began to lead me up some steep stairs. At the small landing, I felt some of them staring still, and I whipped around to glare at the mass of men. They all immediately began to revisit their suppers and talk loudly. I smiled slightly. None of them were as terrifying as the being from which I ran.

As I smiled, however, I noticed one face I recognized, one face that brought feelings to the surface I'd long since tried to bury. I had not seen him for several years, but I would know his face anywhere. He stood with one hand in his pocket and one hand to his mouth covering a hateful sneer, staring straight at me, standing out like a picture against the others. The corner of the room cast a shadow over his features, but did not make him unrecognizable. His familiar dark, slanting eyebrows made me shudder. I had no trouble believing he had turned into a criminal and that that could have been the reason for his sudden disappearance years ago. What had he to run from? Creditors? Or family? Why had he come back now?

I knew he was an only child, for I'd never heard of him having siblings. And I knew his wife had passed away in mysterious circumstances, bearing no children. I also knew he had inherited his parent's property and wealth when his parents were carried away with scarlet fever. They had been well known for refusing to help those in need and doing nothing save amusing themselves inside their own home. No one even knew what the interior of their estate looked like. So quiet they were, so peculiar, so very secular to the point of rude and dismissive.

Without my conscious permission, my mind remembered the feelings I'd had for him before his marriage. My heart thrilled in spite of myself, then sank in quick succession as I forced the feelings out again. I lowered my gaze and quickly followed the innkeeper up the remaining stairs.

After a fine supper and some help from a maid into my sleeping clothes, I was soon left alone, but sleep did not come easily. Nightmares came to me by night consistently now, and nothing I did could ease them. I kept imagining steady footsteps treading up the stairs in the darkness—slow, but sure, footsteps in a dogged pursuit. Perhaps it was because of the hostile man, or perhaps because I was in a new place, but my dreams were more surreal than ever . . .

I was a child again, and I stood in the sitting room in my mother's house, watching my father read. I often found him in the library, poring over yet another leather-bound tome. His broad shoulders and fine chin seemed almost regal when reading, and his face was exactly the type you could always find in a library. I focused intently on his face, trying to break his attention so he could appreciate the new dress Mother had bought for me, but he was absorbed in a book. Beowulf. *His hair swayed to one side as he watched Beowulf the hero face the monster Grendel once again in his mind's eye.*

At long last he looked up and grinned so hugely his eyes nearly disappeared.

"You look so lovely, Catherine," he said, smiling at me. I giggled in appreciation as he returned, still smiling, to his poem. I continued to twirl around the room until I found myself by the fire. It was unseasonably cold and the fire was so comforting. I watched as the flames danced, as I did, in the comfort of Father's presence.

When morning came and I awoke, I ordered my breakfast with solemnity. Even remembering my real name in a dream made me nervous. I must remember to use my new name, Anna, or I might be found out.

Preparing myself for the day was surprisingly difficult. Mother had always employed a maid to do my hair and powder. Now that I was alone, I did my best with a braid and a fresh, plain muslin dress with pounds of undergarments beneath—though I did leave one layer of a slip in the room, hoping to make my entry into the chaise less humiliating. I trotted down the stairs to the door and found the dining hall mostly empty, to my relief. I was not so apprehensive about the mass of vulgar men as much as I was of the one who had glared so defiantly last night. I climbed into my waiting chaise and we made our way to the main London dock.

Simple and poor as I was becoming, I had never felt so much freedom until then, because those who are free can spend their wealth in ways that please them. If they choose to donate a hundred pounds to a beggar on the street, they could. Or they may choose to spend it on a hideous hat that undoubtedly all the ladies would adore. Regardless, they are free to choose. I propped my head on my folded arms on the open window of the vehicle. I, now, was free as well. And freedom had never smelled so sweet. In my joy, I leaned my face out the small window and breathed deep the smell of it all. All around me was joy and acceptance. I relished it.

All too suddenly we reached the dock. James, from the office, was there to greet me. I was glad to see that five thousand pounds at least produced a welcome. Behind him stood three old, rigid men whom I assumed to be his pleased superiors.

"Good morning, Miss!" he exclaimed as he opened my door and let down the steps himself.

"Anna," I maintained with a smile.

"Oh." He hesitated, remembering my vulgarity. "Yes. Well, Miss Anna, unless you would like for me to inform you of your destination, I shall escort you to the ship myself."

I shook my head. Truly, I did not wish to know my destination.

James turned to his company. "Miss Anna, this is Mr. Bradbury, Mr. Crawford, and Mr. Martins," he stated indicating each man individually. This poor man was desperately grasping onto fragments of broken etiquette. I could not help but enjoy his attempts.

"Well, you are a stalwart bunch, I'll give you that," I pronounced with amusement. "However, I will only be introduced with first names." The wall of bleak men was unsurprised. James must have informed them of my eccentric behavior.

"Miss Anna," James began hesitantly, "This is David, Jeffrey, and Jonathan." Each man bowed in turn.

"And it is absolutely lovely to meet you," I returned with a fervent handshake to each. "Goodness!" I pointed at David, whose bright gold cuff links could blind the eyes if placed in the correct angle. "Don't you know one unfortunate wind or shove of a workman could send you overboard? And with those weights, surely you would never resurface!"

Mr. Bradbury squirmed in unease and placed both wrists firmly behind his back.

I took James's arm and began walking, but found myself gazing at the ships as I passed. Of all the ships along the line, my assigned ship seemed to be the largest. The *Madras* was her name, and I stopped to admire her splendor and strength. James told me she was used primarily for transporting goods; however, the captain of the ship was allowing a few passengers aboard for this voyage. He was not known to allow women before, but I suspected it had something to do with the five thousand pounds I had given him.

"Ah! The lady of the hour!" My attention was drawn to a stern face approaching us.

James cleared his throat gruffly. "Missus Mary Livingstone, may I present Miss Anna." He seemed slightly embarrassed at having no surname to introduce me with. She curtsied in response. "Missus Livingstone was born and raised on the land you are sailing to!" he added proudly.

"It is a treat, indeed, to meet you, Miss Anna." she said with a small, wise grin.

In an instant, I knew I would like her. It did not appear that she was born in a foreign land, with her white skin and smart bonnet. She was rather short, yet hardy, with a blunted nose. Her hair was raven black and forced back into a simple and strict bun, yet she smelled of freshly baked bread and hardworking mornings. She had two small children in tow, both peering at me from behind her skirts. Neither of them could be older than four years of age.

"My husband is David, whom we are traveling to join," she continued, "and the children are Robert and Agnes, respectively." She gestured to each child as they peeked behind her skirts. The oldest, whom she had introduced as Robert, gave me a small wave. "I hope you will call us by our first names as well." She agreed with a no-nonsense tone. "We travel alone, I'm afraid, so I'm glad for your company."

"The pleasure is truly mine," I replied. I cannot convey how much I enjoyed her frankness. She said what she meant, and I knew I would always respect a being like her.

I turned to James. "Do you know how we are to board the ship?" I asked as I craned my neck around, searching for access. "I confess I do not see any type of ramp or access at all.".

"The ramp is up, my dear. Do you not see the wooden board?"

I looked again at the ship and saw a long, feeble-looking board, whose width could be no more than a few feet, reaching from the dock to the ship's side.

"I see," I murmured warily. I had no experience with heights or narrow spaces, and I suddenly felt nervous. Nevertheless, faith would not have sent me forward if I were meant to be stopped by a wooden board, so I held firm.

I confess I held my breath as each tiny soul bravely walked up the board. Mary and her children must have been frequent travelers, for the children bounced up the board without a look of fear, but if they had fallen, they would have found themselves in deep water. They were so small. I would have no way to fish them out if they fell in, except perhaps jumping in myself. Could they swim? Could *I* swim? Would the weight of my dress drown me if I tried? My heart leapt in my chest in genuine panic.

However, my fears were unwarranted—everyone made it across safely. Mary then made her way to the top, after informing me I could leave my belongings with a small group of crew members just outside the ship. It would not be a herculean task for them, since all I had taken with me were a few books, four dresses, and undergarments.

Suddenly, I was alone on the dock, staring at the long, flimsy gangplank in front of me. It seemed like a very long way to go, and the water beneath seemed to beckon me to fall and feed its hungry depths. I took a single step, then a deep breath in, a step, and a deep breath out, all the while forcing myself not to stare at the black water. Several times I considered turning back, but then I remembered that even small children had conquered this. If they could do it, I could do it.

Eventually, I reached the top. I stood on the edge of the ship and could finally see past the commotion of the crew and into the endless waters. A strong, sweet breeze came over me as if in congratulation. I breathed in deep the sea air I had always loved. I had made it. I felt I could conquer any obstacle the world had to offer. I truly was strong enough.

Someone held a hand out to assist me, breaking my reverie. I felt almost sad to get onto the ship. Here on the edge between London and the sea, I had no obligation to move forward or back. I was on the verge of adventure and I was happy for it, but standing on this ledge, I need not take any action other than breathing. I was completely liberated.

After a time, I heard Robert, the oldest of Mary's children, snicker at my exuberance. I scowled, taking the impatient hand that was still waiting, and jumped to the deck. The little children clapped at my accomplishment, and I curtsied dramatically. I smiled and turned to thank the owner of the hand that helped me down. And now I regretted not having turned back, because the man, who now fiercely grasped my hand, was the scowling man from the inn.

"Welcome aboard, Miss Kensington," he muttered sternly.

I retrieved my hand quickly from the man and gasped. I froze and stared. He had revealed my surname. Was he here to take me back? Would he disclose my full name to everyone or force me to return to the living nightmare? Was I safe? Panic coursed through me.

"Miss Anna," Mary interjected, "this is Captain Dunna. Captain, Miss Anna."

Captain? Dunna? But I knew him as Benjamin Ashmore. Had he changed his name also?

The captain bowed, and I curtsied automatically, still keeping an eye on him. The introduction was hardly warranted, since he knew more of my name and my past than Mary, and I knew him. I knew his broad, menacing shoulders and hands could have easily crushed me, but as a few seconds lapsed and he didn't force me back to land, I began to relax in the smallest degree. His gesture was polite, yet the hardened expression in his eyes could have cut steel. He was obviously unhappy at my being on board. I was equally unhappy at this coincidence—and also confused.

"Captain?" I asked hesitantly.

"First Mate Anderson will show you to your cabins," he announced, gesturing to the elderly man standing directly to his left, then nodded to us before walking steadily to the ship's helm. I stared after him in wonder and confusion.

"Surely next time you could employ a wider ramp," Mary called after him. "Miss Anna is not used to such a narrow climb."

I flushed in embarrassment.

The captain's chin reached over his shoulder as he peered in our direction. "If she is afraid of a narrow board, I should not have allowed her on the ship at all." He exited.

Afraid of a board? I was certainly not afraid of the board, but of the water beneath! Had I not made it on board unscathed? Didn't I deserve praise instead of censure? And I doubted he would deny my passage because of fright, when my five thousand pounds were most certainly, at least partially, in his pocket. I started toward him, eager to speak my mind.

First Mate Anderson stepped directly in front of me, and I jerked my eyes up to meet his. He had large bushy eyebrows, and his skin told a tale of many years on sea. His eyes, though, were open and kind, and halted my anger. He gave me his arm and escorted us to our cabins.

The Livingstones had a small cabin with several cots to share between them, and I was situated in the cabin directly next to them. It was a simple and small space, filled densely with not only my luggage but also supplies needed for the ship. There was precious little space to maneuver around the room. Directly ahead of me there was a row of low cupboards, on top of which a thin mattress was placed. To one side there was a washing basin with a tall pitcher of fresh water. The pitcher was held with grooves in the counter so as not to tip over when the ship swung with the waves. To the other side and above me hung several items stored for the use of the crewmen, I supposed. A ladder, several pots and pans, and a few wicker baskets hung precariously. It was more crowded than I was used to, but it represented the new life I was taking on and I was glad for it. We had a few hours to collect ourselves and organize our things while the men set sail, so I found myself with time to ponder in my little space.

I was forcibly struck with questions I could not answer. Of all the places in the world, this was the very last place I thought to find an Ashmore. And what of his name? Why had he changed it?

I found myself remembering odd moments that had passed between us years before.

During balls and social gatherings, he would stand in a corner as if physically pinned to the wall from both sides. He always looked as if he had smelled something unpleasant. It was all too easy to be distracted by his dark, evil eyes, menacing expression, and rakish, unkempt, black hair. In quiet circles around the ballroom, if there were ever talk of violent city news, several pairs of eyes would move slowly to his corner in suspicion.

The only person to recommend him had been his wife, Marianne. I had not gained many friends in my youth, but she had been one of them—a sweet, amiable girl. When circumstance allowed, we were often found on the library floor, digging through book after book of beautiful dresses, fashionable hats, and new gloves. In our later years, though, we drifted apart. Soon she was the envied girl with a small fortune, doted on by every male in the room. She was rumored to have received several offers from wealthy men, yet had refused them all. She enjoyed living life without constraints. We did speak on occasion, and I still enjoyed her company. We simply didn't have much to talk about anymore.

One memory in particular stood out to me. Marianne and I had secured a spot to ourselves on a sofa in the grand hallways of Almack's. She had been married for a few months now, but still seemed the same happy girl to me. I was glad to see it.

She was in the midst of sharing a particularly amusing story with me when her arm was suddenly jerked far above her head and she was jolted from her seat into a standing position. Her husband stood not an inch from her frightened face, with malice set in his brow.

"You wretch," he whispered harshly. No one in the room could hear him, save myself.

"My dear," she said, trying to sound cheerful. "My dear, you're hurting me."

"I have just found out how you have been occupied today," he pushed the words out through gritted teeth. "Hats, dresses, shawls. And, of course, the bill has been laid to my door. Where will it end?"

"You gave me a monthly allowance, sir," she spoke boldly, trying to defend herself with a quivering chin. "I was only spending what you yourself had given me."

He took hold of both her delicate arms and shook her violently. "You are materialistic to your very core!" He spoke in shouting whispers, directly next to her ear. "You return those things, and all the other frivolous things you have purchased, or you will feel my glove on your cheek. My love for you is quickly diminishing, Marianne."

She visibly sank in her chair. She knew I could hear him, and her embarrassment must have been extreme. She had never known much money before she had married this man. Was he supposing she would use her allowance on gruel and hard biscuits? I ached to defend her, but could not find the words. I was not accustomed to standing up to accusers of any kind.

He took a step away from her at long last, then ripped the shawl from her shaking hands. "I'll return this piece myself. You may find another means of returning home. Goodnight."

He then exited the building, to my great relief.

Marianne sat quietly next to me again and wept for a few minutes.

She was carried away by illness only four months after the scene at Almack's. We were not allowed to attend her funeral, nor say goodbye to her in any way; her husband would not allow it. One could wonder if it was illness that had killed her after all.

In my wonderment and bitter regret, I dozed off just as Mary's children had done.

I was looking into the dancing flames in Father's office and lost track of time. Suddenly, Mother came into the room and screamed. It was only then I realized the flames had surrounded me. Flames were crawling up my back and had begun to kiss my bare arm. I looked to my parents in panic. Their figures froze in my sight. Father had started to stand from his chair and vault toward me, but he was too far away in the large room. Mother was much closer. She had seen the flames at once and had come running at a full gallop that would make Father's grey geldings proud. For a small, infinitesimal moment, as my mother rushed toward me, I dreamt that she was coming to rescue me. Maybe she was rushing toward me in pure love and genuine concern. I stepped toward her in response. I spread my arms as wide as they would stretch to cling to my mother, my breath of life, as moss clings hard to a tree.

I woke with a sob and clutched my arm. In my moment of absolute misery and terror, I heard that sweet voice again. My mind repeated the words that had spurred my faith and flight. The words of my angel.

"Run, Anna! Oh, please, run."

Chapter 2

I startled to the sound of four-year-old Robert knocking on my door.

"Miss Anna?" he began loudly, "Mama says you are to get ready for supper now. You have slept too much and Momma says we want to see you now!"

I laughed shakily.

"Thank you, Sir Robert," I responded.

He giggled happily and ran away yelling to his mother along the way that he had delivered her message in a fine way. Had he said supper time? I had slept the day away! And I had awoken such a mess. My dress was wrinkled beyond immediate repair and I had been laying in such a position that I was sure my hair resembled that of Medusa. I found a new dress and did my very best with such obstinate hair. There would be no one to help me with these tasks any longer. The thought actually made me glad.

Once I was as presentable as I could manage, and smothered in layers upon layers of undergarments, I emerged from my cabin and walked up the steps to the main deck. The sun was beginning to set on the water as the waves continued their conversations. I stopped amid the bustling crew members to appreciate the sun's final dive below the horizon. The sea reflects what we are feeling, I believe. If someone was afraid, they must have looked on this as the sun abandoning them to the dark. But as bright and unknown as my future was, and with the echo of the voice still ringing in my ears, I felt in the sun's dive a calm assurance. After a long day of mundane duties and forced circulations, it finally got to rest, as I now rested. I sighed.

"I suppose you have been informed that your supper will be served in my cabin." A sharp voice interrupted my reverie.

I spun around to face Captain Dunna—or so he was calling himself. He held the same stance and glare as he wore at every function I had ever witnessed him. It took me a moment to recover from my surprise and respond.

"Yes, Captain, I will attend," I said.

"Then you will attend now," he said. "We are waiting on your presence." Then he held out his arm to me. I knew that I must move to the cabin immediately. However, in that moment, I was suddenly unsure of what I was to do. Finally, in my confusion, I stretched my hand forth and, for reasons that are still unclear to me, placed it atop his own.

Of course, the traditional way to take an arm was through the crux near the elbow. Placing the hand on top of another was sometimes used in dances, of which we certainly were not doing. Sometimes, in the presence of the queen, duchesses were known to do it. My mind knew all these things and reviewed them while he stared at me as if I were incapable of proper thought.

Yet I did not move my hand. After a moment, he simply started toward his cabin and I flushed every time someone stopped to stare and mentally question our position. I was too stubborn to relinquish, and possibly he too exasperated to move my hand himself, and we slowly and oddly made our way to supper.

As we stepped inside, I saw that the space consisted of the management of the ship all clad in their handsome uniforms. They all stood in readiness. One in particular stood at the back of Mary's chair, waiting to assist her. The captain led me to my seat to the right of his own at the head of the table. The ladies sat with assistance.

Robert peeked around a broad shoulder to wave hello to me from a small table to the side, which was set up especially for the children. I smiled and winked at him.

The captain spoke. "If you please, Miss Kensington, Missus Livingstone," he began, "I would be honored to introduce to you my set of worthy men." He then named off every man's name and title, and they each bowed in turn. The men sat and the meal began.

After only a small breakfast, I was sure I could consume as much as any man there. The table was covered in beef, pork, tarts, and fresh fruit. Decorum dictated that I speak to the persons on my left and right at meals, but I was determined to leave the polite world behind. As a result, I took great pleasure in observing the young man across and two chairs down from me, whose name I had remembered.

"Lieutenant Warley, isn't it?" I inquired sweetly. I nearly had to shout to be heard across the din of the supper table. I kept a steady gaze on him so he was sure I was speaking to him and no one else.

He glanced around himself for a moment in slight shock, looking for guidance as to how to respond to this odd female. He had light hair and a fair complexion. I guessed him to be about my age, and also, remarkably handsome.

"Yes, ma'am," he responded, finally.

"And from where do you hail, sir? Is this your first time at sea?" I persisted.

Several of the men around the table looked at me in shock at raising my voice above a whisper. I smiled as I cut my meat.

"No, Miss, I have been out to sea with Captain Dunna once before." He paused, embarrassed and unsure. "I am from Wales."

"Wales is very fine." I smiled. "Do you know Cardiff? I feel sure we have a common friend in Miss Groves."

"Miss Groves of Cardiff near Charles Street?" he asked incredulously.

"The very same," I said, laughing. I could not help but notice the lines that had been formed on his face from his frequent laughter, and the stunning blue of his eyes. "She is a friend of mine. We made some very smart mud pies together as children."

He couldn't help but smile. "It is an arduous task that must be accomplished by someone of intellect," he speculated. "Did you have a special technique?" Several of the senior officers glanced at him in disapproval.

"Yes! You see, the best mud cake is made with a very particularly handled twig. Without a proper twig, I should be completely lost." I waved my hands dramatically. The children were beginning to giggle.

"And what if no twig can be found?" he inquired seriously. "What then?"

"Then I should have to console myself with the use of some sturdy weeds." I postulated solemnly.

The children could not contain themselves any longer and burst into laughter at such silly dinner conversation.

Seeing an end to our philosophies on mud, he began a fresh subject. "And what brings you on a ship like this, Miss Anna? I hope you have family waiting at our berth."

I was about to answer when that sharp voice rudely interrupted.

"No," the captain said bluntly. "Miss Kensington has no family outside of London. She journeys with us for a prime youth adventure." The captain looked to me as if he had just stated a well-known fact or the state of the weather.

"You see," he continued as he leaned closer to Lieutenant Warley, "she is running from an undesirable match." Lieutenant Warley looked down, suddenly uncomfortable.

He then turned to me. "What was it that you disliked about him?" the Captain asked. "Was there not enough wealth? Was he unpopular? Or was he simply not handsome enough?"

All conversation had stopped. I could feel everyone staring either at the captain or at me. The sea men's eyebrows were all raised in sudden surprise. Even Mary looked on in expectation. The children sensed real tension and had stopped their soft squabbles. As for me, I stared at him with intensity at his bold accusations. Is that what people thought of me? That I was running from a man? I had never experienced before such a noble and presumptuous speech against my character. I was unwilling to simply let it pass submissively.

"I run from no man," I said, turning to look him straight in the face. "Even if a man has no wealth, good looks, or respectable personality, I will still sit next to him at the supper table."

The men's eyebrows rose even further and a proud smile broke out on Mary's face. The captain broke eye contact with me first and turned to his guests with a mock grin.

"Well then! Let us toast to those of us humble enough to sit in the presence of such company." He rose his glass to toast and a few men raised their glasses with a mumble. The captain drank from his glass, gave me one last long glare, and took his leave from the table.

All was silent as I reflected on the unreasonable hate, masked by fake cordiality, that burned in his eyes. It was sickeningly familiar.

Supper dismissed informally and I was drawn to the deck by the sight of a bright moon reflecting off the water. I tugged my shawl around me as I gazed at the scenery. The moon was so big I could see gray spots on her surface. My mind wandered.

When I had reached Mother, she did not dive for the raging fire crawling up my back. She held me back. She hit my face. Over and over she slapped me as the flames tore at my tender arm. I whimpered quietly. Father finally reached us and threw Mother back while he used the unburnt folds of my dress to extinguish the remaining flames that held me in a powerful grasp.

Father embraced me and held me tight. I could see Mother over his shoulder, seething with rage. Her breath came in short, heavy gasps.

"What an inconsiderate, stupid child I have! I buy a new dress and you destroy it within minutes! You careless, idiotic creature!"

Tears started to come down my cheeks. My arm hurt so badly, but that was not why I wept.

"I'm sorry, Mother. I am so sorry," I sobbed. Father finally released me and examined my arm, then picked me up and escorted me past Mother and upstairs. Mother screamed in fury that I was meant to go to church with her in that dress and that we would be late. Mother screamed until her voice was gone. Father nursed my arm and pretended the house was silent. With my arm bandaged, tears dried, and a new plain dress on, we spent the afternoon cracking nuts together in his room.

Mother spent the day in church.

"Never apologize to her," Father said when we were together, through gritted teeth and clenched jaw.

I stared at him in surprise, while his eyes were downcast.

He brought his gaze to mine.

"Never," he repeated.

"Miss Anna?" I heard behind me. I turned slightly to see my visitor. Lieutenant Warley stood with perfect posture and spotless uniform.

"I hope you'll forgive me for addressing you with your given name," he said clumsily, "Missus Livingstone said it is what you prefer."

"It is," I responded.

He quickly nodded. His smile flashed for a moment and then faltered. "I feel I must apologize for instigating an argument," he said, "I should not have inquired so boldly as to your situation."

"No, sir, please," I begged. "I feel sure it must be burning in everyone's curiosity. I am glad you felt comfortable enough to ask me."

"Still, I am to blame, in part, for distressing you," he insisted. As unfounded as his guilt was, I knew there would be no convincing him to the contrary.

"Very well, I shall blame you entirely if you wish," I suggested with a smile.

He returned my smile in kind. "I will gladly take all the blame." He joined me on the ledge of the ship. A soft breeze blew the hair from his eyes.

"It is not that I wish to remain a mystery," I tried to explain. He turned to face me. "And the captain was right. I am running, but only in faith, not in fear, nor solely for adventure's sake."

I had spoken to the sea as he watched me. Finishing my vague explanation, I looked to him. His gaze was so direct. I was suddenly uncomfortable, but a part of my rebellious mind spoke loudly. *I need not be uncomfortable in a man's presence. Lieutenant Warley is obviously a good man, and thoroughly respectable. If I am to live this way, I shall have to make my own decisions on what is proper and what is not.*

Conversation with Lieutenant Warley came effortlessly. We spoke of his upbringing in Wales and how his mother and father had met. She came from a wealthy family, her father a duke. She had met her future husband at a ball, where he was dressed in his bright red soldier's uniform. Their eyes met across a busy ballroom floor and they could barely be separated when the time came for company to be dismissed. He traveled all over Europe with the militia, while they wrote letters in secret. Three years from their meeting, he approached her father to ask for her hand in marriage. The duke vehemently refused, and his father and mother promptly removed to Gretna Green for their elopement, unashamed at being in love. He seemed slightly embarrassed at sharing the story with me, but I found it delightful.

"And how did they live?" I asked, "I assume your grandfather, the duke, cut her off."

"Yes, he did," he answered, "they had a small income from my father's work in the militia. And Mother sold the jewelry and fineries she had on her person at the time. They made a small living, and she learned how to become a gardener, chef, and mother."

"I should love to meet her," I said.

"I would love that as well," he agreed quickly. I looked away for a moment. Had I unwittingly declared myself to him? I had only meant I should like to meet her because of her story! She had thrown away worldly ties just as I wished to throw away mine. She embodied hope. I certainly did not wish to meet her so that I could wed her son. But I supposed there was nothing to do about it now. The only danger was in him thinking I had any intention of returning to Europe.

"How long will we be at sea?" I asked.

"Ah yes," he replied, remembering something. "Missus Livingstone told me you have no desire to know our heading. I will not tell you where we travel, though you may likely guess, but it will take us three months to arrive there. I hear Captain Dunna has made it in two!"

"So you have not been employed by him long?" I inquired.

"No, my only other voyage with him was to India," he replied. "But the captain is known for his unworldly speeds, and I am happy to serve him."

"Just as he seems glad to be served," I contested sarcastically.

He turned to me and asked, "Would you pardon me if I asked if you knew him before now?"

"Yes, certainly." I paused, remembering when I knew him as Mr. Ashmore. Articulating the resentment I felt for him was possibly too much for one conversation. I chose a stale answer. "I only knew him in passing."

"He seems a good man to me," he reflected. "Strict to a point, but good."

I had not the heart to quash his optimism. "Perhaps."

The night finally grew too brisk to continue conversation. I moved toward my cabin, but was halted by several of the sailors scrubbing the deck on their hands and knees. I was on the verge of asking to pass, but my thoughts were interrupted.

"Aye, men! Move out of the way! Lady coming through!" Warley shouted.

The men shuffled out of the way, and I hurried through the space with my head down and my cheeks flaming hot. Did he think I was not capable of finding a way? Is that how he perceived me? Incapable, delicate, weak? Or did he simply want to exert his own authority? He certainly did not help my relationship with the men, painting me as a feeble female. I reached my cabin, irked from the experience.

As I began to get ready for another night of dreaded sleep, I decided I had finally reached my limit. I simply could not bear the insatiable itching any longer. I bolted my door as firmly as the little latch was able and tore the wig from my head at long last. My father's plan had been to pass me off as a boy on a long voyage, but that plan had turned cold and Mother bought me a fine piece of hair to cover my shorn scalp.

I gently placed the long piece of hair on my cot and ran my fingernails through the short stubble with satisfaction. It was all I could manage, in the last forty-eight hours, to not tear the loathsome creature off my head. After two weeks of having to wear it, I was still not comfortable with the pins and products it took to make it look natural against my face. Why I wore it, I did not know. It was a representation of everything I disliked in the world. I suppose I simply did not wish to answer the questions my hairless head would raise.

While still scratching my aching scalp, I laid in my cot. As my fingers massaged, I tried to tell myself that I did not need to dream.

Whether the dreams were good or bad, I had no more need of them. I was a new person. I was finally the maker of my own destiny. Thus arguing with myself, I finally dozed off.

"Leaving?" I asked hesitantly. "On holiday?"

"A very long holiday," my father said, smiling widely.

"Leaving Mother's house?" I looked around the library in which we were seated.

He lifted my chin with a single, broad finger, and then reached up to tap my nose.

"I have become aware of a new and exciting situation. Are you prepared to know where we will be making our new home?" he asked eagerly. He reminded me of a schoolboy.

I had to giggle at his eagerness. "All right. Where are we going, Papa?" I asked, not quite believing. "Australia? India? Scotland?"

In a hushed tone, he said, "America."

I sat up in my small bed, my face streaked with tears, and looked out my tiny window. The moon was so bright it lit up my cabin. There was enough light that I could find my worn handkerchief in my belongings. I knew there was no chance of peaceful sleep now.

I stood to dress myself for the day and found myself speculating. Who was the person who had decided that women should wear all these layers? Undoubtedly it had been a man. I did not want to spend hours dressing in my cabin. I wanted to spend them breathing in the pure air of my new existence. I had no desire to impress anyone aboard, save Mary. And I knew that making myself into a hard laborer would impress her most.

Having thus decided, I dressed myself in a simple cap sleeve dress, with minimal undergarments. I was sorely tempted to leave behind my wig. Nothing would have made me more happy than to throw it into the teeming deep. But I did not want to answer all questions all at once. Maybe, in time, I could discard it and say I had cut my hair because of the heat. For the time being, I sat in front of a small mirror to place the horrid thing atop my head.

Sullen, and already itching, I emerged from my cabin and up to the deck. The scene of the setting moon on the ocean was as fine and grand as I had been hoping. The ocean was incredibly still. No waves broke against the sides of the ship as the air strolled, brisk and soothing. I walked alone alongside the entire length of the *Madras*. Suddenly, I realized I was not alone. The captain was standing with his back to me at the helm. I turned to walk away, but just then, he spoke.

"You need not leave for my sake, Miss Kensington. I am only supervising the crew." He gestured above with a single hand.

At least six men were working far above the ship in the sails without making a single sound. They jumped so effortlessly between beams and ropes, I would never have known they were present. I was momentarily embarrassed by my lack of common sense. Did I suppose the ship simply glided along without effort to the correct destination?

"Ah, I see." I looked from the crew back to the captain whose back was still turned. From this angle, I could truly observe him. He was as tall as I remembered, perhaps in his early forties now, and had unkempt black hair that once endeared him to me. Parts of his hair were graying around the temple and at the nape of his neck. I could see why young men like Lieutenant Warley could admire him. If he held a firm stance, demanded control, and made hasty voyages across a troubled ocean, I suppose any aspiring young man could not help but be impressed.

"Miss Livingstone tells me you have no desire to know our destination," he said suddenly.

"That is true," I responded curtly, looking away. There was a long pause. I assumed he was waiting for me to elaborate, which I had no intention of doing.

He decided to elaborate for me. "It must seem romantic to so young a person to simply board a ship and see where the wind takes her."

He certainly was skilled in false information.

"Certainly it must be, but that is not why I came," I countered simply, through clenched teeth. "Age is no guarantee for whimsy."

He finally turned to me. Somehow his brows came closer together than at supper. I continued in irritation. "It must be difficult, for *you*, Ashmore, to have women aboard the ship. Especially aboard the deck and not locked away beneath, where they cannot be heard or seen," I sneered. "James told me you rarely allow the creatures aboard the *Madras*. I suppose courtesy is something men could do without, whenever given the opportunity."

"So women are the standard for proper behavior, then? Is it your experience, Miss Kensington, that all women are mild mannered in every provoking situation?"

I stared with wide eyes. Silence grew black and thick between us. My heart panicked. How much did he know?

"I suppose not," I said finally, crossing my arms.

He noted my gestures with a blank expression.

"In truth, I do not know if there are many who are consistently calm," he said quietly.

I could not help but stare. He was speaking and his eyes were not burning anger into me. He spoke in hushed tones, which baffled me. I felt as if all my tender nerves were suddenly on display for him to see, and I did not know how he had access to them so easily.

"I knew only one," I responded.

"A woman, I presume," he guessed mockingly.

I stared at him warily and said nothing. This was too tender a subject.

He continued. "I suppose you think men of your acquaintance to be sordid, stupid figures who are only good for fetching cups of punch or calling forth fine carriages."

"I know only one," I repeated with a grin. He grunted in response. I departed. I would return to my cabin until the sun reappeared.

Chapter 3

When the sun had risen, I emerged from my cabin at the precise moment Mary and her children were emerging from theirs. Mary directed us all to a small mess hall where we would be eating the same meal as the crew. This was from special direction from the captain. He did not like the idea of passengers eating separately from the men who were responsible for their safety. I was not worried. I had survived on all kinds of food in the dark corners of my childhood home.

The mess hall was compact, with tight rows of chairs, stools, and short tables. The ceiling was particularly low, and Mary and I had to hunch over while holding our dented tin trays. We were presented with dense biscuits, salted pork, and dark tea, a stark contrast with last night's fine supper.

"Our dinner last night was a celebratory one," Mary explained. "This will be our fare for the majority of the voyage." She paused. "We shall see how your stomach tolerates it."

I had to smile at her kindness. She thought I was used to nothing but fine foods. I did not mind the biscuit. The children and I dipped them in our tea and chatted away amiably. Mary scrutinized me, waiting for me to excuse myself in disgust, or to refuse to eat further. I could not tell her I had seen worse than this. I kept my eyes down and thanked God I was on the sea.

I spent most of my day aboard the *Madras* helping Mary in any way I was able. The nature of the voyage bade us stay in the cabins below deck most of the time. The crew had much work to do and the deck was not used as a social setting. Although I still made my way up in the early mornings and late nights, I did not know if the sailors and captain were happy about it. I wondered if my monetary contribution had something to do with their generosity. Mary said she had voyaged several times before and had never been allowed on deck as much as this.

I was not very helpful to Mary in several respects. I had never washed clothing before. I was at a loss as how to wash children as well. I did not even know how to tie Robert's shoelaces. However, I had an advantage in knowing how to sew. I would hardly be an English lady of quality without the ability to embroider a pretty cushion. I took on the task of darning all socks and garments, and even using other scavenged fabric to create new tunics for the children.

Mary was a blunt person, but conversation came easily with her. We spoke, briefly, of her upbringing in a different country than England, her meeting Mr. Livingstone, and of both of her precious children. Her relationship with her husband was deep and long-lasting. However, he had dedicated himself to missionary work, medical work, and exploration of the land of our destination. Mary was always so kind to not mention where exactly we were destined.

I could see that raising two children alone would be very difficult, but Mary made it look effortless and joyful. Robert helped her with Agnes and was a happy and well-disciplined boy. Mary once said I had only to look at Robert to see her husband, just as you only had to look at the toddler Agnes to see her. What joy and marvelous light I did behold in this small family! Obviously, the children were in great need of a father and Mary in need of a husband, yet they supported his adventures with perfect solemnity and responsibility. It was as if they took each step he took, every breath he inhaled, only from a physical distance. They were a family, tied together eternally by love, and they amazed me daily.

On many nights, I would sink grateful into my cot, exhausted by a long day of helping Mary and playing with the children. Agnes, especially, needed my constant and full attention. Yet in those nights of exhaustion, in that moment directly before dreaming, I felt, in a word, joyful. Completely and fully elated. I was *useful* to the world. In an entire day of assisting others, I had lost myself. No one had complimented my dress, nor admired my stitches. This one simple fact made me nearly giddy with pride. My dresses began to show holes and wear and were covered in Robert's breakfast and Agnes's accidents. I had never been so horribly dirty, yet I had never felt so needed and content. The hard work of the day made the rest of my soul that much more wholesome and lovely. With those moments of fulfillment, I was at long last able to face my dreams with courage. And a good thing too. The nightmares seemed more vivid than before.

Father and I strolled, hand in hand, down a narrow path in the forest behind Mother's house. The tall pines stood as sentinels on every side, pointing toward a dark and celestial sky. Although the way was dim and the sounds that came to my ears were ominous and strange, I had no need to know our destination. Father was with me and Mother was far away. There was nothing else in the world I wanted.

However, even as a small girl, I knew Mother needed far more than these simple pleasures. Mother needed carriages, morning calls, and expensive clothes in order to be content. If Mother alone had raised me, what kind of person would I be? Would I be as obsessed with material gain as she? Would I hold any stock in human compassion? The path we took became more extensive, treacherous, and difficult to maneuver. Father did not speak as sweat streamed from his temples. Every step became more difficult and heart-wrenching than the last. Our feet plodded heavy on the unforgiving earth.

How long could we go on this way?

I awoke by simply opening my eyes. I gained no solace from holding Father's hand through the night, no rest for my eyes from seeing his face. Only restlessness. I sat up and began to prepare for another day. I had come to find that my body awoke at four a.m. daily and needed no encouragement to wake.

The time on the *Madras* was akin to raindrops coursing down a glass window. Every day we began at the top of the pane. The same food, the same conversation, the same companions. Slowly we trickled down the glass with some little deviation in our daily course, until finally we made it to the end of our day and began the next at the top of the glass again.

That morning, I took meticulous care in applying my frivolous wig. I wished again that I could go without it. At this point my hair had grown a touch. It would feel so wonderful to be able to leave the bothersome thing behind and feel the sea wind through my own hair. But every day, I went through irritating pain.

At last, pinned, pinched, and presentable, I mounted the deck.

In my morning wanderings, I had not seen the captain since last we spoke. I tried to convince myself that he did not avoid me on purpose. Lieutenant Warley mentioned that the captain was not always called upon to supervise the men. In any case, I was glad to be alone in those dismal mornings. The first mate typically acknowledged me with a friendly nod, and I would proceed to spend the rest of the morning with the moon. I could tell we were making good distance in the two months we'd spent on sea—the stars were beginning to alter their design in the sky. When the sun rose, I would sometimes try my hand at drawing waves breaking against the Madras. I was attempting a sketch when a voice spoke.

"That is a very interesting drawing, Miss Anna," Lieutenant Warley complimented.

"Oh!" I exclaimed, taken by surprise. "Thank you, sir." I had sketched the helm of the ship with waves crashing up the sides.

"It has been fortunate we have not met any unfavorable weather," he said, facing the sea.

"Yes," I responded. "Indeed fortunate."

"Have you ever been on a ship during a storm, Miss Anna?" he asked.

"No. I have only ever been on small boats with Sir Albernon and my brother."

"I should have known you knew Sir Albernon!" he spoke, delighted. "How is the gentleman?"

"I am not sure I would have ever called him a gentleman," I countered, laughing. "He cares only about his own social standing, and I have seen him on several occasions kick stray dogs and whip his horses mercilessly! He is the epitome of pretentious manners. I cannot say I should be at a loss at never seeing him again."

Lieutenant Warley was silent. I admit, I had stunned myself as well. Why did I feel the need to put him in his place? I had never spoken so uncivilly about anyone. Yet, I could not apologize for such a speech. If I was going to rid myself of polite society, I should feel no guilt in exposing a man who was unkind and foul.

"I, myself, have always known him to be a gentleman," he attempted.

"Yes, I am sure you would," I agreed. "He is always at his best when around fellow men. However, when in the presence of women and animals, he can be the very devil."

My mind clicked in satisfaction in using the word *devil*. Mother would have punished me for using that word.

"I see," was all he muttered.

We stood there silent, watching the waves and the rising sun in silence. I was not sure I wanted him to speak again. I was sure Lieutenant Warley was feeling awkward, but I dismissed it. The waves provided some happy scenery, which I cherished. I tried to draw some floral decoration on the ship, but the tiny flowers unfortunately reminded me of others . . .

There were five hundred and forty-eight printed flowers on my bedroom walls. I had counted them many times. Each mirrored another in perfectly straight lines until the cut of the paper halted their progression. My door was a dark chestnut, made of sturdy material, yet showing signs of wear in large, progressing cracks. It had been thrown shut several hundred times, and a door could only sustain so much abuse. A large fireplace dominated the space on my left. Its bricks and mortar showed signs of having housed flames, yet those were merely a memory now. Windows dotted the large walls, but Mother had them covered with large sheets of cheap fabric so that the room was dim at noonday. She told others she put up the sheets to protect my fair skin from the sun. I knew better.

I forced my mind to think of other things.

Tall, soft grass frozen mid-sway as Father leaned up against a tree in happy dozing. Big bloated tears running down his weathered cheek in relief as I jumped fence after fence on his horse. He could see the freedom in my countenance. I had been taught to ride a horse from a very young age. Father's horse would not permit me to ride side saddle as Mother would have wanted—I rode astride like a man.

A realization came to me. All of my happy memories had two things in common. They involved Father, and they did not involve any frivolous thing. All of my joys came from the outdoors, from learning, from Father. No balls I had attended, nor beautiful dresses I wore, no handsome suitors who had escorted me elicited this kind of joy from me. I took part in social events but simply performed the actions required of me. Mother's reign of terror had not allowed me to even consider neglecting a social function. I suppose I felt since I was a woman, I should enjoy those things. No one would listen to a girl go on about how much she detested balls, and if I had, I surely would have made myself a social outcast. Mother would have been livid.

I had pretended to enjoy parties to protect myself from her. Father had been so easy to please I had not needed to try, but I had put on the pretty dress and pounds of undergarments to please Mother, and did so without question. Too scared to consider doing what pleased me instead. The one person who was incapable of affection, I had hurt myself to please. Suddenly, I hated the dress I wore. I hated the mannerisms and etiquette I kept up for her sake.

I hated my wig.

"Excuse me," I said quietly.

I made my way to my cabin in quick steps. Once there, I ripped the pest from my head and stared at my reflection in the mirror.

This was Anna.

This was who I was meant to be.

I decided, with the removal of the wig, that I would more fully follow my new manners and not heed the stares and questions. I enjoyed this new version of myself. This Anna spoke whatever came into her mind. It was almost a reckless kind of happiness. And who would stop me, except God? Until then, I would strive to not be rude to someone directly, but I would not allow others to force me into every social nicety.

Ignoring the gazes of those around me, however, proved very difficult. Every single crew member stopped in his tracks at my passing. I thought men weren't supposed to notice hair. Of course, they had little idea that my hair had been even shorter weeks ago. They thought a girl had just cut all of her beautiful, glossy locks in exchange for short, spiked, boyish hair. Surely they thought me mad. All I could do was walk right past them. After a few minutes, with the feeling of the wind finally playing with my scalp, it was easy to ignore them.

I returned to my sketching next to Lieutenant Warley. He gazed wide-eyed at my state, but I had no words to explain it. I simply continued to sketch a storm-wrecked ship.

"How—" he began. I chanced a glance up to his face. He blinked once every second. He shook his head while holding out his hands. He must be searching for some clue as to why I would return this way. I had bewildered him. I pressed my lips together to contain my laughter.

He tried again.

"Why—" he muttered, still searching for meaning around him. "Why did you just cut your hair? Did I possibly say something to upset you?"

"Lieutenant," I said between bouts of giggles, "I did not, just now, cut my hair." I spoke slowly, willing him to understand. "It has been short for some time, you just helped me to realize that I didn't need the wig anymore."

He simply stared. "I do not understand," he said miserably. I pitied his confusion.

"It has been short for some time," I repeated. "Mother had that piece of hair made for me to avoid questions."

"Why would she allow you to cut your hair in the first place?" he asked, still bewildered.

There was no way I could explain and have him understand fully. Father had cut my hair so that we might leave England discreetly. I was known for my auburn hair that was long enough to touch the ground if it were not pinned up. He felt if I could be passed as a boy we might leave without raising awareness.

"She thought it may be the new fashion," I lied through tense eyebrows, "and when she realized it did not suit me, she bought me the wig." The irony of this situation sickened me. I had cut my hair to escape her, then she had forced the wig on me after she had won.

"Oh," he pronounced finally. "You could have informed me of this before you shocked me so."

"And be spared this reaction? I think not," I said, smiling.

He smiled back wearily and left me to my sketch.

"Miss Kensington," a voice interrupted my peace.

I turned around to survey the captain, although it was unnecessary. He was the only one aboard whom I did not correct when he used my surname. I felt more comfortable calling him "captain" than I did calling him "Mr. Ashmore."

"Good morning," I said without curtsy, bow, or proper etiquette.

I felt sure he would move along the deck, surveying his crew. He did neither of these things, but stood stationary and glared. Finally, he spoke.

"Why is your hair short?" he demanded.

I could not fathom his interest. In reality, his question made me angry.

"Why?" I asked curtly. He seemed confused. "I mean, why would you ask about my hair?" I clarified.

He simply glared at me.

"It is my own head, is it not?"

He began a new topic. "I feel the need to inform you, Miss Kensington, that we are three weeks from our berth." I did not react. He continued. "Would you like to know your future home?" His voice was mocking.

"I have no desire to know our destination, Sir, as I have told you." And it was true. I was happy helping Mary and the children and waking to the bright moon every morning. Although I still had nightmares, somehow they seemed easier to handle on the sea, with the moon here to comfort me. At some point I would have to prepare myself for landing, I would have to come back to the harsh world in time, but for now I could brush it aside.

"There may be preparations you can perform that would make your arrival easier," he persisted. "There may be an opportunity there befitting a lady. I cannot tell you the details if I am held back by your childish wish to remain aloof."

His tone and the way he said "lady" were identical to my mother's. He was condemning, what he supposed to be, childish ignorance. What right did he have? Why did he feel the need to correct me in my direction? Why could he not let me continue on my course?

I was tempted to react in obedience and fear, as the two reactions were always partners with me. It would be sensible of me to prepare myself for our landing. I could have faith without being completely blind to my surroundings. Certainly Father would not have set sail to America without first making some arrangements for us either on land or at sea. In truth, I had been slightly curious as to my future home.

But I could not do it. I could not concede to this man who represented the world I ran from. I had been burdened by his kind for my entire existence. Years and years of balls and parties where fatherly patrons would criticize me on the cut of my dress or the slouch in my shoulders. They had never considered that, because of their remark, Mother would attempt to beat the slouch out of me when we returned home. Those ignorant and nosy fops took no notice of my desires or well-being. No genuine concern had filled their eyes as they lectured me on how a lady should not eat too many cakes at these events. Did they know that Mother was starving me? That I was not allowed any kind of food superior to my brother's? It was taken from me at every turn with a slap to my cheek. And did they even bother to think that my mother's supposed grace and kindness were merely a grand performance for their benefit?

No. Their need for propriety outweighed my needs entirely. There was not anything I needed, not food, nor clothes, nor shelter, nor faith that could supersede their need for dignity. And here was the living embodiment of those men.

I raised my eyes, and they felt like burning hot marbles. My existence had filled my body with sorrow, but perhaps now I could burn it out with anger.

"If I have any desire to stay aloof, it is in my desire to stay as far away from you as this ship will allow," I said. He straightened his posture, and I continued. "When we land, I shall endeavor to cross the *entire* continent we arrive on, in pursuit of becoming more *aloof*." His jaw had turned hard and his eyes mirrored the hate in my own, but I could not yield. "You can keep your haughty contempt, for I have no use of it. You are worthless! Leave me alone!"

My speech was over. And I was overwhelmed by it. My goal to avoid insulting someone directly to their face was now crumbled. Was this a strength in me now? Or a weakness?

The captain's gaze had not diverted from me. He took a moment to watch my red face as I took deep breaths to settle myself, then he began.

"There is nothing I could have wished for more than this. If you could have but told me sooner, I could have been saved the torture of this situation. Pray, carry out your plan, get as far from me as the continent will allow, even there will not be far enough to separate me from the anguish you have caused."

"Anguish *I* have caused?" I screamed. "I had not spoken a word to you before we entered this ship. What responsibility do I hold for your anger?"

"I should ask the same of you," he retorted, stepping closer. "You have no reason to dislike me, other than your natural temperament, raised by a frivolous mother and a prideful, insipid father."

"Stop," I whispered. I felt as though a large block of iron had just been placed on my chest. He said exactly what could hurt me most. And he found it so quickly, for which I hated him all the more. That anyone could think my idol in this horrible earth proud or insipid left me immediately depressed at the state of the world. How could anyone imagine that Father was proud? They could not see him for the angel that he was. He had fought long and hard to shield me and had ultimately failed. And this is what the world thought of him— they thought he was too prideful.

The captain stared at me angrily and seemed to be about to speak again. I found words.

"My father was perfect." My voice rose. "And frivolous is not a sufficient word for the other." A wretched sob escaped me. I realized suddenly that my head had drooped and I had made this last retort to the long wooden boards of the deck. Large tears of anger and misery welled in my eyes.

I didn't bother looking up. There was nothing I wanted more than the deck to swallow me up and bury me in the sea. The captain was similar to my mother; he hated simply for the pleasure he got from hating. For this I need not look up. I knew the familiar sneer of that countenance.

Chapter 4

The Captain

I had been angry many times as a captain. And yet I knew that she did not cower in fear of me. I knew when I first saw her that she had no real pride left in her, only a haughty show. And yet this girl, who moments ago had told me everything she disliked about me, was now bent over in a perfect example of awful humility. My own trials seemed like nothing. Although the deaths and hatred in my life had left me hollow and incomplete, it had not, as of yet, reduced me to the pitiful state in which it had left this girl.

When I saw her at the inn she was defiant and proud like her father. Yet she had seemed sleepless, drained, even ill. Her eyes had dark, swollen pockets and her hands shook as if life would be taken from her at any moment. I did not think any being could be so thin and fragile yet so disdainfully arrogant. She had become stronger the further we traveled from England, but now she was back to her destitute state. I had to know what grief, or situations, could overcome a person to make them appear in this strange way.

"What did she do to you?" I asked.

Another tearless sob escaped from her. Her face turned upward to lock eyes with mine. At least now the fire had been extinguished from them. She contemplated her answer for a moment while I waited.

"Perhaps someday I will tell someone the whole of it," she whispered. The words were uttered in such an earnest and lonely plea that despite my negative feelings toward her, I found myself wishing, against reason, against logic, that if it were possible, she could confide in me and not perish from the burden. Just then, I noticed a change come over her. She straightened her posture suddenly and became rigid. Her eyes became defiant once again as she yelled, "But it sure as hell will not be you!"

She stomped heavily down the starboard side and down into her cabin. I heard her door slam with fervor. It was wildly disconcerting, but somehow, I could not keep my lips from moving into a smile.

"Captain!" Anderson announced himself.

I turned to face him, irritated. "What is it?"

"Murphy has just reported from the riggings, sir," he stammered.

I braced myself.

"Storm."

I whirled around to stare into the darkened clouds I had been monitoring for days. They had been following us closely. I had hoped they would pass us by, but in vain.

"Prepare the men," I instructed and Anderson departed, yelling his orders to the crew. The frenzy of preparation began.

I ignored the instant response his directions brought about. Crew men sprinted and leapt for their positions. I headed to the cabins, however, because my first responsibility was to warn the passengers.

I took the steps down to the lower barracks and stepped directly into Miss Kensington's cabin without knocking. It irritated me still that she received her own cabin when passengers usually had to share the same space between ten or twenty of them. She was not even aware, I was sure, that she was being treated so well. And all because of her money, which would surely run out soon. My irritation showed as I stepped into her quarters, but she did not see me.

In the corner of her space, she was balled up as tightly as humanly possible. Both hands held the side of her head, intertwined in the short clumps of hair, as she sat perfectly still and silent. Suddenly I felt acutely uncomfortable. I should not have entered.

I had stepped into the lair of a demon.

What could possibly possess a mind to render the body this way? Surely she was exaggerating her troubles in an effort to stand out. There was not enough terror in all of London to force on her this anxious misery. All this I tried to convince myself of, and yet, the logic could not reach my instinct. The demon was screaming inside of her. Perhaps demons afflict many people and the weak scream while the strong stay silent.

The storm was moving. I had to act quickly.

"Miss Kensington, a storm is breaking," I said.

She responded immediately. Her head rose and she stood at attention.

"A storm?" she asked, almost too quiet to hear. "Is it dangerous?"

"It is if you come out of your cabin," I said. "You must remain here until I come to fetch you."

"Oh." Her small face lowered in an anxious expression. She clasped her hands together and looked around her as if the walls would cave in immediately. I had never seen her afraid before.

"You could ask Missus Livingstone if you might share her space," I ventured.

Miss Kensington stared at me with widened eyes, then slowly nodded.

"Gather a few things," I stated. She grabbed only a few items and then followed me out the door. I knocked on Missus Livingstone's door.

Little Robert opened the door with a terrified look on his face. I was about to inquire after their well-being when Miss Kensington jumped between us. In an instant, her arms were around Robert. I turned my attention from them to peer inside the room. Mrs. Livingstone was as white and worn as old sails. *Dysentery.* I knew it well. She lunged for a pail and lurched up gruesome contents from her stomach. Her children sat around the cabin with wide, crying eyes, but their mother was unable to comfort them.

Miss Kensington strode into the room with Robert in her arms, as if she weren't the weakest person aboard the ship. She gathered the children around her and soothed them while pulling back Mrs. Livingstone's hair with calm, collected hands. She was absolutely bewildering.

"Miss Kensington," I began. "The storm will be heavy and will come upon us in no less than an hour. You need to prepare yourself and the children. I must, of a necessity, lock this cabin door until the storm has passed. The rocking of the boat will be drastic and it is unsafe for any of you to be outside of this cabin, or up in your cots, until it has passed. Do you understand?"

"I understand," she spoke clear as day. No sign of her fright remained.

"Stay calm and try to rest," I said to them all. I nodded to Robert in assurance.

After the door was secure I leapt aboard the deck. Anderson would be commended for his speed and discipline. The ship and crew members were in place and prepared for anything. I took a deep breath of satisfaction.

This is why I had become a captain.

Chapter 5

ANNA

Mary was terribly ill. Robert said that she had been sick for days, but had politely excused herself when it became too much to bear. Now she could barely move. Her eyes stared in the general direction of her children, no doubt wanting to watch after them, but being completely unable to do anything but watch.

I had never cared for the sick before. I had visited the sick with Father but he had never allowed me to minister to them. He said my health was his first priority. Now I had only my instincts to rely on. I prayed they would be enough.

In Mary's low water basin, I used the fresh water to rinse and apply a cold wash rag to her neck and forehead. I suddenly wished her doctor husband were traveling with us. She had a high fever. The children were frightened at the sight of her.

Soon, the ship began to rock back and forth so fiercely that little Agnes would have surely been thrown off the cot if Robert had not been there to rescue her again and again. I understood now why the captain had warned us to stay off the cots. The rocking could throw a grown man across the room. Our trunks crashed and broke open again and again. I prepared Mary on a low, makeshift bed on the floor, surrounded by any padding I could find to keep her still. When I was sure she would not roll from the rocking of the boat, I moved to Agnes and Robert and gave them fierce embraces. As I pulled back and looked into their eyes, I remembered from my depths, a song that might soothe them.

"Shall we sing?" I asked quietly. Robert nodded quickly. I placed him on one knee and Agnes on the other as I sat on the floor near Mary's head. Robert was perfectly still, except his shoulders shook in tight sobs. It was so tragic how grown up he was expected to be. I reached a hand out and stroked his head while I sang a song from my childhood.

> There's a lady called Victoria
> who keeps a little school,
> containing many clever boys
> and many a little fool.
> The school is down in Westminster
> an old established one.
> The scholars full of business too
> and often full of fun.

I sang to the children until my voice was hoarse and I simply whispered the words. They fell asleep in my arms, and I would not lay them down. There was no guarantee of survival, nothing to cling to but hope and each other.

The rocking and pitching of the ship was more extreme than I would have supposed. Constantly during the day I would have to brace us against the close walls of the cabin with my legs to keep us from ending up in one giant mound of sleeping flesh. The storm regularly jerked us from our positions, however, despite my efforts.

What I had not expected was the noise! I had never experienced anything this loud before. Mother had certainly yelled before, and her voice was shrill, piercing even, but it was nothing to the roar of a furious sea.

I wondered what would happen to us if the *Madras* were to sink. Would we drown? Suffocate? I remembered the captain had locked the door. Suffocate, then. Perhaps it was the merciful way to die. The thought made my heart race. Robert woke and took his head off my chest to look at me in a questioning way. He could sense my panic. I shook my head at him and held him to me. I could remain calm for him. Slowly my heart slowed and I drifted into a fitful sleep . . .

My worn, and nearly lifeless, frame sat rigid on the front pew of a large cathedral. The bench was hard and uncomfortable to rest on, especially considering I had been there for many hours. Yet I did not move an inch. I had no need to readjust or position myself in an effort to become more comfortable. My body was useless to me now, and my mind wandered as I stared blankly ahead. My spirit had become separated from my body the moment Father had passed away.

A dull, droning voice was giving an elaborate speech of a man I never knew. The man he described was nothing like my father. No one in this tightly packed cathedral knew him above half. They were present because this was the fashionable place to be: the funeral of a duke.

A sharp, familiar elbow lodged between my ribs. I looked around myself. The man had finished talking and my part had come to place the roses on Father's casket. It had become the latest thing for the daughters to lay flowers on the casket of their fathers. The minds of these people were truly backwards.

Unspeakable agony began its journey in my stomach and climbed slowly up to my heart, crushing it without mercy. My mind was numb as I stood and walked, dazed, toward the wooden box that held all my freedom locked tightly inside. Mother would not allow an open casket.

I have no real recollection of climbing the small steps. Hundreds of mute spectators watched my every move, unfeeling. I placed red and white roses on the black box. My tears created a pattern around the pretty set. I had tied them with a blue ribbon, the color of a land we would never know, in painful irony.

At once, my mind was alert. My eyes opened slowly while my arms remained immovable in their position around the little ones. I turned my gaze slowly to the door. The captain was dominating the small door frame in an effort to assess our situation. His exhausted blue eyes had dark patches underneath them and his shoulders were hunched.

"How is Mrs. Livingstone?" he whispered.

I reached over to feel Mary's head.

"She has slept most of this time. Her fever is lessened," I said quietly.

Suddenly I realized it was silent outside.

"The storm has passed," I said amazed.

"Yes," the captain replied. "Not more than a half hour ago."

"What time is it?" I asked

"It is morning. Back to the time I left you. Almost twenty-four hours," he stated.

Twenty-four hours. I had been singing and sleeping a shorter time than I had thought. Gratitude swelled in my throat.

"Thank you for keeping them safe," I murmured, breathing a sigh of relief.

The captain gave me a strange look, and then left the cabin without locking the door. I assumed we were free to move about.

As gently as I was able, I laid Agnes and Robert in the family's cot and departed. I desperately needed to breathe some fresh air. The cabin had become muggy and thick in such a small enclosed space. All I could smell was the evidence of Mary's illness.

I mounted the deck and surveyed the disaster. Several of the sails had broken down and were laying in piles of disarray on the deck. The sailmaker was working on mending them in a flooded corner. He could not avoid the water at his feet, however. The deck was covered in at least six inches of murky liquid. Most of the crew worked with pails, buckets or anything that would contain the mess to throw it over the side.

The sea was uncommonly still. An uneasy, scared, and restless, feeling had settled upon the crew members. I moved to the mess hall and encountered the crew man who was mostly in control of the supplies.

"Good sir," I said, "where is the ship's physician?"

"Physician?" he repeated "There is no doctor on board, Miss. Captain works as ship's doctor when needed, but he is with First Mate Anderson now."

"Anderson?" I inquired. "What happened? Is he all right?"

"A beam, thrown by the wind, pommeled him in the stomach," he described grimly. "We got the beam out all right, but the captain said a large wooden chip remains in his gut."

Poor, unfortunate Anderson. The effects of the storm had been more severe than I had realized. I recalled my mission.

"Mary Livingstone is sick with dysentery. Do you happen to know something that would help her?"

"Arrowroot," he replied quickly. "It is in these biscuits. And she'll also be needing beef tea, which I would be happy to help you with, Miss." He handed me the arrowroot biscuits and tipped his cap in my direction.

"I would be ever so grateful," I told him truly. "I shall be back for the tea."

I rushed to Mary's cabin and lifted her head onto my lap. Robert was playing a clapping game with his sister. I shook their mother slightly and gave her the biscuit, bit by bit, until it was fully consumed. She rolled back to her former position a little more content, I thought.

Next my attentions turned to the children. They had not eaten for a day, and yet they did not complain. They were warriors among men. I toted them both together with me and we mounted the stairs. I retrieved for them our typical breakfast. As the crewman handed the large bowl of tea for Mary, I did not think it looked like a tea at all, but rather like soup. I left Agnes with Robert as I took it to Mary and awoke her again to spoon-feed the contents to her.

After Mary and the children were all fed, I ventured out onto the ship, past those who were working to fix the sails, and in the direction of the captain's cabin.

As I slowly stepped toward the captain's door, inhuman groans caught my ears. I raised my hand to turn the knob when I heard the captain's frantic voice and Anderson's terrible sounds.

"More hands to me NOW!"

I pushed the door open.

Blood covered the floor surrounding the captain and his patient. A lantern hung disturbingly still above their heads. Captain had both hands on First Mate Anderson's stomach as he twisted and turned gruesomely. A large block of wood was in Anderson's mouth to hold in his sounds, but it wasn't working. His gray hair crumpled back and forth on his sweaty brow as he thrashed his head in an effort to stand the pain. A young lieutenant stood, frozen in shock, his hands holding him upright against the operating table as the captain dug for the foreign object in Anderson's belly. A fog of nausea swept over me as I braced myself on the doorframe. The captain's feet slipped in the thickness of the blood on the floor.

"Salt!" he ordered, "we need salt!"

My mind could not unravel these simple words. Salt? In the wound, possibly? I looked around myself, searching for salt.

"Now, man!" the captain hollered as he continued to push on the first mate's stomach, but the lieutenant stood in silence, seemingly unable to move.

My mind recalled a time when a thin layer of ice had covered the front steps of my mother's house. A footman had used salt to make the area more easily traversable.

I leapt at a large bag that I hoped would contain what the captain sought. My guess was fortunate. I took large handfuls of salt and threw them at the Captain's feet and then at the feet of the frozen lieutenant. The pools of blood instantly soaked up the salt during its first few doses, but after a time, the captain could stand without slipping. To cover more space, and because First Mate Anderson's cries were becoming more desperate, I took the bag by the corners and threw it to the ground with full force. The bag spilled forth its remaining contents and I kicked them around the room. Through all this, the captain's eyes were focused on something in Anderson's gut and he had not perceived me. It is my belief, to this day, that this captain originated the phrase "curse like a sailor." The young lieutenant would not move no matter what threats or warnings were shouted at him from the captain.

I grabbed the arm of the lieutenant and threw him, possibly harder than the situation warranted, into a small sofa against the wall of the cabin. He did not even blink. He would do Anderson no good by being catatonic, so I stood in his place.

"Take this," the captain said. He held up long prongs for me to take, which were covered in dark blood. I took them mechanically. At the sight of my white hand, the captain finally looked up.

"No, no, NO!" His voice became progressively louder as he shouted. Fire burned in his eyes.

"Stop! Please!" I cried above the screams of the first mate. "No arguments now. Help him! I beg of you!" The sweet old man twisting in such terrible pain afflicted my feelings greatly. Tears of frustration coursed down my cheeks.

He flexed his jaw and glared at me. After a pregnant moment, he returned to his work.

"Whiskey," he said gruffly. I glanced around the room in a daze. My mind had become stupefied from the sight of so much blood. The room tilted on its side and would not right itself. I stamped my foot in frustration. At last, I could see a tall bottle of the stuff on his desk. I dashed for it and held Anderson's head up only slightly, giving him several small gulps. After I finished, the captain spoke.

"In the wound as well."

I glanced up at him, afraid. He did not return my gaze. I swallowed thickly. Before this, I had not seen blood, save my own, and I had never seen innards. I did not know if I had the strength to see the effects of the whiskey on Anderson's already suffering midsection. I felt so very sick from the sight and smell, but at the same time, I saw I was needed. I tipped the bottle and closed my eyes for a moment as Anderson's cries were seared into my memory. I then used the awful stuff to wash the captain's hands. Anderson continued screaming wretchedly.

Finally, the captain saw what he had been searching for. It was a large splint of wood, perhaps the width of his hand. He retrieved the long prongs from me and pulled the wood out. Once it was free from Anderson's gut, he moved to a reading table where the majority of the beam sat. He moved delicately as he placed the missing piece into the beam. It was a perfect fit. No other shards were missing. He closed his eyes and breathed in deeply, then returned to Anderson and me.

"I'm going to put him back together," he said. "You are going to have to watch and use the whiskey to clean."

I nodded emphatically. There could be no mistakes. He gestured to his desk.

"Get the needle and thread."

I went to retrieve the items. When I saw them, I had to breathe calmly several times before I could function again. Several hooks, needles, and other metal contraptions were laid out on a leather patch. So many odd shaped metals used for medical practices I knew nothing about. The needle and thread alone looked as if they were used for horses and cattle, they were so frighteningly thick. I returned with the items.

"You'll hold his sides together," he commanded. "Squeeze his middle tightly so I can have both hands free."

A sob escaped me. I dreaded the thought of coming into such close contact with Anderson's mutilated insides. The captain's head spun around to survey me with distaste.

"Anyone within the sound of my voice come to me now!" he boomed. But no one was close. All were busy with the mending of the ship, and quite possibly could not hear him over the cries of Anderson. After a few moments of silent sobs and wretches into my arm, I was somewhat calm again. Anderson's cries pushed me forward. I reached across the table to place one hand on the other side of him. I used my other arm and the rest of my body to hold the other half of the man as the captain began stitching. The old man's skin was terribly cold and clammy. However, compared to the captain digging through his middle, the stitching must not have been as painful. First Mate Anderson finally quieted, as the whiskey took its affect.

I was close to the Captain as he took small and deliberate stitches into Anderson's skin. To avoid looking down into Anderson's belly, I focused on the captain's face. Why did he need to know what I'd suffered? He knew my mother, couldn't he perceive what an evil disposition she could have? Why could no one see it and understand? Did he truly fall victim to her falsehoods? How could he? He seemed capable and intelligent, yet he fell to her guile as swiftly as the rest. He must be a fool just like the rest of them.

Several times, he stopped sewing, closed his eyes, and took a long and deep breath in, and then slowly out again. Then he would continue stitching. I did not feel any amount of breathing would calm me. I was still panicked and angry, but I tried to keep from shaking.

I knew he was doing what was necessary for Anderson. I knew he did not mean to torture him or make him uncomfortable. This was his only chance of survival. Still I wondered if he cared as much for Anderson as I did, and if he didn't want my help because I was a woman or because it was *me*.

The last stitch was administered, another dose of whiskey given to Anderson, and clean linens wrapped around his middle. I finally sat next to the shocked lieutenant on the sofa, craning my head as far away from the captain, and the smell, as I could manage. I closed my eyes as long minutes ticked by on the captain's clock. Hate, fear, and sickness consumed me.

Father loosened the bandage on my upper arm and inspected the burns. There were several small ones, all circled around one that was very large. I craned my neck to look away. In truth, the burns didn't hurt any longer. I simply could not look on the physical evidence that my mother did not love me, that she never had loved me. She was as happy to be rid of me as she would be a parasite. She would rather I be consumed in an awful fire than to burn one of her purchases. I could not keep the tears from my eyes.

Father thought I was crying in pain. "It is all right," he soothed. "They are even better now than they were yesterday. There may be a small scar, but you need not worry."

I turned to face him in anguish.

"Why does she hate me, Father? Why does she hurt me?" I sobbed uncontrollably. The motions shook my weak frame.

I remember Father's face clearly: helplessness, hurt, and rage.

If wooden splints were lodged inside of me, would she have worked at all to retrieve them? Would she have cared if the wood moved slowly along my veins and finally reached my heart? Perhaps she cared naught for small burns, but what if I had been in real danger? Would she have rushed to save me? I had asked questions like these thousands of times, although I knew the answer.

No. She would not move to save me, even if my life were in danger.

I opened my eyes to escape my mind. The tears ran, liberated, down my cheeks.

My gaze wandered listless around the room and almost subconsciously locked with the captain's across the room. He held a much different expression.

Pity.

Chapter 6

Days began to blend together as we were all lost in hard work. The sailmaker and crewmen hardly slept as they repaired the sails and mast. Slowly, the flooring of the *Madras* became dry again and signs of the storm began to pass.

Mary continued to improve. There were two more nights of terrible illness and delirium, but soon she was herself again. The reunion of the children with their true mother pulled at my heart. Mary thanked me for my help. She said although it was a terrible ordeal, she felt stronger and more lively for it. As for myself, despite being part of a traumatic surgery, on a battered ship in the middle of an ocean, I confess I had never been so happy.

First Mate Anderson spent long days recovering and leaving the captain bereft of his fine whiskey. From time to time, I would seek him out in the comfort of his cabin. He was so still, I wondered if I would find him dead on one of my visits. The risk of infection still threatened, a tall, dark figure in the corner that could steal him away.

Once, I pushed the door open to peek inside and saw the captain sitting on a small chair in a corner, his head in his hands. My mind imagined the worst. He may still have been upset with me for helping when he had wanted someone with experience. I may not have done the job well enough, and Anderson may be suffering because of it. Anderson made a movement and the captain jumped from his seat to administer to him. I quietly exited. I would never have imagined the captain in a sick room.

In the midst of all of this, the *Madras* was not moving in the slightest. Lieutenant Warley reassured us by saying it was natural to be motionless after a storm. Still, it was an unsettling feeling being on a ship that did not rock or pull with the waves. We hardly spoke. We hardly moved. We prayed for change.

A quiet panic had settled on the citizens of our small island, and my mind began to wander. What would happen to a ship without wind nor waves? What if we had discovered some section of sea that never moved, never progressed? Soon we would be out of food, and starvation and sickness would begin. Would the crew find someone to blame? I suppose if I thought one person were responsible for hurting Mary and her family, I might be tempted to throw them overboard, no matter their history or innocence.

Three full days passed. The crew busied themselves with scrubbing the deck again and again. Mary toted a metal wash basin to the deck and filled it with water, allowing it to be warmed by the sun. Robert and Agnes splashed in the small space until they were perfectly clean and giggling. It was wonderful to watch. Mary and I also took turns with the basin in the cabins, using the tub to wash our scalps and faces.

That evening, Mary and I sat on the deck, all cleaned and dry, supervising as the children played at hide-and-seek. The crew did not approve, but did not interfere with our fun. Mary and I sat in easy conversation while I darned my worn dress and she knitted a proper shirt for Agnes.

Suddenly Robert came up to the deck in a panic.

"Momma! Momma! Help Agnes! She's stuck!" he yelled, breathless. Mary dropped her knitting and ran to the place Robert directed. I followed close behind. Robert huddled by the closed door of a storage closet with tears in his eyes. On the other side of the door I could hear Agnes pounding and scratching on the wooden panels of the door. Apparently, Agnes had hidden in the closet and had pulled down the wooden latch to lock the door, but now the latch would not let up and she could not escape the darkness.

The flooding from the storm must have warped the door, or damaged the latch. Mary instructed Robert to find a crewmember, and as Robert went away, Mary attempted to soothe Agnes from the other side of the door with no success. The little girl was frantic and likely filled with slivers and splinters from pounding the door.

My mind flashed to a childhood memory without my consent.

I was locked in my bedroom, unable to escape. Somewhere outside, people I loved were being hurt. I screamed again and again, but no amount of cries would reach my mother's stone-cold ears. She had abandoned me, and no one in the world could come to my aid.

Dark terror filled my heart as I remembered the solitude. Within this mortal frame, being locked in a room was the most helpless I had ever felt.

I refused to believe that there was no one to rescue Agnes. Her cries echoed my own. Every abuse, every unkindness, and every piece of neglect came at me all at once. There was no room that could contain my anger, no walls, doors, or any barrier that could control the hostility that filled me.

I found my voice and rushed to the rough wood of the door.

"Get back! Move away!" I screamed. My voice was warning Agnes. My heart was threatening my mother.

I rushed at the door, breaking the warped latch with my shoulder. I stood in the small closet, breathing heavily for a moment before I rushed to Agnes and savagely held her in my arms as she wept on my shoulder. Luckily, she had heeded my warning and had moved out of the way. We sobbed together, and Mary looked at me with new understanding on her face.

After what seemed a long, healing eternity, we broke apart and Agnes went to her mother. I still felt the pulsing strength rejuvenating every muscle in me. I felt as if I could move a mountain by sheer force, or dig at the wood under my feet and reach the ocean. The fervor in my muscles could pull this ship through hurricanes.

Only then did I look down the hall. I saw some of the ship's management and a handful of crew members looking on with somber faces. They had seen me crash through the door and sob with Agnes. I must have looked savage. The captain stood at the front of the group, staring.

The men gave me a wide berth as I entered my cabin and closed the door. I wanted to scream. But I knew the entire crew was standing just outside. I bit a quilt in my agitation and attempted to stay quiet as I bitterly sobbed away my childhood. The event that I had worked hardest to suppress clawed its way to the surface . . .

Father and I walked in the forest until we came upon a small, decrepit cottage on our estate. A man who had once worked as Father's steward had recently passed away, and Father had gone to visit his widow. Mother had tried to keep it from Father, but a footman had betrayed her trust and slipped him a note. Now, walking into the woods, it was as if I were stepping into another reality. I had not known there was anyone living in this part of the estate. Father knocked, and when there was no reply, he let himself in.

The space inside was no bigger than my bed. That was one thing Mother had always given me, a nice bedroom. She did not want there to be any solid evidence that she treated me badly in case anyone were to suspect her. Now I would gladly drag my bed and all my possessions to this small dwelling with nothing but my shaky hands.

This woman had nothing. Literally nothing.

In a corner of the room a rough hole had been drilled out of the dirt to make a small fire pit, which had obviously not seen fire for weeks, despite the freezing cold. Another corner had been dug out to be used as a latrine. The smell frightened me in a way I didn't think I could ever be frightened. I didn't know people lived this way.

As we stepped into the dwelling, she lifted her eyes from her lap and into my father's face and smiled weakly. "Praise be to God, who is truly merciful," she whispered.

I saw then that she did indeed have something to call her own.

A child.

The baby girl cooed and smiled at us from the crook of her mother's arm. Father began to inquire in hushed tones if she had any family or friends who could take her in. I only heard bits of their conversation. My eyes were fixed on the little girl. How could someone so small be surviving on the living her mother was making? How had they survived? Later, it was discovered Mother had taken their possessions as soon as the steward had passed. The young mother resembled a bare skeleton a tutor had shown me once in a book. There was no flesh left to rest on her weary bones. The baby was not starving, but looked like she soon might be.

Instinctively, I reached my hands out to hold the girl.

"May I hold her?" I asked.

The mother consented and handed me the precious bundle. Father instructed me to play with the little girl in the other corner while he saw to the mother. While the baby girl and I played and bounced, Father set up a situation for the mother and child in a cottage closer to the main house, one he knew was well insulated for the coming winter. He would supply food and water there until he could find her a more stable situation.

"Thank you, dear Duke," she murmured humbly.

Father picked up her frail form and carried her to the cottage while I carried the little girl.

The baby's name was Anna.

I knew the ending to this story. My mind had betrayed me and let the flood gates open. Was it my anger that had broken the dam? I was too tired to speculate. There was still nothing I could do but curl up as tightly as my limbs would allow me and cry till my body was bereft of moisture.

After many hours, I peeked timidly out the door of my cabin. It was morning again. I was uncertain how to approach everyone after such an emotional scene. The captain was waiting for me on the deck.

"Good morning, Miss Kensington," he greeted me.

"Good morning, sir," I responded as cordially as I could. I was amazed at my weariness. I was too tired to be angry or confused with him.

"I hope, Miss Kensington, that you did not sustain any injury," he said.

I was taken aback.

"What?" I asked plainly, dazed into a slight trance. Had his eyes always been that blue?

He stared at me confused, then stammered.

"The door." He gestured automatically toward the general direction of the closet door Agnes had been trapped in not hours ago. Apparently not knowing what else to say to jog my memory.

"Oh," I recollected. "No, I am not injured."

"That is good news," he said hesitantly.

I turned my attention to the ocean. I couldn't think of anything to say.

"She was not in any real danger, you know," the captain said suddenly. "Only afraid of a closed space."

"I am well aware," I said, looking away.

"And still you felt the need to rescue her?" he asked.

I nodded.

"Why?"

I stared into his blue eyes. What had made him so sincere? Perhaps he could only respect women with fierce brute strength. I smiled weakly at the thought. His eyes questioned my smile and then I remembered his inquiry.

"Because . . . no one was there to save me," I said. I was too tired to realize I was now confessing.

"But her mother was there," the captain said, persisting. "And I was on my way. Why did you rush?"

I considered his question for a moment.

"I suppose because of my own memories," I said. "I hardly remember actually breaking the door, I just remember the need to save her." I paused and looked up at him. He looked slightly angry all of a sudden.

A realization hit me. "Oh!" I spluttered quickly. "Oh, I am sorry, Captain, I just now realize I quite possibly broke the door beyond repair. Oh, I—I do apologize," I stammered, embarrassed. "I will have it replaced, I promise you."

"No," he scoffed as I looked up, "that is not why I am angry."

I felt as if I were missing some large part of our conversation, and I looked at him, perplexed. He shook himself physically before he continued.

"Miss Kensington, I must apologize for our conversation before the storm," he paused. "If you are in need of some kind of explanation, and if a confession would encourage your forgiveness, then I would say that, I too, was pushed forward by my memories."

I stared at him in disbelief. What was happening?

He seemed agitated and uncomfortable waiting for my response. Finally, I said, "All my life, at every party I was forced to attend, I've been told how to stand, eat, behave. I suppose when you advised me, I retaliated to you in the way I wish I should have retaliated to all those who would belittle and direct me heedlessly."

He looked up into my face, and I could have gasped out loud at the intensity of his gaze. Then he looked down at his shoes and nodded softly.

"Thank you, Miss Kensington," he bowed, eyes still downcast. "There is nothing to forgive in your words if they were meant for those who have abused you."

"Thank you," was all I could say.

Sometimes it was difficult to separate my memories from what was happening in the moment. But I didn't think even my distorted head could have come up with that conversation.

He abruptly changed the subject. "I hope you will forgive me if I feel I must persist in endeavoring to help you when we reach our destination." He paused. "The country we are arriving into is . . . unforgiving. You will need every resource available to you to survive there." My heart gave a small leap of fear at the use of the word *survive*. "Please allow me to disclose our destination and how we, Mrs. Livingstone and I, can help you."

I considered his words for a moment.

"Well then," I said hesitantly, "where are we going, Captain?"

He did not smile. "Africa."

I gasped, and a light wind brushed my face. The *Madras* was moving again. A promise of good things to come. Through clouds of uncertainty, I could feel God smile.

Soon everyone was bustling, preparing for our final leg into our berth. Is there anyone more eager than those who have been stagnant and suddenly given motion? It appeared sailors are particularly keen on movement. Their excitement was exhilarating! Grown men leapt as nimbly as monkeys to the top sails to release them from captivity, then swung down on ropes as if they were vines. What a spectacle they made!

The captain ordered a special treat to be delivered to us all. The ship's cook had made delectable doughnuts, covered in sugar, to celebrate our voyage's end. The cook had been holding out on us, and had been saying we were out of sugar for days now. The children, Mary, and I took our first bite all at once. After weeks of biscuits, stale tea, and stew, I was sure I had never had anything more delightful in all of London. I closed my eyes to savor the bite.

I felt relief knowing a bright future was ahead of me, but I was still so very tired from all the emotions that had coursed through me. I dragged my feet behind me as I left the mess hall and out onto the deck to spend some time in the sun before it set.

Chapter 7

It had taken us twelve weeks to sail from London to a town in the south of Africa called Durban. My ignorance of the continent on Africa was immense. I could tell you every cut of the sleeve Her Majesty, the Queen of England, had ever worn, but I could not tell you a thing about an entire continent of souls. Since Mother was so concerned with my privacy, I never had a tutor or teacher for longer than six months at a time. None of them had enlightened my mind on this subject.

As I prepared myself for the day, I wondered at the mysteries that lay ahead of me. The captain, Mary, and Lieutenant Warley had been informing me of what they knew of the continent. Mary was the most helpful, having been born and raised in a place called Kuruman, not far from Durban. Her parents were missionaries like her husband. They established Kuruman as a mission and raised it from the ground up. There were gardens, fruit trees, economy, and even roads.

She surprised me at her pride in the town having roads. Weren't there roads everywhere?

The captain focused on informing me of the dangers of Africa. There were wild animals in abundance. People died every day from animal attacks, starvation, and a lack of water. Not to mention the slave trade that was growing in strength and range. The stories he told me added to my nightmares. Now, in my dreams, after Mother had terrorized me, I would be taken screaming from Father by heartless, cruel men and made to work alongside little children in hot, dry fields. When I would push the captain to know how he came to know these things, he would avoid the question or simply walk away.

Lieutenant Warley focused on the positive, as usual. He talked about how there are numerous different terrains and they are all beautiful in their own way. There are mountains, plains, gorges, and waterfalls. The people are family oriented and adore their children. In the city you can see them making and selling jewelry with their little ones strapped to their backs and a giant load of fruit on their heads. I told Warley I had a teacher once as a child that made me balance a book on my head to try and teach me balance and grace. That made him laugh.

"Wait until you see the amount these women balance. You'll be astonished, I promise you."

"And when will I get to see this balancing act?"

Lieutenant Warley estimated we would land at high noon the next day. We had been seeing land for some time now, but continued onto the port for which we were destined. What would these people think of my now tattered clothes and short hair? What if they were unkind? I knew they were not expecting me. How would they react to a new obligation, someone who was absolutely useless in practical living?

It did not take me long to collect my few items. I carried them myself and mounted the deck for the last time. The captain was standing on the helm, staring out in the water.

I stood on the deck with all that I owned lying at my feet. Mary and the children stood with me. All of us looked toward that small piece of land that would soon be home. I had no plans to return to my native country. In fact, if I returned to London, it would have to be through extreme force. I would move forward. Even if moving forward was difficult, it would prove easier than moving backward.

Soon we could see Durban. As we slid into view, the city draped in front of us like a smooth curtain being drawn at evening. I was amazed that the town came directly up to the water. There was one detail that took me off guard—the town was absolutely ordinary. The buildings were short, low to the ground, in a typical brick design.

Small windows remained open, I guessed, most of the time. Flowers were on verandas, mothers walked along the beach with their children, vendors and market places lined the narrow streets. When the captain had told me we were landing in Africa, my mind's eye had imagined large bonfires with natives in full celebratory dress performing traditional dances along the shores. Durban was small, but seemingly hospitable. I breathed a sigh of relief. And there were several women with the fruit on their heads! I smiled in appreciation.

In the midst of my speculations, I was particularly drawn to one face. A tall, lanky man was walking toward the shore. He wore a loose white smock against strong shoulders and simple trousers above bare feet. He was calm and dedicated and seemed to me about fifty years of age. As we drew closer, I could see a distinct determination in his face, as if walking were the most important of his day-to-day functions. I had never experienced such determination in anything I had ever done. What was his existence like? Was he well treated by others? Was he a leader? What were his experiences? Surely no one could reach his age and not accompany heartache with some happiness. His mind must be filled with memories that I could not begin to guess at. He was utterly unique. All this I noticed after I realized his skin was the blackest I had ever seen.

I liked him.

A wind built up and swept across my face. God had directed me to this exact spot for a purpose. Whether that purpose was known to me or not, did not matter in the slightest! Knowing that I was in the place God meant me to be in this very moment filled my aching heart. I could have stayed in that moment for all eternity, feeling loved and honored.

"There he is! There he is!" Robert jerked at my hand as he shouted at an incredible volume.

I broke my gaze and turned it into the general direction of Robert's exclamations. A sturdy man stood on the very edge of the beach. His broad rimmed hat covered his weathered face and shook as he waved his arm in anticipation of the *Madras's* occupants.

"Daddy!" Robert called.

Mary's head cocked affectionately to the side as she surveyed her husband.

"David," she pronounced reverently.

Fortunately, Robert did not have to sit idle for long. A heavy anchor plunged into the deep and at long last, we were there. Several crew members manned smaller ships to take us to shore.

Standing a small distance behind David was the middle-aged man with dark skin I had seen walking along the beach. He had dark curly hair that was cropped short and I could see even from several yards away was beginning to gray at the temples. He wore a hat like David's, which effectively protected him from the rays of the sun. He wore a white tunic and trousers in simple, light colors. I got the distinct impression that he was not a servant or slave to David, but a loyal companion, an impression that was confirmed later. A distinct nod passed between him and Mary, a mutual respect, almost a kinship.

David squatted down to the level of his running children and caught them up in his arms. Robert squeezed his father so fiercely his arms shook with the excitement. Memories of reunions identical to this, with my father, played over in my mind. I felt more happiness for Robert than sadness for myself. Perhaps I had finally found some measure of healing.

Agnes caught up at long last and timidly hugged David, whom she had not seen for a year. It was possible she was simply mirroring Robert's excitement at seeing their father. I wondered if she remembered him at all. She was already inspecting him uneasily, a wary eye set on his large, brown mustache. Out of David's eyes came large tears—in response, I supposed, to their grown faces. Suddenly, he stood and turned all his attention to Mary. In that moment I felt intrusive to their privacy, even standing five yards away. What love and tenderness passed between them in a single glance! The world could have passed away in fire around them and I felt convinced they would not arrest their gaze until they were ready. Trust and compassion flowed between them like a strong and steady beacon of light. I knew that many things were going to be new and foreign to me on this new continent, yet this was the most foreign of all: true, real love between a man and a woman.

I ducked my head away in embarrassment. The sun was straight above me and the shine glistened off the water while the *Madras* looked stalwart on the soft current. It was peculiar to look on the ship from this position. It had come through the storm unharmed, and possibly even better than when it had started the journey, and it was satisfying. Improved. Sturdy.

I thought of our misery during some moments of the voyage. If only I could have reached back in time and told everyone on board that we were going to arrive here safely! If only I could have assured Mary's children that Mary would get sick, but she would heal! If only I could have touched the long planks of the *Madras* and told her she would make it here in one piece. But then, what faith would we have needed? Would we really have been better off flipping the pages and arriving at the last pages of the story?

Several more boats were coming back to the dock with other loads of supplies and passengers.

"Anna," Mary said to call me back. I turned my attention to her.

"May I introduce you to my husband, David Livingstone," she introduced him. "And to our good friend and fellow missionary, Mebalwe." She gestured to the native man who stepped forward to shake my hand warmly. When he smiled, his eyes sparkled. I smiled warmly at him and David.

"It is such a pleasure to meet you, David and Mebalwe," I spoke formally.

Mebalwe did not speak English, so David translated my greeting and he smiled again.

David shook my hand. "The pleasure is all mine, Anna. Mary was telling me of your help to my family during a storm and some illness. I can say I am very grateful to you."

"I am hoping, sir, that your gratitude may assist me," I hedged.

He looked at me perplexed. Mary interceded.

"Anna is needing a place to stay, I had hoped she might accompany us to Kolobeng, and be a help to us in our work."

"Kolobeng is not a safe place for single women," David responded.

"Anna is becoming incredibly capable," Mary defended me. "Her practical skills will need to be improved, but I feel sure she will be ready to help me with my duties. I should like some help."

David was looking doubtful as he looked at my hands. They had not seen hard work. I tucked them behind my back.

"I do not mean to put you in a difficult situation, sir," I said. "If there was any other occupation open to me I would take it." I looked at Agnes in his arms. "Even then, sir, I should be saddened to leave these children and Mary."

He regarded me differently, turning something over in his mind.

"You see, my dear," Mary spoke to her spouse, "she is determined. As am I."

David mulled it over in his mind for a moment.

"Miss Anna and I have something in common," he said, surprising me. "She and I have trouble being separated from this group." He smiled. "Let me speak with Mary." Mary took his arm and led him a way off.

I began to gather all of our luggage and the children around me. Mebalwe quickly jumped to my aid, and together we took slow trips to the wagon with the children until the wagon was full and we were ready to embark. I could sense already that Mebalwe was a very easy soul to be around. There was one last trunk to be loaded and when I reached for it, Mebalwe waved his hand at me. For a moment I thought he was saying "hello," but then he rushed over and took the trunk from my hands, loading it in the wagon himself.

Robert, Agnes, and Mebalwe settled down in the shade of the wagon. I was amazed as Robert began rattling off in their common native language of Sechuana.

"I must tell Mebalwe of my many travels," Robert explained to me. I smiled as I walked toward the crew to say goodbye.

A small group of the crewman walked directly toward me. I had only spoken with them in passing, but I was ashamed to say I did not know many of their names. Several of them took off their caps as they approached. I thanked them for their service with a handshake.

"Thank you for your hard work, gentlemen! I do indeed appreciate your efforts!"

Nothing. No expression, no words, no response whatsoever to my voice. Their fatigue must finally be showing, I thought. I turned to the man who had given me arrowroot for Mary, and repeated my thanks to him.

"I appreciate your help when Mary was sick. I never got a chance to thank you." He, at least, had an expression. His face was afraid. I turned perplexed to Lieutenant Warley, who had made his way to my side.

"Anna," Lieutenant Warley began, "the crew and I would like you to return with us."

"Return?" I turned to witness the men whose opinion was being stated for them. They all nodded solemnly.

"We have all discussed it," he continued. "We have, each of us, seen what this country does to grown men. We cannot bear the guilt that would come with allowing a young girl to traverse this land with no prior experience. Please return to England and we will all work to find you a new situation there."

"But Mary—" I defended, "Mary has led most of her life here, and she believes me to be capable."

"It is not that we doubt your strength, Anna," Warley expressed. "It is that this land *changes* people. It is different for Mary because she was born here. You cannot possibly imagine what you are going to be subjected to. We will protect you if you would allow it. We will make London a safe place for you again."

He was so confident, so sure that he could confront and fight that silent monster from which I fled. The man whom I trusted most in the world could not halt her. No one ever would. No man could defeat a dragon that didn't roar.

Every person besides Father and myself had thought her perfectly amiable. Several times I had tried to confide in my closest friends at the abuse I endured at home and they had laughed me to scorn. Several said that I must be wrong, that Mother was the most agreeable woman in town!

I felt some disbelief at these men's sudden need to protect me, but I also felt appreciation. Men whose names I had not even bothered remembering had communed together to defend me.

"I cannot tell you how grateful I am," I told them, my eyes threatening to overflow. I took a moment to collect myself. "I run from oppression. It cannot be killed, but I am indeed grateful to you for offering to try."

I looked into their faces, willing them to understand. They did. One crewman whom I had always taken for one of the most intimidating creatures I had ever beheld was biting the inside of his lip in an effort to not appear emotional.

"Then we would like to give you this, ma'am," one sailor spoke as he stepped toward me. He placed in my hand a white bracelet, made with the fine white line I had seen them use on the *Madras*. The delicate rope had been tied into thousands of minuscule square knots to form a sort of lace pattern. A small buckle held the piece together.

"Thank you," I said, breathless. I took my time with each man now, shaking his hand in mine and then laying another hand atop theirs.

"Please do try to stay out of harm's way," Lieutenant Warley said fretfully.

"I will not be running into the face of trouble, that much I will promise you," I returned.

He smiled weakly as he shook my hand.

Suddenly, the captain was beside me. I turned to him.

"And you, Captain? Are you not worried about this English damsel being swept up in her African adventures?" I gestured dramatically. No one laughed.

He peered down on me for five heavy seconds, and then looked away as he spoke.

"Do not watch the hopo," was all he said.

"The hopo . . . ?" I looked questioningly to Lieutenant Warley, who shrugged his shoulders. "What is the hopo?"

"Just don't watch," he responded curtly. His entire frame turned with a jerk and he tromped down the beach, his broad shoulders unmoving. I stared after him for a moment before I turned back to Warley to bid adieu.

David and Mary arrived at the wagon at the precise moment I did. I had seen my share of large carriages, but I imagined this cart could fit Mother's entire chaise in its depths. It was enormous—a fact I would be grateful for in the coming weeks. It was driven by ten oxen, in two lines ahead of us. If I had any trepidation as to the size of the wagon, it was nothing in comparison to the size of the oxen. What large beasts they were! I had never been near one before, and the sheer mass of them was truly startling to me. Mary began to load Agnes into the wagon with Robert right behind her.

"Do you think," I asked Robert as I ducked down to his level, "if that ox were to sneeze, and I were nearby, he would crush me as he would a dried leaf?"

Robert laughed in delight. "Oxen are nice, Anna! Look!" Without warning he ran up next to the closest ox and placed both hands on its belly in an attempt at a hug, although his little arms could not reach even a fourth of the animal's waist.

"Oh yes, very nice. I see. Now come back," I urged. He laughed at my nerves.

Turning around, we noticed a small group of individuals observing us in a peculiar way. There were three men, a woman, and a boy that had to be about Robert's age. None of them were smiling. They stood with proud postures although their clothes suggested hard work and long hours in the heat. Their eyes were as frightened and hostile as I had ever seen. All of their attention was focused on us, contempt heavy in the air. I looked down at my dress, thinking maybe I had become immodest or unclean.

"Hello," I ventured. In reaction to my greeting, there were several responses. Robert inched closer to me and buried his face in my skirts, Mebalwe took a step to place himself between us and the strangers, and Mary and David turned around at the sound of my voice. In the midst of the group of strangers, a man edged his way to the front, his face old and his thin fingers clenching his removed coat.

He was their leader, I was sure.

The strangers looked at me with anger. Even the child seemed hostile. They did not return my greeting. Instead, the leader turned around and they all followed suit, walking in the opposite direction.

I stared after them. Mebalwe watched them with a cautious look. David hurried after them.

"Abraham," he spoke loud enough for the man with the thin fingers to hear. He trotted a couple steps and tried to step in their way but they simply brushed past him. David stopped his efforts and sighed, then turned to us.

"It's time to go."

The children and I nestled in between pieces of luggage and supplies in the bed of the wagon, David and Mary sat up near the front lip of the vehicle, and Mebalwe walked alongside, encouraging and directing the oxen. I watched southern Africa slide by me like a picture. Immediately after the dock and the beach was the push and pull of the city. I was surprised to find ours was not the largest wagon in the area. Massive oxen and ever larger wagons squeezed in between aisles of buildings. The locals barely noticed the giant animals maneuvering their way around. When approached by one, they simply moved out of its way. It was not peculiar to them, but I admit I held my breath for fear they would be hurt by the beasts. Did they not worry that the ox would misstep and crush them instantly? Eventually, I forced myself to breathe evenly despite the panic I felt.

As the wagon went along, the sun was sometimes blocked by the shade of a large tavern or a place of lodging. No material covered the bare road, and the dirt swirled around us in patterns that would have been entertaining if they didn't make breathing more difficult.

Then there were the women Lieutenant Warley had spoken of. I thought he had exaggerated when he spoke of the load they carried on their heads, but now I saw he had understated the truth. A young lady, who could not have been larger than me, and certainly looked my same age, was dressed in many colorful layers draped over her shoulders and across her hips. Beads dangled at her wrists and ankles above her feet, which were bare. On top of her black hair she held several giant bowls stacked in layers, each filled to the brim with produce. Their situation seemed so precarious. I waited to see the fruits and vegetables topple to the ground, but not a single article fell.

When we came closer, I could see she also had something strapped to her chest. For a few long moments, she released the bowls she had been holding upright with her hands, and allowed the tower to balance on top of her seemingly minuscule frame. She peered down to the package she held in front. A small mess of black hair appeared from under the folds of her blouse. A sweet child had been nursing while this extraordinary woman had carried a massive weight all balanced on top of her head. And she had kept walking while she performed all this! I could not balance a single volume of text atop my head, and here this woman, an industrious mother, surpassed the skill of every poise teacher I had ever had. As we passed directly in front of her, I realized too late that my eyes and mouth were wide open. Seeing my aghast expression, she mistook my meaning and self-consciously pulled and tugged at her colorful clothing. I attempted to smile to show her it was all right, but she had looked away from me. I felt sick with regret.

As the buildings started to spread and become sparser, we saw a large group of people assembled together with all kinds of knives, guns, and spears. In the crowd I saw the man David had called Abraham. He spotted me peering out the back of the wagon and ran the knife he held from the tip of his thumb to the tip of his longest finger. I moved the children deeper into the wagon so we could not be seen.

As soon as I was confident we were in hearing range of David I asked, "Why are they armed?"

"They are always armed," he said. "But I believe today they go to fight Dingane."

"And who is Dingane?" I asked.

"A man," was all he said.

There were no trails to speak of after we left the small town of Durban, only small footpaths that we followed. There were small hills all around, but nothing that would be too difficult to climb. Small shrubs came together in sparse bunches along the horizon, but would just as quickly disappear and leave nothing but sand. It was not uncommon for me to see several different types of ground in one day. The land changed its mind so frequently.

During the day, David, Mary, and Mebalwe would take turns walking. It would take us two weeks to reach the village of David and Mary's good friend. His name was Sechele, Chief of the Bakwena.

"And what is he like, I wonder?" I turned to the children with a smile. "Does he have a broad chest like this?" I acted the part of a broad-chested chief. Their laughter was contagious. "A stern expression like so? Or does he possibly wear a giant headdress like this?" I spoke as I picked Agnes from my lap and sat her atop my head. She had no fear and gave a wide grin, which made her brother roar with giggles.

David and Mary were also smiling as they drove the slow oxen.

"Sechele is a very singular person to be sure," David joined in on my banter.

"Sechele," I repeated thoughtfully. "It is a very nice name."

"He is a nice man," David responded without hesitation. "He will have a great many questions to ask you, Miss Anna. He is fascinated by all things English."

"Truly?" I asked stunned. I hoped that meant there was a greater chance of him finding me amiable and allowing me to stay in Kolobeng. "What else interests him?" I asked.

"Everything else interests him, Miss Anna." He laughed, as did Mary. "He has a keen interest in learning. When I met him he had no knowledge of reading or the alphabet. He learned the alphabet in one day and has never relented! Mary's father translated the bible into Sechuana for him, and his copy is so used and worn it is in desperate need of repair. He is my most eager student of the gospel, sitting at the very front of every sermon I give. He is in constant need of information. He is forever memorizing and quoting the Old Testament!"

"And his character?" I probed.

"Excellent," he responded instantly. "He is charitable and does his best to see to the needs of all his subjects, as well as any visitors."

I was surprised, but pleased. However, my mind was still wound around the memory of that small band of grief-stricken souls we had seen earlier. If I had been in London, asking about a sensitive subject such as this would lead to instant censure. In a new country, however, I felt determined to form a new set of social protocol. Since I was curious, I asked, "David, who were those people? The ones who would not speak to us?"

He surveyed me over his shoulder for a moment, perhaps discerning whether I was sincere or merely morbidly curious. Finally, he relented. "They are the Boers," he said. "They are of Dutch descent, born and raised in Cape Town far from here. They have just finished a grueling trek lasting many days to get here."

"Boers," I said, committing it to memory. "Why did they make the trek?"

"They do not agree with the British laws put in place in the Cape Colony," he said matter-of-factly. "They had hoped to move into the interior of Africa and establish their own colony. It is not going well for them, I fear. They did not intend to end up here."

He paused for a long moment.

"Where were they hoping to go?" I ventured.

"I suppose they were expecting to find a land of milk and honey," he speculated. "One where they could have a peaceful existence of wealth and prosperity and not have to answer to any government but their own."

"And does such a place exist?" I questioned.

I could sense a tragedy in his voice as he spoke. His tone brought an end to our conversation. "No, Miss Anna," he said. "There is no such place."

Chapter 8

Although we were destined to spend two exhaustive weeks in close quarters, we did not feel the effects of it that day. The children were happy to be reunited with David, as was Mary. And I was content to see them joyful. If Mary and the children felt the dizziness and nausea that I felt, they did not admit it. Transitioning from sea travel to land was proving difficult for me. I could not help but feel that the water was still beneath me, tossing me about.

We watched for any animals on the trail, and when we spotted any, Robert would ask David to give them details of the beast. I was very grateful for this because I had yet to see an animal I recognized. A small herd of what David called gnus leapt past the window in the back of the wagon, our temporary apartment. I jumped up and craned my head out the back of the wagon to survey them longer.

I had never seen a truly wild animal before. I had seen small squirrels and birds in the forest behind Mother's house, to be sure, but the closest I had ever come to seeing a really wild animal in London were the stray dogs that wandered about the streets. To be sure, man needed to separate himself from large carnivorous animals as a means of survival. But why separate from the others? Without quite knowing why, it suddenly seemed to me this separation from nature had endangered a large part of man's existence and identity.

I had imagined Africa as considerably more hot and uncomfortable than what I was accustomed to, even blistering. To me, though, the heat was actually quite manageable, even as the sun bore down on the fabric tent. I knew my health must have passed Mary's mind, for she surveyed me from the corner of her eye at times. However, I had experienced the heat that comes as a result of twelve layers of clothing in a crowded ballroom, with every fire lit to boast the prominence of the host. In a small wagon, we at least had openings at the front and the rear to alleviate the warmth. I continued to wear my simple muslin dress, so the balance of temperature was fine in my mind. The swelter was much more feasible when it came from above instead of within.

This life, by means of oxen travel, was not altogether disagreeable. From my perspective, we were on a long ride with occasional picnics. The children and I, and at times Mary, would doze in the bed of the wagon while David drove for long hours. I had my fair share of smiles, hugs, and games from the children. When we stopped, only once a day, to prepare and consume our rations, I helped Mary in whatever way I was able. While Mary prepared lunch, David would hunt whatever he could find. Occasionally he would take Robert with him, the latter so proud of this high honor that he would strut back into camp as if they had caught an elephant, when in fact they mostly came with birds.

I came to think of Mebalwe as a warrior. He never came into the shade of the wagon, even when he spent the most time working. He remained in the sun while he herded oxen, hunted game, set up camp, and a myriad of other duties I did not understand. All the while, sweat poured from his brow and he would brush it away, unaffected.

When the sun began her descent into rest, David would stop the wagon at last. This first night, we made a small camp in a large, empty space. I was continually amazed at how open this land was. It was not cluttered with buildings as London was. The large empty spaces called to me to throw off my shoes and run as fast and long as I was able.

It was then that Mary confronted me. Suddenly she was next to me with a determined face.

"Miss Anna," she began, "if you are going to make your way here, it is time you took on some responsibility."

I was surprised.

"Mary," I gasped, "haven't I been helping you?"

"Oh, you have been helping," she agreed, "but I need you to be independent of any other person. Being self-sufficient will take much more than the simple chores you have been conducting. It is time to learn how to take care of yourself."

I had never been so shocked in my life. Had I not been taking care of myself, eating those foods that were good for me and looking after my own safety and hygiene?

"What else is there?" I asked her, bewildered.

Mary actually laughed.

"Oh, Anna," she said, true pity and foresight in her voice.

I had always felt independent from any other person. I always told myself that I didn't need another soul to survive. The reality of it, as I came to know in time, was that I didn't know what independence truly was.

"We will begin with fire making," Mary declared, "then move straight into cooking and baking. It will do you no good to catch or receive food without the knowledge of how to prepare it. David and Robert are out hunting now. You and I will be the ones to prepare the animal for the fire."

"Prepare . . . the animal?" I said hesitantly.

"You will see," she replied tersely. "Now, building a fire is a critical skill for all individuals. How do you suppose we will make the fire, Anna?"

Of course, I knew the answer. And yet I didn't. Wood was involved, I was sure. But how did it ignite?

"I don't know," was all I could say.

"Friction, Miss Anna. We will need friction to begin the fire with some light material like grass, then the fire will move to the wood, if it can be found. We will burn whatever can be burnt. We'll use wood today, but for example, buffalo chips make excellent fires."

"Chips?" I asked, puzzled.

"Buffalo droppings, Anna," she elaborated.

"We're going to burn the droppings?" I asked. "Why?"

"Because they can burn," she said without a smile.

I stared at her, dazed.

Mary picked up a bundle of wood that she'd gathered from a stop earlier in the day, and handed me two long pieces of wood, obviously whittled to some specific use.

"These seem special," I guessed.

"Yes. They are the tools we are going to use to build your fire."

We moved some distance from the wagon, and then without a moment's hesitation Mary knelt down in the dirt. I looked around bewildered. I crouched down beside her awkwardly in a subtle attempt to keep my dress clean.

"Now," Mary began, "we start with the hand drill." She gestured to the two pieces of wood she had me holding. "Take the thicker piece, the board, and place it on the ground. There you are. Now you are going to take the spindle, like this, and roll it between your hands while pushing down." She demonstrated this for me proficiently, the drill obeying her every gesture. She made it look easy. This would be simpler than I had imagined!

"All right!" I spoke, enthusiastic, "I believe I can do that!"

Mary smiled at me knowingly. "Try to start slow," she advised, "there's no need to use all of your energy at once."

I nodded, but her warning was unnecessary. This would surely be the easiest thing to learn.

"When you can get some sufficient smoke, we will place your coal in this." She displayed a small pile of leaves and dry grass, like a pillow, she had collected.

"Thank you, Mary," I said dismissively.

"Don't thank me just yet." She patted my knee and stood to tend to her children.

I looked down at my newly acquired spindle and board. This is what stood between me and independence.

I began to roll the spindle between my palms, as instructed. I started slowly, following Mary's advice, and my hands slowly moved downward as hers had done. I could then move my hands to the top of the spindle and begin again. I was lucky the wood was soft and was not rough on my skin, because the wood did not obey me as it had with Mary. The pieces felt awkward and uncomfortable. Where

Mary had simply rolled the rod between her hands, I had a difficult time of keeping the rod straight and in the same position. The board at the bottom would shift and my hand drill would slip to another unblackened section where it would do no good. All too quickly I began to sweat and breathe heavily.

I was beginning to worry that there was no smoke or fire as of yet. I looked up to Mary in slight confusion.

"Continue," she advised.

Again and again I placed my hands at the top of the spindle and rolled them down to the center of the rod, but it did not seem anything was happening. I was sure I had mirrored Mary's movements exactly.

"You must go faster," Mary called out to me from across the camp. She had washed and changed her two little ones by the time I had exhausted all my energy on one task. I felt disheartened.

I whisked the rod between my hands more aggressively, and now with more stubborn determination. My arms began to give way to the strain. My back begged me to sit down. The ground had looked uninviting, but now seemed like a haven. *However*, I thought, *I might be close to accomplishing my task*. I couldn't give up now.

I continued turning the thin rod between my now aching hands. Maybe I could gain an advantage by distracting my mind. I tried to look around me for something else to draw my attention. There were short shrubs scattered around the plain, along with other low, dry vegetation along the ground that I did not recognize. There was nothing in my sight that registered a memory, or that held enough intrigue to interest me. My mind did, however, take hold of the idea of breaking this rod against my knee until it was nothing but splinters.

The ache was becoming unbearable in my legs, back, and arms. I could not continue in this way for much longer, and no smoke was rising from the wretched set of tools. I must either continue in stubborn pain or relent and bear the consequences of a messy dress.

Given the circumstances, the choice became much easier.

My knees crashed to the ground in sweet relief. Instantly, muscles that had been bellowing now relaxed. I stretched and straightened my back as I continued to spin the rod.

Finally, at the point where I was determined to live my life without warmth if it meant this type of agony, a small pillar of smoke emerged from the base.

"Mary!" I cried out. She was at my side in an instant. Carefully she pulled the base from the ground to reveal a small black mound of coal. The smoke wavered and faltered slightly as she transferred the precious bit to our pillow of leaves. I held my breath in agonizing hope that it had not diminished.

It had.

Mary handed the tools back to me with a nod. When I reached for them, my hand shook. Mary saw, but said nothing.

This time when I began to twist, my muscles actually jerked in protest. I had never worked them this way. It was true, then, that I had been mostly stagnant my whole existence. This thought made me angry and I attacked the spindle as I had not hitherto done.

Suddenly, smoke appeared again and this time the pillow Mary held burst into a small, yet exquisite, flame. It crackled and spat as Mary placed it gently underneath the pieces of wood she had arranged so meticulously. Instantly I felt the warmth from the small fire.

If there were rooftops to be stood upon, I would have been shouting from them. A task which had appeared so simple and mundane at first had become, to me, a colossal achievement. How many people had gone without fire because they did not know how to create it? I would have wandered in that same darkness, but I had conquered and now had light, heat, and a tool by which I could sustain life. My frame swelled with pride. I was a woman of the frontier.

Mary was kind enough to teach me in small increments—one step at a time. That night she allowed me to sit by my triumphant achievement as she took the skinned birds from David and prepared them on the coals that resulted from the fire. I tried to watch her movements and commit them to memory.

We all nibbled on pieces of Mary's cooked bird and some strips of dried meat that David called *biltong*. It was small cuts out of cattle or antelope, sprinkled with salt and exposed to the hot sun, and could sustain a person between hunting wild animals. It was quite good, and the salt was especially gratifying.

I helped Mary in preparing the children for bed, and watched as she nestled them into their small tent and sang a simple song. I drifted away from them, feeling out of place, back to the fire where David and Mebalwe sat silently, comfortable in each other's presence. I rested to David's left, a little ways off so that I could leave him undisturbed. Soon, however, he spoke and surprised me.

"What are you running from?" he asked simply. He did not even look at me. The fire played patterns on his face, his mustache making funny shadows on his chin.

"I am not running from anything. On the contrary, I am running toward something."

That got his attention. "What is that?"

"I cannot tell you," I answered honestly. "I do not know."

He grunted.

I smiled. "Perhaps instead you could answer some questions for me."

"I guessed you would have some questions," he confirmed.

"What happened to the Boers?" I spoke frankly.

His eyebrows raised as he turned to me.

"Perhaps that is not the question you should be asking. I had thought you would want to know where you will be living, what you will be doing to occupy your time, or how you will survive in a terrain that has already claimed many, many lives."

"Oh," I said, reconsidering, "I had supposed I would take that all in one day at a time. There are so many things I know nothing about. The recent history of this continent seemed like a good place to start."

David acknowledged my speech with a grunt.

"You may be right," he consented. "The Boers, as I said, were white settlers of Dutch descent who left the Cape to find their land of milk and honey. There were unwise in their search."

"Because you said there is no land of milk and honey," I repeated what he told me before.

"Certainly there was that," he agreed. "But more than that, they mistook open land as free land. They saw a wide-open space and thought to claim it as their own property without any thought to the centuries of chiefs and tribes that had occupied that area in the past, or who were *currently* living on it. It happened more than once that a Boer would begin plowing a field while a native was plowing on the other side. They took no thought to their journey except to find a place where they would be free from government restrictions."

"Government restrictions?" I asked. "What restrictions were they opposed to?"

"There were several regulations the Dutch did not agree with such as property taxation. But, in truth, the main area of concern was with the keeping of slaves." An edge of hardness had come into his voice.

"Then," I said, "the Boers desired to keep their slaves."

He looked at me, then nodded. "Yes. They were anxious indeed. A surprising number of Boers fail to see anything wrong with the way they treat the natives. Some maintain that it wasn't loss of slave labor that drove them from Cape Town, but the British threat to their position of authority over the Africans. They saw a distinct difference. But there is no difference."

He began to speak more freely with me. "The Boers live out their lives as if they were on the pages of the Old Testament. The African is Ham, the dark-skinned son of Noah, cursed into slavery. Their flight from the English in Europe was the Exodus of the Children of Israel, the African interior their Promised Land by covenant with God. To them, all actions are justified, all brutality and bloodshed mandated—even ordained."

"Of course, there is certainly an economic issue with the freeing of slaves. Suddenly large ranch owners have no more labor to work their land, no hands to plow the field. With the release of slaves, one has satisfied the demand of one's conscience, but a large work force, previously relied upon, is suddenly relinquished. You do have to consider the influence on the economy.

"But to my knowledge, the British did as well as they could in that regard. Small steps were taken to bridge the gap the change would form. The Boers were informed well in advance that the slaves would be freed. But how do you transition a large group of people from something that has been ingrained into their culture? When the emancipation law finally came into effect, plows were dropped in fields without a glance back. All slaves instantly migrated from this lifestyle into a new. The Boers offered to pay the slaves to return, but they would not return to their former masters. As much as the British enforced the laws of mistreating slaves, I believe the fact that they would not return speaks volumes to how they were treated behind doors."

"So you are opposed to the slave trade," I guessed.

"If Africans behaved like savages, it was the slave trade that made them do so," he said, with a touch of fierceness. "I find I cannot be morally sound and be in favor of slavery. The slave trade ought to be a source of burning shame to every civilized being who does not help to put it down. I know that God certainly disapproves. I am simply attempting to see the good in the Boers. I wonder sometimes if it is warranted."

"And so the Boers simply left their homes?" I asked bewildered. "They left their homes because they could not keep slaves?"

"Oh, there is more to it, Miss Anna," he continued calmly. "You see, after the release of the slaves, some of the natives took it upon themselves to redeem past slaves. Looting and thievery abounded. Some would simply walk onto Boer property and take away cattle, or chickens or anything they desired. The Boers applied to the government but claimed they would do nothing." I noted that David didn't seem to believe that statement. "They are self-proclaimed pioneers. They must move forward, even if moving forward is detrimental to themselves and to the natives." The fire played off the broad angles of his masculine face, casting harsh shadows across his cheekbones.

"Is that why they dislike you," I asked quietly, "because you took the side of the natives?"

"No, Miss Anna." He almost smiled. "They believe I have used my missionary work as a facade, and have, in reality, been supplying rifles to my friend, Sechele, and to his people."

"Have you?" I asked interested.

He did not look at me, but smiled at the ground. "No Miss Anna. I have not. I do not deny it openly, however, because it is useful for others to believe it is true. I know the Boer's fear of guns in African hands is as useful to the Bakwena as the guns themselves. It prevents the Boers from treating the Bakwena as they do many others under their domination. Some arms and ammunition are a necessity in this terrain as lions and other carnivorous animals roam here, and they are certainly more effective than spears. But it makes little difference to a group of men who are feeling particularly hostile in their vulnerability."

I considered that.

"What happened," I asked, "on their trek? Why were they so dejected?"

"That is a story I would not like to retell at all, let alone late at night with a full day ahead of me," he said with a smile.

I smiled back. "We do have another long day tomorrow, don't we?"

"I think you will get used to them," he responded. "Now, do you know how to put out a fire?" he questioned.

"With water?" I guessed.

He shook his head. "No. We don't waste water here, Anna, not for anything." He then took giant mounds of dirt in his hands and smothered the fire effectively. Soon we were all nestled around the bed of the wagon in our tents, ready to sleep away the darkness. I shared a tent with Agnes, wiggling myself into the small space to sleep with my back to her, listening to her small steady breathing.

I had time to think before I slept. It had been fascinating to hear David speak. Even down to the fine details, he spoke in an air that would indicate that he spoke fact with every syllable that escaped his lips. Perhaps he did! He did not waste time with pleasantries nor did he bore his companions with polite conversation. He continuously had only one course with a sense of absolute certainty. There were no forks in the roads of David's mind. I had never, nor ever would again, meet someone who was so confident in their honesty.

The darkness was not gone when I awoke.

I sat up amidst my small band and instantly felt the effects of yesterday's fire making. Every muscle from the top of my shoulders to the tips of my red fingers torqued in pain at my every movement. Simply lifting my hand to remove the blanket from my legs was excruciating. Mary saw my discomfort and looked away.

Another day passed in like manner. Mary began to lean on me more heavily as the days went on. I had only been in the wagon for an hour when Mary's voice beckoned me from the front.

"Miss Anna, step down and have Mebalwe show you how to direct the oxen." She relayed her instructions to Mebalwe in her native Sechuana. A sudden shot of adrenaline shot to my fingers as I thought of walking next to the giant animals, but I swallowed hard and jumped out of the moving wagon. I walked as confident as I could muster to Mebalwe. He handed me a long wooden stick similar to his own. He communicated to me through simple panto-mime that I should watch him. He walked beside the rows of oxen and softly tapped their sides and feet with the stick. Gradually, he moved to the other side and did the same. The idea was to gently guide them along and keep them in their straight lines. One of the ox acted up and Mebalwe shoved against its shoulder with his own to push it back in line and exercise some authority. I wondered how an ox would react to my small frame pushing against it. I wondered if I would have any more affect than the hundreds of flies the oxen ignored so easily. I would soon find out, for Mebalwe gestured to me to begin guiding.

The grass had gotten considerably higher as I had observed Mebalwe's methods. I worked hard to step high with my knees so as to make good time with the wagon, but the effect was making me fatigued very quickly. Nevertheless, this was the sort of activity I felt I was obligated to become accustomed to. I tapped the leg of one ox and the animal jerked his head back so quickly and violently that I jumped back and dropped my stick in the tall grass. It took me sev-eral moments to find it again, and when I did, I looked at Mebalwe for instructions. He creased his forehead and gave me a hard nod. I was to try again. This time I was a bit more frustrated and hit the ox a bit harder than was necessary. He moved back in line as if I had just asked him politely. I would soon, gratefully, find that oxen do not measure pain in the same way as me. I moved around the yoke of oxen, tapping and pushing their sides and feet with my stick. One ox began to act out by rearing its head and stamping its feet. I rammed against its shoulder as mightily as I could in my small figure. In a move that surprised me entirely, the ox quickly jumped in the opposite direction of me and I suddenly found myself at its feet. It didn't take long for the inevitable to happen. One of his mighty hooves came down on my hand.

I heard several loud cracks and snaps.

As soon as he had moved on I rolled far out of its reach and cradled my hand to my chest. My mind couldn't focus. Images seemed hazy to my eyes. Somewhere in my mind I knew that the pain, when it set in, would be excruciating. For now, though, I felt only surprise.

Mebalwe and David were upon me very quickly, jabbering in calm Sechuana, and David slid an arm underneath me to steady me. "Stand up, Miss Anna," David instructed as he lifted me on to my feet. "That's it," he said soothingly, complimenting my simple effort. They kept looking at my face to assess my reaction, but the real pain had not set in yet. I was simply feeling embarrassed for getting in the way of a moving ox.

David sat me in the shade of the wagon with a drink of water, and slowly, I came back to myself as the pain began. As I'd imagined, the pain was immense, and waves of nausea threatened to overcome me when I looked at my injury, but I stayed silent, pulling myself inward to the space within myself I'd discovered long ago.

After a time, when he was sure I was calm and no longer suffering from shock, he took my hand in both of his. Considering the rough look of his own hands, he was surprisingly gentle. He touched and pulled slowly on all the bones in my hands. He did not have to tell me it was broken, only in how many *places* it was broken.

"We will have to adjust the bones in your hand, Miss Anna," he explained.

I did not need the details. I had had many broken bones before. "Proceed," I said simply.

He looked at me warily, possibly wondering if I was some unearthly thing. Maybe I was. I looked away as he adjusted two of my fingers back into their rightful place. The pain was excruciating as always, I pursed my lips and jumped slightly with each bone. I felt, as I had always felt, that as soon as the bones were back in place, my mind felt more settled but my hand felt worse.

David made very nice small splints for my two fingers and bandaged the rest of my hand professionally. Robert and Agnes had jumped down from the wagon to see the commotion, and they watched attentively as David bandaged my hand. Agnes was especially sympathetic as she repeated, "Anna hand hurt," enough times that Robert finally asked her for some quiet.

As soon as my hand was safe and covered, I stood on my own and thanked David profusely. He still regarded me strangely. Mebalwe came upon us in that moment and spoke something in Sechuana. In response, Mary nodded, a look of concern on her face.

I cocked my head in question.

"He says you must be strong to not make a sound when stepped on by a full-grown ox," Mary translated. Mebalwe gave me that same expression as David, as if they did not know how to react to me.

I shrugged, not knowing what other reaction to give.

I could see Mary tried to contain the swell of sympathy she sometimes felt when I revealed too much of my history. David and Mebalwe merely nodded.

Suddenly I was embarrassed, and excused myself to get another drink of water.

Chapter 9

A few hours later, Mary and I collected roots and tubers as we walked alongside the moving wagon. She said this was one of the responsibilities the women of the Bakwena took on. Mary showed me how to dig in the earth and pull out the ones that would benefit the body most. She pointed out to me which were wholesome and which were detrimental. I took care to use my good hand, as the other pulsed painfully with surplus blood.

As we rummaged, we spoke.

"What are your responsibilities in Sechele's village, Mary?"

"Not much," she responded modestly. "I take care of my family, attend David's sermons, and help in the village where I am needed."

"I feel certain you do a great deal more than that," I prodded. "You're so accustomed to the work load that you do not feel it upon your back."

Her smile did not reach her eyes.

"Do you help with David's medical practice?" I probed.

"Of course—"

David interrupted with a loud, "Hark!"

Mary and Mebalwe froze in their tracks and Mary's hand instantly grasped my elbow to keep me stationary. I needed no incentive to remain still—not only because David's voice was as loud as a boat whistle, but because I could see the reason for the stop.

Lions.

An entire pride of them lay under the shade of several trees some distance ahead of us. They had not been visible to the eye until we were too close for comfort. Luckily the children were inside the wagon at the time.

"Get into the wagon," David spoke to Mary and me. "Move slowly." Mebalwe stayed with his hand on the head of the ox at the forefront.

I realized, with a knot in my stomach, that oxen must look like a fine meal to a pack of lions. If they were hungry, we may encounter them. In a frantic moment, I realized if I had to fight a lion, or any other beast or enemy, I now was weak and slightly injured. I would be no help whatsoever.

Mary and I cautiously moved to the back of the wagon and climbed inside. To our relief, Robert and Agnes were asleep with angel faces. We moved closer to the front next to David so that we could keep an eye on the situation.

David was absolutely, immovably focused. His eyes would not be taken from the pride any more than his heart from his chest. I looked at him for a moment and then continued my stare as well. David had moved the cart to veer hard right in an effort to not appear hostile.

"If they attack it will be that female there," he spoke, his eyes never leaving a particular lioness that strode back and forth in front of her family.

Slowly and painfully we moved away from the animals and back into the open, delicious air of the late afternoon. After some time, David and Mary's forms seemed to relax and she went to perch next to him on the front of the wagon. About the same time, the children awoke and began to move about.

Robert approached the adults.

"May we go searching for frogs?" he asked eagerly. They had remained blissfully unaware of all that had passed. Despite my lingering fear, I had to smile at his sweet ignorance.

"Stay in the wagon for only an hour longer," David responded casually, not a hint of stress in his voice. "We will stop for the night soon."

Once we stopped, I quickly realized the fire building had become my full responsibility. As Mary handed the spindle and board to me, I thought not only of the pain beating from my hand, but the already present ache in my arms, legs, and back from last night's fire and today's walking and excitement. Not to mention, the hurt that would come if I attempted this task again.

"Please don't make me do this, Mary," I begged. "My hand and arms hurt so badly, can't you help me?"

Mary put her hand on my good one.

"It is necessary that you work against the pain of the body to make it stronger so that you may be a strong African woman," she explained. "It will hurt, Miss Anna. But does that make it bad?"

I had started to cry, but nevertheless I turned away and began the job.

Mary and I were right. There was pain. I felt sure that if it weren't for my crushed hand, I would have been faster tonight. I used the side of my hand that the ox had missed, and used its strength to rub against the spindle as quickly as I could manage. I stopped several times to rub my screaming arms and cradle my throbbing hand to my chest. The tears did not come from sadness, but from pain. They cascaded down my face and halted my progress by making my board slightly damp.

I knew now that no help would come. All three of my companions seemed determined to limit their pity. I knew their neglect was actually out of concern. They were determined I should be strong to face whatever was coming next in our journey.

After an hour of struggling, I finally came to the conclusion that I had to either ignore the pain and make the fire or give up and admit defeat. What a pathetic sight I would be if I gave up the fight so soon into the journey! No. Defeat was not acceptable. And so, as I spun my wood between my battered hands, the pain came, and it came strong, harder than before. But in my mind, I dismissed the need to feel and pushed through.

That tiny spark was the most gratifying sight seen in the history of women. All three of my adult companions suddenly rushed to my side and secured the small flame to the wood they'd prepared.

Although the new, deeper pain in my hand would have to be addressed, in that moment I could not help but laugh at the sweet nature of my team. They had succeeded in their own task of not helping me with the spark, but they could not possibly contain their feelings any longer when the job had been accomplished. I cried fresh tears for such caring friends.

David and Robert, who had left partway through the fire making, came into camp with two large birds they had caught together. I was allotted a few moments to rest and inspect my bandages before dinner preparations began, but then Mary beckoned me to her, and I obeyed.

Without ceremony or hesitation, Mary used her butcher cleaver to take the heads off the animals. She then brought the bodies to me and started to show me how to pull the feathers out. However, the sight of their headless bodies overcame me in an instant and I bolted for some low, nearby bushes where I relieved myself of my lunch. When I was finished, I came back to Mary, who looked truly annoyed.

"Are you done?" she asked me impatiently.

I was bewildered. I had had no control over it. Yet I had disappointed Mary, so I answered simply.

"Yes."

She continued where she left off and I held back my remaining nausea. Soon the body was in my hands and I was pulling viciously at the feathers, apologizing to it repeatedly in my mind.

Mary put the birds in a pot on my fire and I excused myself from dinner. I was no longer hungry.

Dinner cooked, roots gathered, and all tools cleaned and put away, I emerged from my hiding place. No one commented on either my disappearance or reappearance.

Now that the fear of today's situation had passed, David sat calmly by the fire, drinking his tea. I wanted to talk some more with him, and I was as interested in the Boers as he was disinterested in talking about them. He relinquished some facts, however.

"The majority of them that are in my acquaintance were under the direction of a certain man, Piet Retief. He once took charge of a group of about thirty wagons a couple months into their trek. He was a gambler at heart, and had recently lost his fortune in a business risk, but was certainly charismatic enough for the position."

"Was?" I asked, picking up on the past tense.

David paused and sighed heavily. I sensed that this was the story he hadn't wanted to tell me.

"Piet struck a deal with a barbarian Zulu chief by the name of Dingane, whose village lies on the eastern coast, near where you landed not two days ago. Chief Dingane told Piet if he would retrieve some of his stolen cattle, he would allow him and his group to settle on his land. He even signed a treaty of sorts, allowing the settlers to have a portion of his land once the cattle were retrieved. Piet and his boys delivered the cattle to Dingane, after which the chief invited them to a great feast. Then Chief Dingane politely asked the men to leave their modern weapons at home, claiming his home to be a sacred place."

I gasped audibly.

"I am glad to see you understand the danger in such a scheme, Miss Anna. Piet took one hundred men with him to the feast, including his son, thinking that more than enough protection and expecting to be welcomed and praised. And the feast went well enough, until Dingane's men killed every last one of them."

David was angry now.

"So that is why they are so acutely miserable," I guessed. "Because a hundred of their men were killed by this Dingane?"

"Dingane did not stop there." David shook his head. "The women and children of the hundred men were left unprotected not six miles from the place. Only a handful survived, including two young girls, who had been stabbed more than thirty times between them."

My heart was in my stomach.

"One of the men who survived the attack ran ahead to another group of Boers who were then able to fight off the Zulu warriors. Abraham was one of those men, and his courage in the ensuing fight is what has made him the new leader. But the fighting left him very bitter and violent.

"Obviously, I do not condone Dingane's actions," David said quickly. "He is the vilest and evilest of creatures. However, I also don't condone acting a fool—which Piet certainly did. He thought he could simply wander into the terrains of Africa with absolutely no knowledge of the centuries of organization and management by these chiefs! Any man could be in Dingane's presence for a moment and discern the evil that plays host in his mind. The Boers have a never-ending pride that will be the death of them if they do not change."

"Still," I declared, growing emotional, "he must be stopped."

"That is what the Boers are working on," he stated. "But I fear they see all natives as the enemy now instead of just Dingane. They hate Sechele, nearly as much as they hate the Zulu, simply because his skin is the same shade. There is great danger in a people who think that way." He eyed me in a peculiar way, perhaps asking whether I, too, shared those feelings.

"Chief Sechele is not a heathen chief?" I asked confidently.

"You may ask him yourself. We will be arriving in only a few short days."

"And what is he like?" I inquired.

"My friend Sechele," David began quietly. "Sechele is wound tightly around the traditions of his people. His enthusiasm for the Bible is outstanding, but he has yet to be baptized. I have known him and preached to him for three years this October. The conflict is in Sechele's soul, drawn forward by new ideals but pulled back by the entanglements forged by a hundred generations. His higher self delights in the Law of God, but a different law wars within, leaving him captive to his lower self."

I pretended to understand what he meant.

"He is an excellent leader, but he had a tragic childhood. His father was killed by his uncles when he was just a boy. Sechele was saved but was forced to wander the deserts of Africa until his adulthood. If there is anyone that could teach you about surviving here on your own, Miss Anna, it would be Sechele."

"And do you know what he will have me do?" I wondered. "What will occupy my time?"

"I imagine you will work as a help to my Mary," he stated confidently. "But the rest of the time, you will be learning how to be a useful part of the human race here."

I nodded solemnly. I had come to realize that I was not truly useful yet. Not here.

David looked around himself, unsteady.

"Leave the fire blazing tonight, Miss Anna," he requested. "Hopefully it will help us in keeping the beasts away." With that, he stood up and took up his bed with Mary. I was left out in the open, with my eyes blinded by a bright fire and a sure knowledge of vicious carnivores in the area. I stepped slowly from the fire and fell asleep quickly as safe as I could be inside a small fabric tent.

Mary shook me awake. The pain that accompanied consciousness was overwhelming. Every muscle in my body begged me to crawl back into the cramped space. I sighed and snuck out of the small space to face the day. It wasn't going to start well.

"Three oxen have wandered off in the night despite being tied," was the first thing I heard from David. I envied Agnes her warm bed as I shivered in the cold morning haze. "Mebalwe remembers a small body of water two miles to the east. We'll begin that way."

"And I'm going, am I?" I asked, still befuddled from sleep.

"You are of no use to me here," Mary explained, somewhat more frankly than seemed necessary.

I nodded. Exhaustion had made me passive.

I laced my quickly withering shoes and we started east. The men chattered away in Sechuana while I trudged along trying not to look too pathetic as the rising sun woke me. With my slow gait to hinder us, it took us half an hour to reach the body of water spoken of. Mebalwe looked back at me several times, clearly wishing to simply throw me over his shoulders and sprint to the water. Nevertheless, he resisted and we arrived.

From a distance, it appeared to me a miniature oasis. The greenery that sprung from the water was dark green and spread out around the body of water for several hundred yards. A circle of trees stood together as guards protecting the precious water on every side, and had to be pushed quite hard to be passed by. My hand screamed at me when I forgot its condition in my delirium.

As soon as we could see the water we could see the oxen. Two of the three were directly across from us on the other side of the pond. The third was nowhere to be seen. Mebalwe and David, without speaking, separated from each other and went round opposite sides of the pond to capture the animals from both angles. I followed behind Mebalwe, but some distance further into the brush so as to stay out of the way of his techniques. There was thick foliage around the pond, which David and Mebalwe navigated easily. However, I stumbled my way noisily through the mess of brush and vines. Suddenly, I tripped and landed crudely on my already injured hand, gasping in pain. When I looked up, I stared right into the face of the third, deceased, ox.

I jerked away quickly and jumped to my feet to call to Mebalwe, but he and David were almost to the other oxen and likely would not be deterred. I stood guard over the dead beast while I waited for the men to take notice of me. I tried not to look at the giant corpse, but my morbid curiosity got the best of me. I regretted it instantly. The ox was not only dead, but had obviously been killed by a local carnivore and half eaten, its lower half mostly gone except for bone, cartilage, and a great deal of blood.

Stuttering, I tried to step back but was halted by a tree. I leaned on it until I could breathe without gagging and gasping. Pulling feathers out of birds for Mary now seemed like a much better option. It occurred to me that the animal responsible for the mess may still be present. I clung to the bark and stayed silent.

Soon, Mebalwe was with me and put a comforting hand on my shoulder. I looked up at him, and his face was concerned, but confused. He did not know why I was hiding. I merely pointed at the dead ox. He saw the carnage, then called to David, who had the two oxen in tow. After securing the oxen, the first thing David and Mebalwe did was take out the large knife they each carried with them.

Now it was my turn to be confused. What could we possibly do for the animal now? My observations were quickly replaced by horror as I watched the two men I trusted most in the world begin cutting and slicing the ox's flesh. Only after a moment of watching this horrid spectacle did I realize they were looking for any desirable meat that was left. Although I saw the logic behind it, my nerves could not endure it.

"What?" I cried, flustered. "What are you doing?"

These two men whom I had already grown to admire so greatly looked up at me in surprise, their hands covered in blood, large knives in their hands. They looked to each other. David halted his work, wiped some blood on his trousers and came toward me. I stepped back instinctively. He saw it and slowed.

"Miss Anna," he began slowly, "do you remember me telling you we don't waste water for anything? The same applies with meat. We cannot afford to be wasteful."

"But you did not pause!" I cried desperately. "You are no better than the animals that devoured it!"

"Meat is something of great value here, Anna. Desired above almost anything else. We cannot wait to conduct a funeral for the creature, because of your sensibilities, while the meat spoils. Hundreds of families across this continent, my own included, would suffer much if we were to lose precious meat. Do you value animals more than you value people?"

"Of course not," I defended myself.

"Then you will release your idea that to kill animals is barbaric," he said harshly. "It is an English schoolgirl notion that I have no time or patience for." His expression gave me no room to form an argument. I slowly nodded my submission and he resumed his labor, although Mebalwe had made quick work of it while we argued, not understanding a word.

They had several arm loads of meat to transport back to camp. Mebalwe carried his in his bare arms, blood trickling down to his elbows and down to the ground. They could have carried all the meat back to Mary without my help, but there were the other oxen to consider. They would have to be led back to camp, and my small frame and injured hand would not be enough to hold them if they acted out, so I had to carry meat.

David came over to me slowly and, without a word, placed several cuts of meat one by one into my outstretched arms. I did not look at the meat, only at his face, which was unreadable. I knew that although I had aroused his temper, he was not truly angry with me, only with my customs.

I carried the meat the two miles west, my heart pounding in anguish with every step and my arms burning in agony. I kept my eyes strictly forward, although it was difficult in the face of so many flies. They came from miles around, I was sure, at the smell of the open flesh. Although I succeeded in not looking at what I held, there was no escaping the smell, which I have no need, or desire, to describe or remember.

Mary could see me coming from several hundred yards away, and she could see what I carried. At the edge of the camp she met me and instructed me where to place the meat, a place she had prepared. I set the meat down where she asked. She gave me no time to pity myself.

"Change your dress and then awake the children, Miss Anna," she instructed, "then you may make the coffee while I begin the porridge."

I simply nodded, tears dropping off the tip of my nose.

With my bloodstained clothes off and replaced with clean linens, I woke Robert and Agnes and helped them in their morning routines. Robert did not need much assistance. As of late, he had decided he was a man like his father and Mebalwe. He conceded to my helping him with his shirt buttons, but only with the face of a true martyr. Next I awoke Agnes, and the smile and fierce hug she gave me almost made up for the entire morning. With her dressed and ready, we stepped out of our tent to face another day together.

Since we had left the port, we had not seen another living soul, besides the variety of animals. The children and I watched for beasts eagerly. Each time we saw a new one, I would ask them the noise it made and they would both repeat it instantly, with excellent skill. Mary had taught them well. I found myself delighted to pass the time making ridiculous noises with children. Although, when we could see some buffalo in the distance, I asked Robert to make the sound, and he rammed my belly with his small forehead. After that, I was careful of the questions I asked.

We saw such a myriad of forms of life. Elephants were bewildering in their mass, and the more distance between us, the more at ease I felt. Mebalwe brought us a meerkat to see up close, its wide eyes wondering what it was doing trapped in a box. The herds of wild horses I felt I could watch throughout eternity, whereas the rhinoceros seemed awfully dull and lackadaisical. To this statement David vehemently disagreed.

"Caught at the wrong moment in the grass, a rhinoceros could take a man's leg off. They are much quicker than they seem."

"You speak as if you have experienced this," I said.

He shrugged a single shoulder. "I like to explore."

Mary gave him a look of admiration.

We passed through two small villages, and at long last, we saw other humans. David got down from the cart and spoke with small groups of natives at both places. Mary got down only at the latter village, to embrace a woman she recognized, with skin as dark as hers was white. At the same time Mary was with her friend, a chief made his way toward us. I say he was a chief because he strode with authority and had several tall, glorious feathers attached to his dark hair. He was accompanied by eight women, all emotionally attached to him somehow. I was too apprehensive to ask if they were his wives.

He spoke with David for only a few minutes before returning the way he came. He had left David with a parting gift, a small piece of ivory, carved into the shape of a bird with its beak wide open.

"It's lovely," I told him when he showed me the piece.

"The chiefs here give a gift if they are pleased with your entering and exiting their lands. He said he found no fault with me, but would like me all the better if I was not forever preaching and giving sermons."

I looked at the carving again.

"Are you the bird, then?" I asked.

"I suppose so," he replied with a grin. "I suppose this is his formal request to hear less about salvation."

Chapter 10

As soon as the days started to roll together into an indiscernible mass, our trek came to a close. We arrived at Sechele's tribe on the end of the seventh day of travel by wagon. It was a much larger village than I had imagined. As we looked down on the valley atop a hill, I could see hundreds of neatly thatched huts, built with some sort of clay. The huts swirled around each other in small concentrated circles, and a large, triangular wall surrounded the entirety of them. The wall must have been at least seven feet in height, and as we drew near and traveled alongside the wall, I could see it was surprisingly attractive for what must have been done with hands and crude tools. I stretched my hand out the back of the wagon to feel the rough, warm texture of the wall. At regular intervals along the surface, my hand met perfectly round holes, about the size of my hand. I inquired after David to know their purpose.

"They are the width of a musket end," he wiped his brow in the heat. "It allows the tribe members to shoot out of the village while still staying mostly protected."

This struck me as wise. I found myself suddenly wanting to be inside the walls instead of outside.

"For protection against animals?" I asked

"Something like that," David said, then spoke again suddenly. "There he is now."

There, just outside the wall, was a small group of native men, women, and children. In my mind's eye, I was looking for an individual who had similarities to the chief David had met with yesterday, and I could see amongst them was a man a good deal taller than his companions, whose skin was a good deal darker than the rest. It most certainly was Kgosi Sechele, Chief and King of the Bakwena. From afar I could see he was dressed differently than his fellow African leaders. And yet, something was oddly familiar about him.

As we came closer, I recognized the cut of his suit, the style of his boots, the curve of his collar. His cravat was neatly tied, his vest freshly pressed and his high hessian boots polished, if not slightly out of fashion. He was costumed as an Englishman! His buckles and buttons shone in the African sun so brightly, it told me he must have them polished individually and meticulously. The tunic, I knew, was stylish when my father was a youth, and the shirt peeked out at his wrists and neck, the stark white creating a charming contrast to his dark skin. His coat was a worn but pleasing navy blue. His costume was finished by a long, dark walking stick with a shining, white ball on the end.

My jaw dropped slightly. I was always one to enjoy the ridiculous, but I had not imagined an English suit in the midst of all this rough terrain. I looked to Mary in my astonishment and she did not return my gaze. She simply shook her head. In my mind's eye, I had fashioned Sechele in a large feathered hat, a bare chest, and skins about his loins. The African that stood directly in front of us now could stroll the streets of London without a second glance if his skin were white. How had he come to own such clothing? And why would he wear it?

"How?" I asked in bewilderment. I was grateful Mary understood what I was asking.

"Kolobeng gets its supplies from traders that move from the coast to the interior. They are well aware that Sechele is interested in English items and will pay well for them." She cocked her head. "He must be baking in this weather."

As if agreeing with her, some of his companions wore next to nothing, which I could understand more than I could a three piece suit. The others were dressed in plain tunics, hats, and trousers. In place of a walking stick, almost all of them carried long spears, which Mary told me were called *assegais*. The clothing they wore was obviously handmade, but not needing in anything. Almost all had bare feet, but all looked dressed up in a way, to welcome home the missionary doctor.

"Kgosi!" Robert shrieked. It startled me into remembering that, for the children, this was a typical experience. They were returning home. Robert bolted from the back of the wagon to clasp the knees of his chief. Sechele patted him on the back and grinned broadly while murmuring a low hum of soothing Sechuana to him. Agnes wobbled behind in imitation of her brother. When she arrived to Sechele with her arms outstretched, his eyes grew wide and he picked her up gently. I was amazed at his tenderness with her.

"Has he met Agnes before?" I asked Mary as we climbed down the front of the wagon.

"Only when she was new," she answered. "His wife Selemeng is my good friend, and she helped me deliver Agnes. Sechele met her soon after." She paused and smiled in remembering. "I imagine she has grown a touch since then."

David stepped down from his seat and shook Sechele's hand while his other hand clapped him on the back.

"Sechele, my friend," he greeted.

"Ngaka," Sechele called him.

I may have noticed Sechele's clothing first, but let it be understood that he, in no way, looked ridiculous. He was royalty. His back was perfectly straight, his shoulders wide and strong. A hard jaw and a broad forehead were his dominating features. And yet, there was a clear suggestion of humility in him. His face showed lines of laughter, his hands often moved to clasp the shoulder or pat the back of the friends around him. As I observed him, I could see that he was sincere in his kindness yet certain in his authority.

"We are returned home," David explained. "Mebalwe has accompanied me and we have brought my wife and children," he said as he gestured to Mary and the children.

"My heart is glad at the sight of you. Welcome home," Sechele said with an accent most intriguing. "Little Robert, I have been pondering while you were behaving as a great traveler."

He crouched down so he was face-to-face with my little companion. "I shall place a giant hippo on the porch of your house, and you would have to stay there like the cattle in my corral, and you could never leave us again." He clapped a hand on Robert's shoulder in a friendly way and his smile ran from ear to ear. Robert chuckled, as did I.

Mary inquired after her friend.

"Selemeng is dreaming in the shade," Sechele answered her. "She has been planting the garden this day."

"And there is another who has accompanied us." David introduced me as I stepped out of the wagon. I looked up into the face of Sechele. What piercing eyes he had! In an instant I felt if I were dishonest he would instantly be aware of it. He had the power of discernment. He saw through walls and dug out secrets. And so much rested on his opinion of me, if I would be welcome in this corner of the world. In a way, I needed his approval to begin my new life here.

And so, in a slight panic, I did what I had been taught since infancy when meeting a new acquaintance. I bowed my head and curtsied.

There was a slight stir in the company surrounding their chief. They looked around with question, and possible concern, in their faces. I quickly righted myself, worrying that a curtsy may have been the wrong first impression.

Sensing my discomfort, Sechele took two large steps to stand directly in front of me. Then with grace I did not expect in a desert, he bowed himself in half.

"I am pleased to be meeting you," he said, speaking with purposeful articulation now. "I welcome you here. I am Kgosi Sechele, Chief of the Bakwena." He gave me a small smile as he stood straight again.

His manners relieved my nerves so greatly I felt I could burst.

"The pleasure is mine," I choked out. "I am Anna. And I thank you, sir."

Sechele righted himself and his face glowed with a wide grin. He turned and extended his arm to me. I took it, and we walked arm in arm into another corner of the world.

Mebalwe excused himself discreetly, but David, Mary, and the children followed behind us as I saw the village for the first time.

There did not appear to be a single blade of grass out of place. The paths were paved flat and straight by the passage of many feet. Every so often a cow or goat would appear tied to the side of a home, as if it had been born and raised in that very spot, fearing to move and disrupt the cleanliness of such a place. All was orderly and comely. Mothers sat at their open doors and witnessed their chief walk past with a white girl at his arm. As peculiar a situation it seemed to me, the villagers did not seem surprised. I sensed that they knew their chief to be odd, but loved him all the same.

Toward me, however, there was a marked expression of suspicion. Brows furrowed and smiles slackened as they looked upon me. I thought it might have been because I was new and unknown, but as the Livingstones followed me, the villager's expression continued in wariness.

We were all escorted to the center of the village, directly to the door of the chief's own dwelling. In contrast to all the homes in his village, Sechele's home was brick, square, large, painted white with an iron roof, and looked remarkably like a typical English home. Glass windows dotted the face of it, and flowers grew in pots hanging by the sill. A large garden was planted to the left of his front door, perfect rows of unfamiliar plants conformed in symmetrical lines. I shook my head at the spectacle. I could just have easily been in the country outside of London. I had been preparing myself to be accepting and open to new cultures and customs. How could I have imagined that the chief would be anxious to mimic mine?

Directly in front of his home was a large fire pit, which, I was told, was used for grand meetings. Signs of a recent gathering still remained in the sand.

Sechele, remembering something, turned his head and spoke to a man in his native tongue of Sechuana. It sounded like an order. The man ran in the opposite direction to heed his master's demand.

In the same moment, a woman opened the front door of the large home and stepped outside. If I had taken the time to sketch out what my mind's eye had seen as a perfect African queen, I feel certain I would have captured her precisely. She wore traditional African clothing. Beads hung around her neck and wrists. A thin cotton dress covered her frame, and two bold stripes ran from shoulder to shoulder, perhaps representing of the mantle she bore. Looking back, I suppose many of my English constituents would classify her as corpulent, but I found no fault with her. She was strong! Just as an African queen should be.

Distinctive cheekbones accented wise beautiful eyes. A small stern mouth told me she did not allow disobedience. She was majestic, commanding, a leader. Yet something in her face told me her husband persuaded her to laugh, but rarely.

"Anna," Sechele spoke to me and patted my hand in a fatherly way. "I will have you meet my head wife, Selemeng." She and I exchanged a nod of acknowledgement. I wondered why he called her "head wife."

The man whom Sechele had ordered a command returned to our group with an ox. Everyone turned to him expectantly.

"Ah!" Sechele sang happily. "My friend David! Your family and Miss Anna are most welcome. I present this ox!" He gestured to the animal proudly.

This was obviously a welcoming custom. I felt lucky to be witnessing their culture firsthand. This was turning into a regular English setting, only with a slightly more unconventional gift.

I heard Mary speak my name loudly, but I did not turn. Then, Sechele spoke a single word in Sechuana to a man near him. The man drew a giant spear from his side like a sword, and expertly drove the head of the weapon into the neck of the animal. The ox hollered in surprise and shook its head in an attempt to swat the spear away. Several other villagers attacked the ox with their spears and other types of weapons, thrashing and cutting. Soon, the ox was on the ground, dead, and bathed in its own blood.

I witnessed the entire spectacle with my eyes wide, head cocked, and hands clasped politely in front of me, which had been my stance prior to the incident. I had not dared move for fear of offending Sechele or any of his family. Luckily, Mary had turned the children away from the scene, but was not quick enough to turn my head as well. I assured her I was all right. Perhaps I needed to see it. After all, the ox was meant to be our celebratory feast that evening. I couldn't be blind to the facts of living here any longer.

Now I bit my lip and considered what had just passed. Proper thought eluded me. Perhaps there *were* a few key differences between the Bakwena and the polite society of London.

We were escorted into Sechele's home by his wife Selemeng. Thick, colorful rugs welcomed our weary feet as we entered, and it was larger inside than the exterior suggested. The walls were a solid white like the exterior, in contrast with the ebony black floor. The accents of color around the room made the space comfortable and interesting. Many large windows, with real glass, shed light into his receiving room. I noted that each window had thick curtains as well. I could imagine shade was precious here. And, in the small welcoming area in which we stood, there was a massive, mahogany grandfather clock to our right, the most breathtaking piece I had ever come upon.

I could also see into a sublime dining room. A long, gorgeous table capable of seating twelve dominated the space there, covered by a slightly dingy white tablecloth. In front of each chair was a place setting of simple white plates and shining silver utensils. A long, beautifully crafted sideboard sat out of the way, filled with more fragile plates and silverware. Above hung an elegant glass chandelier, more suitable for a ballroom than a home. The clear, delicate ornaments nearly touched the table, so great was its size. How it could have survived in the bed of a wagon I had not the faintest idea. Yet here it was, beautiful, if not peculiar to behold.

Three more younger women appeared beside Selemeng, trying to get a look at the newcomers.

"These are my other wives," Sechele said proudly, "Mokgokong, Modiagape and Motshipi." They all smiled pleasantly, proud to be introduced.

"Oh!" I exclaimed in my surprise. My naivety was astonishing. I had not even thought to ask the question, so engrossed was I in Sechele's English clothing and English home. Trying to recover my composure, I spoke. "It is good to meet all of you."

The three wives grinned amiably, then exited in mass with Selemeng.

I continued to take in the chief's home. I expected to see many books in a home like this, yet there was only one. An open bible sat on a short table beside what must have been his favorite red chair. I could see that Sechele had written in the margins of the pages. One paragraph in Isaiah he had circled entirely in red pencil and written to the side, *Why?*

"Please sit!" he said politely. "Eat!"

"No, Sechele," David began, "you are already feeding us in a few hours, there is no need."

Sechele shrugged and set a bowl of fruit on a short table. The children each took a piece of fruit that was familiar to them, but foreign to me.

I sat in a padded armchair and relished the comfort. I had not realized how hard the wooden benches of the wagon were.

David spoke casually. "And how are the affairs of the village, my friend? Is everything well with you?"

"Oh," he responded in his thick African accent, "we have good rain and my women become fat and shining!"

I could not help letting out a burst of laughter. That caught his attention.

"I will speak at you first, Anna." He turned to smile at me. "What do you plan?"

I straightened my back. This was to be my interview.

"Well, sir," I began, "I have been told Mary needs help in her work." I nodded in Mary's direction. "I should like to apply myself to that role."

As I spoke, Chief Sechele watched me intensely. I had never encountered someone who absorbed details so fully as this unconventional chief. He listened, not only to respond, but to truly hear. Nothing missed the scrutiny of his eyes. When he spoke, his features loosened and he could laugh and make others feel at ease, but as soon as another began speaking, I could sense that he was focused on not only their words but also their true meaning. Listening was a lost art that Sechele had perfected.

"At the school as well?" he questioned. "You taught before?"

"Well, no," I faltered. "I do, however, feel confident in my education. My father was an avid reader like yourself. I have read since I could walk. And I attended a very fine school in my youth."

"You stopped school when you became an old lady?" He asked.

I laughed again. "I am old in mind, if not in body, sir."

He nodded, understanding me.

"And why stop attending to school?" he asked seriously.

"I was . . ." I faltered, ". . . needed at home."

He nodded again.

"I believe I could learn to teach others," I said confidently.

"Yes," he said, smiling. "You may, Anna. Teach school with Mma-Robert. Understand?"

"I understand," I responded grinning, assuming by "Mma-Robert" he meant Mary. "Thank you, sir."

"Now!" Sechele said, "My friend David, I have to discuss with you. Let us walk."

Sechele and David left Mary, the children, and me to rest in Sechele's spacious home. Selemeng and the other three wives reentered the room, each greeting Mary and calling her Mma-Robert, which I was to learn simply meant "mother of Robert." Mary responded to each of them in Sechuana, in which she was fluent. They sat on, and all around, a lovely sofa directly across from me. They ranged from tall to short, fair to coarse. The head wife, Selemeng, was the only one among them who knew some English.

"Miss Anna," she addressed me. "Why your hairs short?"

Selemeng's English was not as developed as her husband's. Nevertheless, I understood.

"Oh!" I responded startled. I had not considered my appearance. Now I realized I must

have been quite a scene compared to what they were used to with English women. How could I explain? I considered telling the truth: *My father cut it short so I would be mistaken for a boy as we escaped England under assumed names and start a new life in America away from my mentally disturbed mother.*

A simpler explanation would have to do.

"I like it." I shrugged as I ran one hand through my quickly growing hair.

Selemeng stared at me with tight lips and a confused expression, then translated for the other wives. I wish I could have framed what I then saw as they all took on the same expression: tight lips, scrutinizing eyes, tilted heads. Four regal African queens perplexed by English fashions. They surveyed me from top to bottom. I moved my hand to attempt to casually cover the hole in my dress that showed my knobby knee. My movement caught their attention and they were puzzled again. I sat in silence for several long, uncomfortable moments.

Thankfully, Sechele and David soon returned. As the Livingstones filed out of Sechele's home one by one thanking him for his hospitality, the chief handed Mary a large beautiful piece of beef, which she accepted graciously. Agnes and Robert were particularly excited about the meat.

While I thanked the chief, the family walked speedily away, but I caught up to them quickly, picking Agnes off the ground and plopping her on my hip with a squeeze. Something they were discussing had them in an excited huddle. I leaned in closer.

"And what did he say after that?" Mary was asking David with an eager expression.

"Well, first, he asked if I had brought back any special medicine to make him a better hunter." He paused and gave us a long face, to which Robert and I laughed and Mary rolled her eyes.

"And then," he began, then stopped and stared off into the African terrain. He turned to look into Mary's face and a smile broke over his face.

"He said he wants to be baptized."

Chapter 11

David related his conversation as we drove the oxen to the Livingstone's home inside the triangle shaped city.

David had been preaching here for six years, and had known Sechele for three of those years, and yet he had never converted a single soul. That surprised me. He seemed to be so convincing in his whole personage. Nonetheless, it was true: Sechele was to be his first baptism.

"He is resolved," David explained. "Despite the consequences, he feels sure baptism is what God wants from him."

"Surely the consequences are not too severe," I ventured.

"Unfortunately they are," David countered. "He will need to give up rain making, a tradition of Bakwena chiefs for centuries. That will certainly not go well. And in addition to that, Sechele has four wives."

I paused.

"Is that," I began, wondering how to phrase my question, "typical here?"

"For a chief it most certainly is typical. Having many wives benefits the tribe in several ways. You have many women who are worthy of being wife to a chief in such a big village, and having a daughter marry Kgosi, even if they are the fourth wife, is a great honor."

"And he is going to take that honor away," Mary said. "If he is to be baptized, he will have to return all wives to their families, save one."

"It is the right thing to do," David confirmed.

This custom was certainly new to me. I remember a lesson where the tutor said that taking several wives was only for the barbarian. But I didn't think of Sechele as a barbarian, especially since he seemed to be very proud of each of his wives.

"What will happen then? Will the people be angry?" I asked.

"He is planning on sending each wife back to her parents with a good deal of valuables and wealth to compensate, in some way, for dismissing them from his presence. He will attempt to convince the families that he found no fault with them."

"But they will not listen," Mary interjected.

"It will be difficult," was all he said in response.

I tried to imagine myself in the place of one of the discarded wives. How would that feel to go from a place of honor and respect back to the place whence you came? Truly, it would be humiliating. Surely people would wonder if you had done something to offend or upset the chief. From what I had witnessed, the chief was the literal and critical center of their community. What happened to those who offended him?

And then there was something deeper.

"Do all of his wives truly love him?" I questioned. "How will he choose?"

"I do not know, Miss Anna," David said wearily.

Sechele's baptism was supposed to be a joyful occasion. I hoped that David's first convert would not be made an outcast of his own society. My mind wandered, and I found myself wondering what the captain would think of the situation. I blinked hard several times, amazed that I would have the thought.

At last, we reached the Livingstone's home. It was plain white and surprisingly wide with narrow windows and two short steps leading up to the front door. A small covered porch before the house looked very welcoming. To the left of the little house was a covered lean-to, which I was sure was Mary's kitchen, full of supplies like bowls, spoons, and pots. To the right of the house was a small corral where ten of the thinnest cattle I had ever witnessed stood quietly chewing cud. The children ran around their familiar home in sweet reunion.

I instantly fell in love. My time in small, dark quarters in a ship and then in the back of an ox-driven wagon allowed me to see this small house with newfound appreciation. It was absolutely stunning. There was a lot of work to do, and a lot of things to learn. I could thrive in responsibility. I felt ready.

The first thing we had to do was prepare and cook the raw meat that Sechele had given Mary. Mary began to prepare the meat and I watched intently.

First she salted the entire piece, but not as much as I'd expected. I wondered why she did not use more salt. Suddenly, it struck me that I did not know where one would buy, or find, salt in this area. Perhaps it came from the traders Mary had described. I wondered if it was expensive. I was afraid salt held more importance than I'd realized.

Mary continued, fetching a long knife from her kitchen supplies still on the wagon. She cut the meat into long and thin strips. After she was finished, she turned to me.

"Start your fire, Anna!" she ordered.

I jumped to my responsibilities. Soon, I had some dry wood and grass collected from around the house and was working with my hand drill and board. I was proud of the fact that building the fire took less time now, though Mary still tapped her foot in impatience. Over the past week on our trek, my hand had become stronger and now bothered me very little while using my spindle and board. David checked it repeatedly during the course of several weeks and was proud to announce I had no lasting damage.

When the fire was roaring, Mary placed the strips of meat into one of her large pots and covered them with water. She then placed the pot on the area of the fire with the most heat.

"How do you know when the meat is finished cooking?" I asked her.

"When the water is gone," she said simply.

I was amazed that if confronted with the need, I now knew how to cook meat. That thought alone brought me satisfaction.

While our meat was cooking, we helped David unload the wagon, along with Mebalwe who had reappeared. Mary then took me to what was to be my quarters. At the top of the stairs we found ourselves in a narrow hallway leading all the way to the back of the house. Before I stepped into the place, I noticed there was a fine layer of sand on every bare surface to be seen.

"Was a window left open?" I wondered aloud.

"No. The house is as air tight as we can make it," Mary answered.

"Then how did the sand get in?" I asked.

She shrugged. "Somehow, it always finds a way."

To the left was a fireplace and a small sitting area. Farther inside to the left was David and Mary's bedroom and a small room meant to be David's library. The walls were covered with books, medical references, dictionaries, encyclopedias, and his own personal journals. Several cases of medicine also rested here. It appeared to me the perfect resting place for David. We followed our path back and took a right to the opposite side of the house, where we found the bedroom I would share with the children. There was nothing spectacular about the space. At least it was larger than my cabin aboard the *Madras*. White walls, highlighted by the sun coming in through the one window, caught my eye. Two small beds lined the room's walls with a large chest sitting at the foot of each. Directly in front of me stood a small table with a bowl and pitcher for washing. It was simple yet splendid. I turned to Mary.

"Robert and Agnes are little enough that they can share one bed," she clarified our sleeping arrangements. "You can feel free to that bed," she said gesturing to the one deeper in the room.

"You know," I began, "I believe there is a special reward in heaven for people like you, Mary. I feel certain that anyone who would take in a lost girl and teach her all of these trades to become independent must surely receive some prize in the end." I smiled.

"I don't work for prize, Miss Anna. If I could tell my Creator I had simply performed a quiet life of service, that would be my reward."

I considered that.

"And David? Will he be content with a simple life of service?"

"Oh no." She shook her head. "David means to make a grand gesture. He is one that feels much is required of him. And he may be right."

"What do you think?" I questioned her.

She paused.

"I think I miss my husband terribly when he is away," she spoke quietly, turning away from me. "That is all I think."

I was not sure I believed her.

"Would he ever consider a life other than this?" I asked.

"I am sure he would not," she said confidently. "Before he left England as a student he was offered a teaching job that would supply us with the income to keep us all comfortable the rest of our days."

"And he did not accept?"

"No, and he was right to refuse," she said. "Teaching was not the object on which he had set his heart. He is best suited for exploration and missionary work. We, neither of us, have ever had a desire to be wealthy. A Kolobeng child, with plenty of food and water, is happier playing in the soil than a rich man is in his mansion of dispensables."

"So you would not live in a grand house in London if given the chance?" I asked.

She shook her head at the question.

"I am African," she said with a small smile.

I grinned at her as she exited the room. The more time I spent with Mary, the more I knew I wanted to emulate her conviction.

Before we had time to fully settle into our home, we were called to the feast of the unfortunate ox. The walk from David and Mary's door to Sechele's was only ten minutes. David pointed in another direction on the way, stating that was the direction of the school in which I would be helping him and Mary.

"You will enjoy the native children, I think. They are fond of Mary, as am I." He looked lovingly at Mary, who shook her head and rolled her eyes. We all shared a laugh.

The celebratory feast was held at the chief's fire pit, or *kotla*, which is to say, his place of gathering. Here, many dinners were consumed and many stories told. The Bakwena were gathering into the area and sitting in a general circle around the fire pit. Our friend the ox was roasting above a roaring fire in preparation.

I looked around at the Bakwena. I was not sure yet how they perceived me—mostly I received confused looks. I felt certain that, at least occasionally, some tribesmen wondered if this little girl was lost and looked as if they were ready to offer me instruction on how to depart. However, I perceived them differently than I guessed they perceived me. They were, in a word, noble. I knew that one singular mother in this wide circle could teach me a thousand skills on survival. Each tribesman and woman had been introduced to, conquered, and moved on from numerous skills I had yet to learn. Their experience showed in their faces. They were confident in their knowledge and experience.

As we began to settle in the circle, I could see the order of things. Sechele's seat was across from us, the ground was covered in blankets for him to sit on. He was not present yet, but his wives were lined along what would be his left. They were comfortable in their positions. I realized they were seated in the same order they had entered the room earlier, possibly in the order in which they were married to Sechele. There was pride in their eyes. They were glad to be the wives of a chief. I cringed as I wondered if they knew they were about to be divorced.

It was soon after these thoughts passed through me, that my eyes noticed what I should have seen from the beginning. All of Sechele's wives, Selemeng excluded, had cut their hair into a short, messy style, each at about an inch and a half long. They periodically ran a single hand through their scalps and smiled to each other. What shocked me further was each had cut a perfect slice out of their beautiful dresses, directly over their left knee, precisely where I had torn mine only days ago. Because they wore skirts with many layers, they purposefully pushed their one knee through the hole.

The sight of them was startling to me. Three regal queens, sitting cross-legged on the ground with short tattered hair and one bare knee coming out of their cotton coverings. I looked to Mary for some kind of explanation. She had her mouth in her handkerchief, quietly holding back laughter. David had noticed them as well and kept finding excuses to touch his cheek or mouth in an effort to cover his smile.

My mouth opened and refused to be closed. Did I have more influence than I realized as a former member of polite society? These wives saw that their husband admired the English, so how could they resist imitating a young woman come to them who was born and raised English? Their dedication to him was endearing. Remembering their possible future, however, I cringed again.

Sechele arrived. The tribespeople stood while he entered, as did we. As he moved through the crowd, he made slow progress while he stopped to talk to several families. Everyone was visibly happier with Sechele near. He seemed to be a beloved chief.

Kgosi Sechele sat and in accordance we took our seats as well. Sechele began to speak in Sechuana with David translating.

"Welcome, my beloved tribesmen, to this welcoming feast for the return of our friends the Livingstones!" he spoke gesturing to David's family. "And a special welcome to their friend, Miss Anna, who will be starting soon as an assistant school teacher." Sechele smiled at me kindly. Every eye around the circle was trained on me. There was a notable stir amongst the crowd. I waved simply. Sechele smiled.

"My dear friend David came when I was younger in the face and smaller in the waist. He came with his faithful friend Mebalwe. At first I was not very fond of Ngaka." The tribe all seemed to take this in stride. "But as he approached he said 'Hail! Sechele, Great Elephant of the Bechuana,' and I liked him the more."

The listeners, including small children, all nodded in approval.

"I commanded the doctor to give my daughter some medicine, for she was ill and thrashing about. He told me only his God could heal through him, and so I allowed him to see my little one."

He turned behind him and wrapped an arm around a teenage girl's waist, then lifted her as if she weighed no more than a leaf and set her on his lap. This was the daughter he spoke of. Her name was Ope. She seemed accustomed to his behavior and giggled while she bit her fingernail.

"I told the white man, 'If you kill my daughter, I will kill you!'"
Ope's smile and my eyes became wider. "But Ngaka said there was
something bad inside her and he had to get it out."

David halted his translation for a moment and whispered to
Mary so that I could hear as well. "Appendicitis."

"But the Lord was with us in His great mercy, for the bad piece
was taken out of her and with only a little rest she was playing again."
The mention of deity was the only time the tribe's people seemed
uncomfortable, fidgeting on their blankets.

"Then the Ngaka gave us the gospel and we were all joyful,
knowing about our Savior and Redeemer Jesus Christ."

The tribe looked even more uncomfortable.

"Eat! Eat!" Sechele spoke suddenly, his story abruptly over.

Sechele had prepared for this feast well. We were served with a
constant stream of peanuts, roasted maize, boiled roots that I was
told were called *manioc*, guavas, and honey, along with the roasted
ox meat that had been so meticulously prepared. My little family and
I ate until our bellies were full.

I noticed a tiny face peering at me from behind Sechele's back.
This would not have gained my attention by itself. Almost all the
faces were still staring at me, but this little face was smiling. I grinned
back. And he giggled and covered his mouth as if I had told a terrific
joke. This made me smile wider. He could not be older than nine
years old. His face held that same wisdom mixed with amusement
that Sechele's held.

Mary noticed my amusement and smiled as well. She turned her
face to me and spoke the boy's name.

"Motsatsi, son of Sechele."

Soon, we were excused and started the walk back home. I carried
Agnes as she slept, full and happy on my shoulder.

The children tucked in, the meat removed from the smolder-
ing fire, and our good nights said, I settled into my first night as a
missionary in the city of Kolobeng. As hot as the day had been, the
evening was delightfully refreshing.

I fell asleep in a new home.

Chapter 12

We started the day, and all the days to follow, at six a.m. We gathered together in the common room amidst all our sleeping rooms for a morning family worship. David would read long passages from the Bible while we sat and contemplated our place in the eternities. These mornings I thoroughly enjoyed. Shortly after, we breakfasted. This meal regularly consisted of porridge made by Mary with my prepared fire, and rusks, which were a simple hard biscuit. Breakfast cleared and dishes cleaned, David, with the occasional assistance from Robert, would go to milk the cows. He once said that all ten of his cows combined could not produce as much milk as one Scottish cow from his boyhood. Nevertheless, we made great use of the milk and cream they produced, and so he accomplished his milking while I began my lessons.

My first lesson in survival was soap making. I confessed to Mary I did not know the first thing about soap, truly. In fact, as I learned, it is made from ashes of a particular plant called saltwort. I made a large fire of saltwort plants, then as it died down, Mary and I retrieved a tray of molds to house the soap. Mary showed me how to use the ashes to make a paste into the molds. They would need to sit for six weeks. The process amazed me. Out of the ashes came the secret to personal hygiene.

Immediately after the soaps were poured into their molds, Mary took me to her small lean-to kitchen on the side of the house. I thought of the massive kitchen at my mother's house where fifty of

Mary's lean-tos could fit inside. Although it could not have been later than eight a.m., a steady stream of perspiration ran the full length down my back.

David ground some wheat for Mary, and she brought all the ingredients together for bread while I watched flabbergasted. Mary knew how to do everything, I was convinced. She showed me how to knead the dough, and I felt confident my fire making had made my arms stronger to help her. Unfortunately, even with my newly acquired strength, Mary had to finish my kneading after only five minutes of my attempts.

I looked around myself for the oven. None could be seen. I took a few steps outside the space and looked on the other side of the shed. Nothing. Just rocks. Mary came up behind me with the pans of raw dough in her hands.

"Follow me, Miss Anna, I will need your assistance," she demanded.

We walked about five minutes from the house before she halted. She had stopped at, what appeared to me, a rock that was slightly bigger than the rest.

"Please lift that large rock, Miss Anna," she said simply.

My mouth gaped open and I stood motionless.

I stuttered, "M-Mary?"

"Do as I tell you," was all the explanation she gave me.

Baffled and hesitant, I leaned over and spread my arms wide over the large mass. Shifting my hands around, I soon found a most fortunate grasp and pulled up with all I had. Surprisingly, the stone came up in my hands and I was able to carry it only a few feet from where it lay. I was happy with myself as I set it down. I would not have guessed I was capable of that. I turned to Mary, who smiled at me in pride.

"Was there a purpose to my Herculean display of strength?" I asked in mock humility. "Or were you simply morbidly curious?"

Mary actually chuckled!

"This is our oven, Miss Anna," Mary explained, at last. She squatted down and placed her pans in a hole the stone had been covering. "The heat is trapped inside the hole when the rock covers it." I ducked down to get a closer look at what the space consisted of. Upon very close inspection, I could see hundreds of minuscule ant trails all around the opening.

"Is it an anthill?" I inquired of her.

"It used to be," she responded. "It has been neglected for years. David discovered it for me when we first arrived in Kolobeng. Isn't he clever?" She smiled.

"The cleverest," I returned, still amazed. Via Mary's instructions, I carefully returned the flat rock and we returned home, allowing the bread to bake for several hours.

Once back in the lean-to, Mary stated it was time for lunch and pulled a large pot of soup, already prepared, from a cupboard in her lean-to. She amazed me again!

"Where did you get that?" I asked, sincerely confused.

"Oh, Anna," she answered, smiling, "I have to be at the beginning, middle, and end of everything. If I had not prepared this meal last night, we would not have anything for lunch right now."

I considered that. I had not thought about what we would eat for lunch the next day. I had not begun to think that far in advance. Not yet. But Mary thought hours, days, months, and years ahead. That was what made her successful.

I peered at the soup. She had finished cooking the meat Sechele had given us, cubed it, and made this soup with it.

"And do you never grow weary?" I implored. "Being at the beginning, middle, and end of everything? You must get frustrated."

She shrugged modestly. "When I first began my life as the wife of a missionary, I had lived with my parents in a more established and stationary missionary center with my nine brothers and sisters constantly around me. After I left them, the solitary nature of mobile missionary work depressed me. After one particularly frustrating day I said to myself, 'Is *this* the sort of work I have left home and friends to spend my life doing in this uncongenial land?'" She paused to shake her head at her past exclamations that I would have thought perfectly justified. She continued. "But I heard a voice within say, 'Ah! If I may be a hewer of wood and a drawer of water for the temple of my God, am I not still blessed and privileged beyond words?'"

"This was a landmark in my life. I realized my chief work is to keep my husband *up*—up from sinking down, down gradually into native style of living—and from losing heart and spirit in that great work, in which I but act as an organ-blower to the musician."

She smiled simply, joyful. I stood in awe. How had I lived to this point and never met anyone like Mary? She was the embodiment of humility and self-denial. She had made herself simply a doorway through which one could see God on the other side.

That night, David held a small sermon, which he invited the entire tribe to. We set out blankets around our little fire near the white house. Mary had prepared biscuits and some vegetable soup. I asked her if she always provided refreshment.

"Neither civilization nor Christianity can be promoted alone," she spoke wisely. "If they are encouraged to strengthen their spirits by strengthening their bodies, I am happy to oblige."

After all the preparations were made, David buried himself in his notes and Bible. Mary sat darning a few socks. Robert and Agnes were throwing a ball back and forth. Slowly, a few members of the tribe came to sit around our fire. I smiled to them in welcome. They timidly grinned back. Sechele arrived last and sat among his people, in no special place of honor. He smiled and joked with the people around him, grasping shoulders and nodding hello to everyone around him. A child came to sit on his lap. I did not know if it was his child or not.

David began his service. He was teaching about the day of judgment straight from his Bible.

"'For surely a day of judgment must come. Where all men must be brought to kneel at the feet of the Savior and report their deeds, whether they be good or whether they be evil.

"'Then I saw a great white throne and Him who sat on it, and the earth and the heaven fled away. And there was found no place for them. And I saw the dead, small and great, standing before God, and books were opened. And another book was opened which is the Book of Life. And the dead were judged according to their works, by the things which were written in the books. The sea gave up the dead who were in it, and Death and hell delivered up the dead who were in them. And they were judged, each one according to his works. Then Death and hell were cast into the lake of fire. This is the second death. And anyone not found written in the Book of Life was cast into the lake of fire.'"

My eyes wandered. I regarded Sechele, who once wore his usual smile, had now become much more serious. As David continued to teach, Sechele became more troubled.

The speech ended, the food gone, and bellies satisfied, everyone turned themselves in the direction of their beds. Sechele stayed behind to speak with David. He was still upset.

"Did your forefathers know of this future judgment?" he asked.

"Yes," David answered.

Sechele shook his head.

"You frighten me. These words make all my bones to shake." He put his hand on David's shoulder as if to steady himself. "My forefathers were living at the same time yours were, and how is it they did not send to tell them about these things? They all passed away in darkness without knowing whither they were going."

David was silent. He had no answer, no solace.

Sechele sent three of his wives home the next morning. David brought the news home. Sechele had sent them all home with many new possessions and fine things. The families of the women, however, were still extremely upset. David did not feel they would act out violently. They were not prone to hostility, especially with the missionaries.

"Which wife did he keep?" I asked.

"Selemeng. She is the wife he married first," David explained. I must have been correct in my assumption at their seating arrangements at the feast. Selemeng was seated closest to Sechele.

"I feel sad to have the children separated in this way," I said.

"Oh, the children will stay with their father," David explained. "It will only be the wives that must return home."

My chest tightened.

"You mean the mothers will be separated from their children?" I asked, incredulous. I looked to Mary to see her reaction—but there was none. I turned back to David.

"It is their way. The mothers would feel even more shame if their children did not get to claim being raised by a chief. I am sure there will be no resistance from them."

He paused for a moment and let me digest this. "It seems with the announcement of his baptism, the biggest concern of the people is that Sechele will no longer perform the rain making ritual," he explained.

"What is rain making exactly?" I asked, interested. "Obviously it must be where they try to summon moisture, but how is it done?"

"Oh, it is a very superstitious practice," he explained. "They will sometimes use charcoal made from burned bats, jackal livers, baboon, and lion hearts to smear on their bodies or on the earth. A traditional dance is performed. It is all out of desperation, I feel."

"But they feel the rain depends on Sechele's ceremony?"

"They do indeed," he said gravely.

"No doubt they will feel much better when Sechele is baptized and the rain continues regardless," Mary commented.

"That may be true," David agreed.

◇◇◇

The baptism was held the first Sunday in October. Despite it being the beginning of their hot season, a large crowd had gathered. A mixture of morbidly curious and vehemently opposed individuals stood together on the banks of the Kolobeng river. Some, I had heard, came to see if Sechele would drink man's brains. Because I could not understand their language, I tried to read the questions on their faces. I felt I had a pretty good idea.

"Why is he doing this to us?" I imagined them asking. "Why forsake our ancestor's traditions?" Betrayal drifted in the air, filling in the cracks of the ever-present confusion and anger. The general mood of the group triggered a feeling of déjà vu in me, but I could not exactly place how this situation was similar to any other I had experienced.

My attention was diverted by one small group of women who sat silently together, but apart from the rest. Sechele's discarded wives.

Before, I had seen them conversing excitedly with one another at the tribal assembly. Now, a word could not be drawn from them. They sat silently, their hair still short from the recent style change, and the evidence of their cut dresses still present, although two of them had sewed the hole back up again. The sight of them broke my heart. Their short hair and torn garments now seemed to be a mark of shame they could not reverse.

Still, there was much to admire them for. If they had not truly loved Sechele, they would surely have moved far away, yet here they sat. Hurt, but present. Supportive, although disgraced. I moved to stand near them. Something inside of me wanted to comfort them, and this was the only method I could conjure.

A low hum of Sechuana pulsed from the crowd, until the participants in the baptism arrived. David held a special communion with Sechele and his children before the ceremony. Now they came toward us, dressed in white. Their happy smiles grew smaller and smaller the closer they came to our little group. I tried to catch their eyes and smile, but they were consumed with the bluntness of the depressed group. Sechele, wearing a cloak David had ordered from Scotland, set out to walk up the hill with Selemeng, who seemed no longer resistant to the new religion. Presumably it suited her to be the only wife left and the queen.

David took Sechele into the water first. A baptismal chair sat immovable in the rushing current, tall, white, and impressively detailed with angels, flowers, and crosses. The chair had arrived only two days ago, despite being ordered from America more than two years ago, and had spent that time being made and then being carted on one ship after another, onto one dock after another, and then onto several wagons, arriving just in time. David and Sechele saw it as a sign that God was pleased. The chair was regal and beautiful, made even more so by the chief sitting so happily on it. Mary and the children smiled proudly at David, and he smiled back. Sechele smiled at his children, who were obviously affected by the mood of the crowd because they stayed silent and unsmiling. The prayer was said, and David doused Sechele in water. Several members of the tribe shouted out in alarm, I whipped around to see one woman kneeling on the ground sobbing as if she had lost a family member. I felt a strange moment of déjà vu as I watched her. A sharp pain came to my heart and my stomach dropped to my knees. The tribe's people felt that Sechele was distancing himself from them. They felt that he was discarding them for no discernible reason.

I could relate to this misery.

I rushed forward instinctively to help her off the ground. As I gently put one hand under her elbow, she jerked away from me and was up on her feet so quickly I jumped in fright.

"*Baloi*!" she spoke quietly, so as to not gather attention from the chief, but so menacingly that I took a step back from her sudden hostility. I looked around myself for some explanation. The people around me simply looked at me with similar expressions. It seemed they agreed with whatever she had called me. I hastily retreated closer to the river and to Mary, my eyes downcast.

As Sechele opened his eyes, the droplets ran off his face one by one. The sun shone off his face and he was solemn and contemplative. David offered his hand, and they stood together in the water a few moments before Sechele nodded. He looked to David and one side of his mouth rose in a half smile. He spoke in Sechuana and David grinned appreciatively. Sechele put one arm around David's shoulders and they exited the river as the comrades they were.

I looked around to my companions. A slight change had overcome a few of them. They seemed relieved, as if they had been expecting an explosion, and now had found themselves safe. A few looked truly touched. For the most part, however, the group remained staunch and unmoving. David continued baptizing Sechele's children as I observed the people. Across our group of about two hundred souls, I recognized a face I had seen once before. David's Boer friend, Abraham, the leader of the band of Boers, stood in our midst. I turned myself to observe him. He was as angry and hostile as before, his wide hat casting a harsh line of shadow on his face. The lines seemed deeper on his face. I felt incredible pity for him and his family. They had been attacked by Dingane and were still healing. He sensed my gaze and turned to me.

"You're a part of the tribe now?" he asked me bluntly.

"Yes, I am trying," I responded.

"Why?"

I tilted my head, pondering.

"I enjoy their company."

He stared at me, emotionless for a moment, then shook his head, turned, and walked away.

I broke my gaze from him and saw Sechele staring at his back. His countenance was saddened.

Now that all of the children were baptized, the group began to scatter. I noticed none of them spoke with the chief. I suppose they didn't know what to say. I approached him, however.

"Congratulations, Kgosi Sechele." I shook his hand. "It is a happy day!" I don't know if I was attempting to convince him or myself.

"Yes!" he agreed, grinning. He patted my hand in a wise sort of way. His attention turned to the small, solemn group of women who remained behind. He turned to me for a moment and excused himself.

He walked over to his former wives and shook each of their hands. He spoke quietly and personally with each one, giving each a piece of his attention. One by one, they departed, a little more contented, I thought. I joined the Livingstones, and Sechele joined us all together.

"We would be honored to have you over for dinner this evening, Sechele," Mary invited him. "We would like to celebrate with you and Selemeng."

"That would be very good, Mma-Robert," he agreed. "I would be happy."

"It is to be a simple affair, Chief. So you need not dress up." She seemed to stress this point with him most sternly. He smiled.

"I will arrive, Mma-Robert. Thank you," he complied.

On our walk home, I asked David what Sechele had said when he emerged from his baptism. He smiled to himself, then told me.

"'God is good. And I am God's.'"

Back at the house, Mary and I began to prepare the chief's celebratory feast while Robert and Agnes enjoyed a chameleon they had found on a tree. They were placing the patient animal on every diverse material they could find to watch it change the color of its skin.

We had come back to a surprise. Mebalwe had delivered a small box of apples and a sack of potatoes.

"Where did he get these?" I asked Mary, amazed.

"Kuruman," she answered as if the answer were implied.

"What is Kuruman?" I asked, truly confounded. "Who sent them?"

"Kuruman is my parents' missionary establishment. They're from my mother," she confirmed affectionately as she displayed the box of apples. Mebalwe smiled.

"Your mother lives only hours away?" I asked bewildered. "Mary, why do we not go to see her?"

"It would take us days in a wagon, Anna," she explained. "It is not essential. We have no time for social visits and I have small children to mind. We will see them at Christmastime, I have no doubt. Now begin peeling these potatoes for me."

I sat mechanically and took the small knife she was handing me. We were quiet for a time while I peeled potatoes and she worked to shred the meat.

"Mary," I began my only question, "is it difficult for you to have your family so close and yet so far away?" I wondered if this was the reason she had kept silent.

She turned to me with a kind smile on her face.

"It is difficult, Miss Anna, but I do try so very hard to speak of my blessings rather than my burdens."

How unlike the rest of the human race Mary was! I had so very much to learn from her quiet dignity. She turned back to her dishes.

Thinking of Mary's goodness and expertise, I was reminded of earlier events.

"Mary," I began again, "what does 'baloi' mean?" I had made sure to memorize the word exactly as the tribeswoman had said it..

She did not turn to look at me. "Witch," she translated simply.

A black anvil sat itself on my chest and refused to be discarded.

Soon, I found myself with a full half hour before dinner began. I knew I needed to prepare myself, for Mary had said tomorrow would be our first day in teaching school together. Surely it was the noblest of callings, I only hoped I could be as noble as the calling.

Mary had already informed me she kept a strict dress code with the children. I assumed she would keep the same standards with me. I had taken special care, until this time, to not put much thought into my appearance. I suppose now I would reconsider that plan since I was to be standing in front of young children as an example, and I did not want any more incidences of cut hair or ripped dresses. Luckily, my other dresses had not ripped yet, but they were still in desperate need of a good scrubbing. I took several simple dresses out to a barrel in the blazing evening sun, where I used as little water as I could to scrub the garments clean.

Once they were cleaned and hung on a line to dry, I turned to the house in time to see Mary step onto the porch to beckon her children inside to wash their hands. What a pretty picture were they! They let the chameleon go free and waved goodbye to it as they scampered into the house. I let them pass in front of me, then turned slightly and became startled by a small tribal boy whom I felt sure had not been in that spot two seconds ago. It was Motsatsi, son of Chief Sechele.

"Oh!" I spoke suddenly, surprised. "I had not seen you, Motsatsi."

"How do you know my name?" he asked, chin raised, eyes squinting.

"Mary told me," I informed him.

"And how did *she* find my name?" he asked curious.

I laughed. "Is your name a big secret, sir?"

"*Very* big," he said seriously.

"Well, if it is a secret, would you be so good as to introduce yourself to me now?" I suggested.

"Very well," he said, very dignified. "I am Motsatsi of the Bakwena! Son of Kgosi Sechele!"

"I am very pleased to meet you, Your Royal Majesty," I bowed deeply. This satisfied him. "Although, you are not the first prince I have met."

"What?" he questioned. "You met another son of a Kgosi? My brother?"

"No, he was the son of the queen of England, Queen Victoria," I clarified.

"And this queen," he inquired, "does she have many cows?"

"I am not sure, Your Royal Highness," I responded, unable to keep from smiling.

He did not seemed impressed if the number of her cows was not widely known.

The rest of his family soon came toward the house in a small group. His mother, Selemeng, was easily recognizable of course. Her way of walking matched her steadiness of character. She seemed born to be a queen. Her head was adorned with a large white hat, and she wore a simple cream colored cotton dress. I imagined she always liked keeping her appearance plain. She led her small children by the hand, of which there were seven, all varying from two to eleven years old. However, even this small extraordinary group could not be as eye-catching as Sechele.

Despite Mary's plea for him to dress casually, here he came marching toward our modest home in a long crimson robe, the brightest red I had seen on this continent swept gracefully behind him as he led his small band to supper. He wore an intricately embroidered vest with a shining white tunic underneath, his legs adorned with black slacks with silver threading. His one hand held a brass poker, which could easily have been mistaken for a royal scepter. All that was lacking was a crown.

I shook my head and smiled in sheer delight of the spectacle. Never could I have imagined Sechele's character, nor portrayed his likeness. He was entirely his own. However, as unique as he was, Mary would not be amused.

Mary emerged that moment from the front door.

"Anna, would you be so good as to—" she was cut short by the site of His Majesty. "Land's sake! Sechele, what did I tell you about your clothing? Couldn't you simply wear a respectable jacket?" She raised her arms, then dropped them, as if heavy, down to her sides.

"What is more respectable than what other kings have worn?" he said with an air of nobility. It seemed a perfectly legitimate question to all around him. The children could not imagine why Mma-Robert was so upset.

"Oh good gracious," she muttered impatiently. "Come inside then, your supper is waiting."

Sechele and Motsatsi ushered the women in the door before them. Soon after, the young prince staunchly climbed the two steps with an immovable chin, and the king swept his cape to the side and followed suit.

Mary had set our modest table with a clean, albeit used, white tablecloth. Worn and old place settings dotted the square for us and our guests. I could not help but instantly prefer this setting to any my mother had spent excruciating months imagining. The adults sat in their places, appointed by Mary, while the children simply sat on blankets on the floor. I noticed Mary sat the adults in the polite English way of separating the spouses from each other. It seemed a silly tradition to me. If I had a husband whom I loved as much as Mary loved David, I should like nothing better than to sit next to him with a full meal ahead of us to hold hands.

David offered a blessing on the food and we began. Mary had made a splendid dinner with the potatoes her mother had sent. Boiled potatoes and boiled meat with a good helping of salt was a better meal than we had had in weeks. Potatoes were, thus far, the pearls of the African desert.

As the food was passed round, Mary began a conversation with the king and queen.

"Kgosi Sechele, how do you feel being newly baptized?" she inquired. I had a slight twinge of guilt knowing they would be speaking English only for my benefit. Everyone else in the room spoke fluent Sechuana.

Sechele took a long moment to respond. David looked up through his bushy eyebrows with just a hint of worry on his face before Sechele finally answered.

"Taller, Mma-Robert. I feel *taller* baptized."

David smiled, extremely pleased, and returned to his supper.

"That is a very apt description, Kgosi Sechele," Mary praised him.

Selemeng sat an unmoving yet silently supportive companion to Sechele. It felt odd and uncomfortable that she had chosen not to be baptized while her husband and all of her children had done so. Still she did not argue or put up a fuss, at least with the missionaries in the room. I wondered what their conversations were like behind closed doors.

"And how do you feel the tribe's people get on?" Mary asked, truly concerned for their happiness. "Have you been treated unkindly?"

Sechele looked surprised. "I shall not be treated unkindly," he said indignantly. "I would disgrace the name of Kgosi if I allowed it."

"Mary meant only that you must feel the uneasiness of the people," David clarified for her. "You must sense it as well as I that the people are feeling hurt."

"You know," Sechele began as he helped himself to a spoonful of potatoes. He swallowed the potatoes and then used his spoon to gesture as he spoke. "When old Kgosis found an interesting thing, the people joined him. If he smiled at hunting, all young men would sharpen their *assegai* and practice until the sun woke up to contest for a place in his hunting party. If the Kgosi was interested in music, all would gather together to sing for him deep into the dark. And yet, I am interested in gospel, and none come to share this with me."

I could feel the hurt, betrayal, and frustration come off of him in waves. An idea struck him suddenly. Turning to David he relayed it.

"Ngaka," he spoke excitedly, "do you imagine these people will ever believe by your merely talking to them? I cannot make them do anything except thrashing them. If you like, I shall call my head men, and with our litopa we will soon make them all believe together!"

I attempted to discreetly hide my mouth behind my napkin. I don't believe I succeeded, however, because Motsatsi gave me a stern glance. Obviously, he found nothing amusing in his father's scheme.

"Although I can appreciate the sentiment behind your offer, Kgosi," David began diplomatically, "I cannot think it right to force conversion."

Sechele nodded, accepting this advice. But soon he had more to say.

"It is only that the Bakwena are lacking in good questions," he said, truly frustrated.

I could not help noticing Selemeng looked particularly irked by this statement. I knew her heart was with her people.

"I understand your frustration, Sechele," David spoke sympathetically. "Who can know better than I? Yet still, we need to hope for the best and keep an eye single to His glory."

Sechele nodded, but then bowed his head, slightly defeated. Any small criticism from David, I would find in the coming months, he would take with great gravity.

I decided to turn the conversation to my curiosity.

"Kgosi Sechele," I addressed him formally, "I would like to hear the story of how you became king. David related to me once that bad men tried to take your title away." I tried to keep my English simple, though I wondered if there was truly a need.

"Yes, they did," he confirmed. "My father, Motswasele, was king of the Bakwena before. He was not the best king of our ancestors," he admitted. "His brothers put him to death in front of his people. Before he died, Father cursed his brothers that they would regret killing, that they would be lost, that ants would devour their land and their cattle. I saw it all. I had ten years."

I was unable to process the image of a ten-year-old boy watching his father be murdered. He continued.

"My mother, and some who were loyal, feared for my life and drew me from that place and took me into wilderness. I wandered for years like a lion without its pride. On the edge of my wanderings, a chief named Sebego gave me cattle, which I named 'Difetlhamolelo.'" He and the Livingstones smiled while I waited for translation. David gave it to me.

"It means 'lighters of the fire.'"

"I light fire of my people's love. I turned the small cattle into fat and then into many, and returned to my people with many cows, as their rightful king. My uncles flew from their huts. They left the wives to run from me. They thought I delivered the curse my father gave them."

I nodded, taking note that the Bakwena feared any sign of witchcraft. I also noted that, in many situations thus far, to have cattle meant you were wealthy.

"Where is your mother now?" I questioned.

"She went to the Lord three years after I am king," he spoke with sadness. "She saw her son have success, instead of drying out in the desert."

I nodded again stupidly. I never knew how to console others with bad news.

"Now, Anna," he effortlessly turned his voice to a more cheerful tone. "I told you my story, now it is time for yours."

I froze.

"What would you like to know, Chief?" I asked warily.

"You lived at London?" he started with a vague question, but the interest burned in his eyes.

"Yes," I spoke slowly, trying to be honest.

"In which circle did you run? Were you servant? A queen?" he guessed.

I chuckled. "Somewhere in between."

David eyed me curiously.

"And what is a London day?" he was anxious to know. "How were you busy?"

A few sarcastic, and also true, answers came to my mind, but I chose the stereotypical London version of a young eligible female. I assumed this would interest him more than my trauma.

"Most people in London wake long after the sun, sometimes eleven or twelve o'clock. Then they receive morning callers, or visitors to their home. Afterwards they are not of much use," I added honestly. "Most of the daylight is used in taking walks, playing silly games, and making yourself ready for the nightly functions of balls or parties."

The look on Sechele's face told me he had absorbed every detail I had shared, caching it away in his mind for future reference. It also told me he wasn't fooled. He knew I had deliberately generalized the question to not include myself specifically.

"Your parents?" he asked simply, but the effect was akin to someone squeezing my heart. "Do they like events?"

Every adult eye was on me. Mary was concerned for me. David was condoning the morbid curiosity, but watching closely. Sechele was absorbed in learning more of English customs. Selemeng put on an air of disinterest, but was betraying herself by watching my face out of the corner of my eye.

"Both dead," I finally said. In an odd way, everyone seemed to relax.

"Then you and I have *two* things the same," Sechele confirmed. "Both orphans, and both have interest in British life." He smiled widely. "I, myself, would like to be a British subject one day."

"You mistake me, good Kgosi," I corrected, "I may have had an interest in British life as a child, but that desire has run thin with me. I should much rather like to be a citizen of the Bakwena."

"And we are honored to have you," he said amiably.

I smiled at his welcome.

Selemeng did not.

Chapter 13

In the morning, I arose a teacher. I felt empowered and ready for the challenge. Although life had left me bereft of several things, it had given me a good education. I washed my face and dampened my hair. I dressed in my clean, yet plain, yellow dress with no adornments. I took a few moments with my reflection to get my short hair to look slightly feminine. I was still lost on how to dress it or make it presentable at this length.

I stepped outside to the sun only just rising. The cool shadows of the night were being drawn into its rays, unable to remain while light shone. Although the heat during the day was turning unbearable, the mornings and evenings of Kolobeng were deliciously refreshing. I had not noticed immediately the presence of David. He stood to the rising sun with his eyes closed, his arms limp at his sides. He sensed my presence and opened his eyes.

"How often have I beheld, in still mornings, scenes the very essence of beauty, and all bathed in a quiet air of delicious warmth. Before the heat of the day has become intense, this forms pictures that can never be forgotten."

After a boyish grin, he donned his hat and moved inside. I tried to see what he saw. I closed my eyes and took a deep breath in. Then I heard Mary preparing breakfast in her lean-to. I finished my breath and went to help her in serving the porridge.

David practically inhaled his breakfast, several pieces attaching themselves to his growing mustache, and rushed out the door with a plan to dig some canals in the Kolobeng for their small garden. Mebalwe had volunteered to help him.

Mary kissed him goodbye while I sat with Robert and Agnes at the table. Agnes still needed occasional help with her spoon. Mary watched David trot away and sighed. Then she spoke almost to herself.

"It grieves one to think of a man so eminently fitted for linguistic preaching, being bound to spend his days in manual labor." She shook her head and then turned to me and my confused expression. "In other missions, the Society will provide an artisan for the work of building, digging, or general repairs and craft. Yet, there is no money for the employment of craftsmen, so he has to do what is necessary with unskilled assistance."

I had never seen Mary envious before. And envious of what? Nothing for herself. She wanted someone to help her husband so he could save souls more effectively. It made me hope that the five thousand pounds I had contributed would somehow reach our mission.

"And yet he seems happy," I tried to comfort her. "He does not seemed begrudged to dig canals while he preaches."

"No," she agreed. "We are the working clergy and make no mistake! David will always prefer poverty and mission service to riches and ease. It's his choice."

Breakfast was eaten and cleaned quickly and soon we were gathering our things to go to school. I had asked Mary if Robert and Agnes were coming with us, but she assured me there was a young sweet girl from the tribe that would watch them while we labored.

A knock at the door introduced the girl spoken of, and Mary allowed her inside and gave her quick and concise instructions in Sechuana. It was obvious this girl had watched the children before, however, because as soon as they saw her their little faces lit up and they cried, "Abeo!" They were obviously content in her company.

Soon, the children were settled and Mary was by my side with her teaching supplies in hand.

"Good morning, Motsatsi," she offered politely.

I had not even perceived him! And yet as I flipped around, there he was directly to my left, staring at me, unamused. I brought a hand to my heart in a vain attempt to slow it.

"Yes," Motsatsi spoke in a slow, droll way. "I am here to escort Mma-Robert and Miss Anna to school on Miss Anna's first day. You will follow me." He turned on his heel and began. Mary looked at me, smiling indulgently.

We followed Motsatsi across another section of the village. He insisted on walking in front to lead his subjects.

Citizens of the Bakwena would notice Motsatsi marching up the road and smile lovingly at him. His silliness was legendary. Soon, they would notice Mary and me following behind and doubt would enter their countenance. It would take some time for Sechele's baptism to die in popular topic, I was sure. With my arrival came the baptism of their chief and, unfortunately, the cessation of rain. At least they did not treat me with physical hostility.

Along the way, Mary pointed out a small tree that held the most radiant and intricate pink flowers I had ever seen! Each flower consisted of hundreds of minuscule sprouts. The smell transported me. I reached out to touch one and it recoiled and closed itself at the touch. Mary smiled.

"It's called mimosa," she said.

Finally reaching the steep hill to the school, we began our slow trod. I suspected from the very beginning that the slow pace of our walk was for my benefit. Although I tried to prove their caution unnecessary, I was winded by the time we made it to the top. Mary and Motsatsi looked on me calmly, unaffected physically by the hill.

"You will get it soon enough," Mary smiled. I tried to smile back through heavy, embarrassing breathing.

One building was used as both school and place of worship. As we entered the meeting house, I noticed instantly there was no flooring. The ground was exposed and raw. Mary entered as comfortable as if she were walking into her own bedroom. One window let in a breeze, to the otherwise stifling square room. Mary marched directly to the left of the small space and placed a few large plates of food on the ground. She had prepared twice-baked bread and a special treat of rhubarb jam for the children, with a pitcher of cow's milk to the side. As soon as all was prepared there, she moved to the head and center of the small space and sat down to read. I sat in a corner opposite her to observe.

Soon, children began to file in. They were dressed considerably different than I had seen them before. Where previously a clutch of strings or a gathering of beads hid their little bodies, now pressed white shirts and creamy clean aprons replaced their native garb. As each student entered, they each took a turn gaining acceptance from Mary. Her small eyes would peer over her book and inspect their clothing. Then if she were to nod, they would be allowed to sit. If she did not nod, she would gesture to them the fault she found with them; an untucked shirt, a loose hem, a hat purposefully askew, which did not please her. Soon, at least fifty small students had arrived and passed inspection. They all sat in the dirt around their beloved Mma-Robert.

She spoke in fluent Sechuana, so I could not understand most of what she said. Once in a great while a student would act out and be visibly reprimanded. The punishment for tardiness or bad behavior in Mary's school was to fetch water from the river. All she did was raise her empty bucket high above her head and state the child's name. The accused would have to march forward in front of his peers and take the bucket from Mma-Robert. By the looks on their sweet, pouting faces, I knew this form of discipline to be ideal. Carrying a heavy bucket for over a half a mile was something all of them wanted to avoid. More often, however, the children were smiling and giggling quietly at her cheerful little antics. Her singing of the Sechuana alphabet was a special treat for them. Sung to the tune of *Auld Lang Syne,* the children's faces would beam. They were especially keen on the treat of knowledge, and it was so obvious they loved their teacher. She was certainly strict with them, but sincerely caring. The food Mary had brought for them remained untouched along the far left wall of the space.

I sat and observed the first day. And how I enjoyed it! Nothing could be better than being around these little ones. School was their highlight where I had seen so many hundreds of children fuss and groan because they had to attend class or study new material. Not these children. They looked forward to Mary's lessons, even if they did pull and tug at their uncomfortable English clothing. Despite their interest in Mary's lessons, quite frequently the students would turn around and stare at me. I expected this. I knew I must look so queer to them. Every time this happened I would smile, wink, or wave, and they would turn back around without a returning gesture.

Mary dismissed class after six short hours. The time seemed to flow by for me, but the children looked slightly weary from sitting so long. Fortunately they had the bread, jam, and milk Mary had brought, and now took part in their refreshment. They hugged their Mma-Robert around the waist as a goodbye and dashed out the door. Soon all had departed and we watched as they tore the ties from their necks, the frocks from their chest's, and the shoes from their feet as they ran down the school hill. They were considerate of Mary's propriety as far as the classroom went, but as soon as they were able, they bolted down the hill at full speed, snatching the pesky clothing away as they went. I have often wished that sight could be frozen in a painting, a sight of perfect freedom.

"And now," Mary spoke, back to business, "you will come with me, Miss Anna, we will visit the village."

"Oh, thank you, Mary!" I thanked her sincerely. "I have been wanting to see more of it!"

Mary didn't smile or react to my enthusiasm at all. She took her large basket and stepped out the door for me to follow.

The walk down the hill, I imagine, was not as liberating when one could not dash off one's clothing. Nevertheless, Mary and I were enjoying being out of the stuffy room and out in the sunshine. A small wind had picked up, so the heat was not unbearable.

Soon down the hill we headed west, in the direction of the town. Mary kept a solemn face, and I followed her quick steps as well as I could. All too quickly, I was out of breath, but she continued even more quickly than before. She had become very determined since leaving the school. I waited to see why this was so.

Passing through the wall we came to a section of Sechele's village that I had not witnessed as of yet. This part of town was considerably more sparsely populated than I had seen thus far. Instead of fully constructed circular huts like the rest of the town, there would be only stationary walls, looking to fall down and collapse at any minute. Sitting up against the wall would be as many beings as could rest their back on the unstable surface, their bare skin absorbing the sunlight with no protection. A man on the far end had been gouged in the eye and could do nothing but sit in the open with a compress to push against the aching socket. A girl who could not have possibly been more than seventeen cradled a small screaming child, whose belly was bulging and distended while his limbs and features were stick thin. He needed water, food, and medicine. What did Mary have in her basket for him?

My horrible memories threatened to overwhelm me as they came pushing back. I found I could barely stand the sight of the hungry children and the suffering adults around them. I wanted to take off my bonnet, my shoes, tear out my hair, anything to give to these people. I must have something to give! But what good would it do? I would help one person, perhaps, when I could have been more frugal and had the ability to serve many! Why had I brought extra clothing in my pack? Why had I not filled it to capacity with food? If I had seen this before I sailed, I surely would have held some grain tightly in my hand the entire ship ride here. Now I had nothing. I was dependent on the Livingstones, with no financial support whatsoever. I had thrown it away. Surely the Missionary Society would have taken two thousand pounds for my passage, or possibly only one! How many supplies could I have bought at the port with such a sum? I could have fed that child. I could have built a communal house. They could have had shelter from the harsh sunlight and severe winds.

I forced myself to look at them, although I was feeling extremely dizzy; overburdened by my idiocy. I soon came to find that Mary was standing next to me, keeping me from falling.

I looked to her with guilt in my eyes and no words to say. I expected another reproach from her, like when I could not stomach the cleaning of our dead birds for dinner. She surprised me.

"I know, Miss Anna," she consoled. "I know."

I forced myself to stand on my own. If I were going to throw away the supplies these poor souls needed, I did not need to take their benefactress as well. I stood apart from Mary and watched as she passed out water and small pieces of bread and meat. She knew I could not do it myself. She passed out several small handfuls of a white dusty material, and I looked at her questioning.

"Salt," she explained.

I swallowed hard. Another substance I had taken for granted. They had no salt. I could not even tell you where my mother's cooks bought salt.

Mary was so wonderful with each one of them. She would hand them something, and of course they would ask for more. But she would touch their arm or face and speak softly in Sechuana, possibly reassuring them she would be back the next day. Soon, they would settle back in their space and slowly eat their piece of bread or attempt to use the blanket she gave them to provide some type of shade.

I confess I do not remember much more of this experience. I watched shocked and immovable, holding back my emotions as Mary passed out supplies to those who were most in need. A woman, whom I had thought quite destitute in comparison with all the polite society I had been accustomed to, was now the most wealthy of us all.

At last we departed and not much time had passed before we were back home. Mary moved directly to her lean-to kitchen to prepare dinner. I stood by her side for a silent moment before speaking.

"Do you need anything of me, Mary?" I whispered through clenched teeth.

She stopped and turned to observe me. What she saw convinced her.

"No," she replied mercifully. "You may go."

I turned on my heel and ran. I kept going until my body screamed against me. I turned a deaf ear to my muscles pleading with me to stop, my lungs begging me to halt my pace, my feet imploring me to save them. But I would not, or could not, stop until I was completely and utterly exhausted and alone, until there was no hope of me continuing. There, finally, I stopped and knelt beside a low tree and sobbed until there was nothing left inside of me.

◇◇◇

I had not realized I had fallen asleep. All I could remember was laying on the ground by the tree and now I was awake. I sat up, perplexed.

"And there you are," a familiar voice said. "Take this, and we begin again." A flask of water was being handed to me and I took it gratefully. I had not realized how desperately thirsty I had become. I drank half of its contents before I remembered the poor people on the other side of the village. I jerked it away from my lips, feeling unworthy of support, and handed it back to the owner.

He took it back and watched me carefully as I tried to straighten my hair and clean my face and hands.

"What are you doing here, Sechele?" I asked somewhat perturbed. "I am well and able to find my way back to the village."

"Then why did you not come when the moon was on her walk?" he said with mockery in his voice.

I jerked up to face him. "Has it been twenty-four hours?" I gasped.

"Ngaka, Mma-Robert and I have been searching for you," he explained. "It took some time. You are five miles away."

"Five miles," I repeated shakily. "Oh, I hate myself for putting you into such trouble! I only wanted to be alone!"

"Perhaps the stress of the change has made you sleepy as an old man who bows his head," he speculated. "Your body is tired, and so slept as long as was needed."

"Why should I sleep when others suffer?" I questioned him openly. "What have I done to deserve sleep and water and endless food, while they go without and are hungry?"

He watched me so intently while I asked these questions. I did not look at him, I could only feel it. He was trying so desperately to understand, and I was speaking in riddles. After a few moments of forming his words carefully, he spoke.

"You have a dark past, Miss Anna, so dark I dare not ask about it," he said carefully. "Would you trade your sorrow for water and food? Would you give your sorrow away?"

It was a provoking thought. It seemed tempting, but if Mother had not abused me, she would have chosen someone else. Would I subject another person to my mother's wrath if it meant I could now obtain food and water?

And another thought: if my mother had never mistreated me, would I have ever come to Africa? Would I have ever met Sechele?

"It is not for us to guess at God's plan for his children," he continued as he watched me pause, "only to be grateful for what he bestows."

I looked up at him and he was in such earnest that I was comforted. I sighed.

"How did you come to be so wise, Sechele?"

His laugh held some self-doubt.

"I sat with the young white man in the shade of a wagon, listening like a babe to his mama, as I was told that those who heard the word of God and did not heed it would be lost, and I was astonished." He was speaking of a younger David, I was sure. "I have clung to the Bible he brought ever since. If there is any wisdom in me it comes from the prophets."

I smiled.

"You have been lucky in your friendship with the Livingstones," I reflected. "If I had only known David and Mary, I should assume the entire race was exemplary."

"You don't believe your kind is good?" he asked curious.

"I don't," I replied without hesitation. "My relations with them, in general, have been foul. Of what I have seen of the world, although it has not been much, the white race is the most selfish and cruel of them all." My anger was turning to every wealthy nation in the world, who were ignorant of what was still fresh in my mind.

Sechele's forehead was creased in familiar lines as he processed what I had said. He nodded his head infinitesimally, letting me know he had heard what I had said. He was so very contemplative and inquisitive. Nothing spoken to him would simply pass through his ears. He pondered words—truly pondered them.

His forehead was still creased as he stood and walked away from me. For a hurt moment, I thought he had simply grown tired of our conversation. Soon, I realized he was heading toward a small patch of thick vines on the African floor some distance away. The terrain here was fascinating how it could transition from sand to vegetation in the most unlikely spots. As he reached the patch, he squatted down and pulled out a knife from his back pocket. He cut an orb-shaped fruit from the vine and started back toward me with it. As soon as I could hear his voice again, he began to explain.

"Last season was especially good for rain," he said. "The river flowed with water—there was no need to hide it. It ran free for all. In these seasons, a special fruit grows. I have some!" He held the fruit up for my observation. "It is the kengwe," he said. "Do you know it?"

"It looks like a watermelon," I ventured.

"Ah!" he said, "And how would you know, Miss Anna, if this was your native watermelon?" his pronunciation of "watermelon" made me smile. "Describe this watermelon to me."

Perhaps something I said had reminded him he had questions about our common vegetation. I collected all my adjectives of the fruit, knowing that if I did not give a complete description he would be disappointed.

"Well, it can be the same size as your kengwe." My pronunciation made him smile too. Apparently both our accents needed some work. "It is green on the outside with lighter stripes. It has a thick husk that when cracked open reveals red or pink insides. It is very juicy! But there are black seeds to be discarded."

"And is it sweet, Miss Anna? Or would your face squint at the taste?" he asked, curious.

"They are mostly sweet. Possibly it would depend on the season and the fruit's ripeness."

"That is very true." He spoke almost as if what I had spoken had disturbed him. I cocked my head and waited for an explanation.

"God put all this fruit on the earth, is that not so?" he said. "And is there ever a variety! Sweet fruit, bitter fruit, fruit that will poison the stomach when eaten too late or too early. But what makes a perfectly tasty fruit, I wonder? How do I know if this fruit will be sweet? How can I know which fruit to pick to feed my children? What makes a fruit delicious?"

I squinted my eyes. "Aren't you aware of all the fruit that grows here, Sechele? David told me you were an expert on living off of the land."

"I am not an expert in kengwe, Miss Anna," he said without false modesty. It was fact. "No one can predict whether this particular fruit will be sour or sweet."

He waited for me, his question still hanging in the air for me.

"Well," I struggled to come up with an answer, "my botany is not very good, but I would say that perhaps whether the fruit is sweet would depend on its environment. The circumstances of its surroundings would determine the taste."

Sechele gave me that wise, amused look that only he could give. "And thus we see, Miss Anna," he concluded, "God did not put sour fruit on the land. It is the fruit's surrounding that determines the worth. Even this kengwe—even when it covers the land for lengths and lengths—it is not always sweet. All this fruit is given the same water, sunlight, and air. Yet some still turn sour."

"And you would have to look inside the fruit, to know if it was sweet," I guessed.

"Yes! Now you understand! But because some of them are sour, my neighbors the Boers call them all "bitter fruit." Naming all of them that way was unwise." He used his knife to cut the piece of fruit in half, revealing a pink interior with small black seeds. He bit into the fruit and smiled.

"This fruit still has seeds to be avoided, imperfections to be seen, but it is mostly sweet. Even the Boers are not all sour," he spoke as he handed me the other half. I stared down at the fruit in my hands, my heart aching.

"And what if the fruit has no chance at being sweet?" I asked softly. "What if the fruit grows up surrounded by fire and no water?"

He chuckled.

"Well, Miss Anna, this is where our parable ends. Because I am certain that God loves his children more than he loves fruit." He ended my lesson with his wide grin. He stood, then strolled off, his hands in his English trousers.

I returned home with my head hung low. I was truly embarrassed by my behavior. I came upon Mary first, outside beating rugs with Agnes at her feet. I approached her timidly.

"I am truly sorry for causing you worry, Mary," I apologized.

My voice had startled her and she jerked around. Seeing my somewhat pathetic state, she nodded sympathetically.

"Sechele brought us a lovely piece of beef." She acted as if I had not spoken, while gesturing to the piece on the veranda. "Will you, please, prepare it and boil it as I showed you?"

I sighed in relief. "With pleasure, Mary. Thank you."

There was no forgiveness like being made useful again.

Chapter 14

Several weeks passed for us in a similar manner. Five days a week Mary taught school and I observed while assisting in any way I could. I became very good at staying cheerful in the face of so many who were upset with me for my rumored witchcraft. It was not uncommon for small groups of men and women to peer at me from the safety of a tree's shade and whisper "baloi" as I walked past.

My only friend, outside of Sechele, Mary, and her family, was Motsatsi. His sweet little temperament could not be dampened by his surroundings. Every day, without fail, he would meet me at the school room door and give me a bright smile. He was a beam of sunshine.

I did my best to move my thoughts to how I may be more useful to Mary. After school, she would take me down into the village where we would distribute what little we had to those who needed it most. These sessions did not prove any easier for me as the weeks went by, but I did not feel the need to run anymore, and I was becoming better at suppressing my deep feelings of remorse.

It was an unfortunate coincidence that no rain had fallen since Sechele's baptism. It fueled the people's hostility toward me, and in a small part toward David and Mary. David had, indeed, been regretting the loss of Sechele's young wives to his congregation. They had been his best pupils, intelligent and eager to learn from the Bible. He had once called them the most amiable females in the town. They strived to understand the importance of their husband's new belief and had been willing to adopt it themselves. They were to have formed the strong nucleus for conversion of the Bakwena people as a whole, or so David thought. He visited each one to express sympathy, but found he could do nothing to offset the conviction that the Christian church had abandoned them. One of the wives had tried to give David back his Bible but he would not take it.

And so it was true, that despite our desperate need for acceptance with the Bakwena, their amiability was sinking with the once booming river. A canal had to be built by David to bring water from the lessening river to our small garden by the house. Several of the tribesmen helped David in his pursuit. Although they wanted little to do with me, it was endearing to see some still felt the desire to assist their doctor in the support of his family. Yet, still, even with the help of David's friends, the lack of rain was starting to affect us. The lack was being felt all over the village. In an effort to find water, several tribesmen ventured out into the terrain to find small ponds or creeks, but the trip would require as much water for drinking as they could bring back, and soon their returning supply was used up.

Mary began to be very careful with our personal water use as well. It was Mary's idea to stop cooking with water all together. Mary showed me how to grill almost anything on a pan over a fire. Only very small amounts were used to wash the hands and face, and the majority of water was used solely for drinking, although I could not help but feel she was limiting our intake of that as well. I witnessed her storing it in small jars in a corner of her bedroom.

"Should we distribute some of these extra jars to the needy families in the village?" I asked her once. "Surely they would like to be storing water as well." I couldn't imagine many of the natives would have glass jars or jugs to use.

"Miss Anna, the Bakwena have been living on these plains for hundreds of years," she explained, somewhat defensively. "They may be at a loss for food, but you can be sure they know better how to preserve water than I."

David was fascinated by all biographical goings on. He would observe and take note of any peculiarity around us. He showed the children and me the large beetles that hid in the shade during the day. As we watched, one brave beetle came out of hiding, attempting to reach another area of shade. The heat and lack of humidity were so extreme it scorched to death within just a couple minutes and laid belly up to the sky in dry defeat. David gathered the small creature up in his gentle hands and carried it back to his study.

After these several weeks of observing her teaching, Mary allowed me to hold a small sewing class to the older girls after the main set of classes had finished. Those who wished to sew like a proper English woman were invited to stay. Despite my unpopularity, the schoolroom was filled. Soon I was standing in front of the large intimidating group.

"Hello," I began timidly. I received no response. Considering my lessons would be in English, and the majority of Bakwena spoke little to no English, my lessons would have to be pantomimed. Instead of speaking further, I picked up a small piece of fabric I had been working on through the afternoon as I sat in the hot schoolroom. With a small square of fabric, a needle, and a small snatch of thread I had torn from one of my dresses, I had sewn a small, yet pleasing flower.

The response was exactly as I had hoped. There were several gasps of approval and several more whose eyes widened in surprise at my skill. Of course, there were still more who stayed obstinately unmoved. I wondered if their legends of witchcraft included sewing flowers.

"This particular flower is especially easy," I spoke excitedly. "There are only a few simple petals so it does not take much time and can be added to all sorts of fabric." When I looked up, I could tell from their expressions that none had understood my rushed English. "I will show you how," I ended lamely. With that, I took a blank square of fabric and held it up as I made the small deliberate stitches, giving visual instruction as I went.

I kept trying to make eye contact with several girls whom I knew shunned me most vehemently. They were quite obstinate in their distrust of me. Several times I would be successful in catching their eyes as I explained my presentation and I would smile shyly. No smile was returned to me. Even those who were obviously absorbed in my demonstration were only interested in the flower and not in the creator.

Through my lesson, Mary kept piping up from the opposite side of the space to chastise the women for some fault, which, try as I might, I could not understand. Mary's booming Sechuana seemed to come at random. I noticed a few of the girls sat in small groups, talking amongst themselves in Sechuana, possibly they were saying inappropriate things. Mary's chastisements seemed to right their wrongs for only a few minutes, and then their unknown omission would repeat itself.

Having finished my demonstration, I handed the little creation to the girl sitting closest to me, her wide eyes rivaled in size only by her mass of hair. It took her a minute to understand my meaning as I offered her this little flower, but slowly she reached up and received it. Though she did not smile at me, she smiled down at the flower and that was enough.

I asked Mary about her scoldings after the class had been dismissed. She heaved a sigh of frustration before she answered me honestly.

"To the average African woman, their only object is to bear children. They were saying, 'A happy, honored woman is one who has many children and is fat.' The women look down on you because you seem weak and small. Ergo, you are not well-fed, not favored by your husband, and therefore not one to be respected."

I thought of London. In polite English circles I had been praised for my petite figure. Whereas older widows who increased in corpulence were the objects of snickering behind gloved hands. Here I was the point of ridicule for my thin frame.

We didn't go down to the village today. When I questioned Mary, she shook me away like a fly. I wondered at this for only a moment before realizing that we had run out of things we could contribute. We walked home slowly.

As we approached home, there was a small crowd just outside the porch, conversing with David. This, in itself, was not unusual. David taught several impromptu sermons in a week, so it could be that. It could also be that they were seeking medical attention. David frequently had a line of patients waiting for him when his day of manual labor was finished. The detail that proved unusual was, as they saw us coming closer, the crowd dispersed, each going their separate ways in haste. We approached David with questions in our eyes.

David smiled sadly. "Come inside, I will tell you."

We followed David inside and removed our bonnets. Mary excused herself for a moment to check on the children and their nanny. All was well, and she returned to hear the news.

"The people were here to beg me to release Sechele." He gave a mocking smirk.

"Release him?" Mary asked for clarification.

"Yes. They said if I could release Sechele from his obligation to be a Christian, then he could perform the rain-making ritual and they could be comfortable again. 'Only release Kgosi Sechele for one hour to make it rain, and then we will come to your church and sing and pray as much as you like,'" he imitated.

"Oh goodness," Mary said truly sympathetic. "What did you tell them?"

"I told them I would be happy to have them in church, but that I could not release Sechele from his baptism, since it was his own choice to do so." He paused, getting ready to repeat what they said to us again, "'We don't like you to speak on the subject of religion. Our empty bellies make us angry. We want rain, and if you argue, we think you don't want it, and our throats make us angry.'" He paused again. "They truly believe Sechele could make rain, but simply refuses to do it because I have convinced him not to! They see him as eccentric to the extreme."

"The drought is becoming troublesome," Mary added. "The Kolobeng river was even lower this morning. Do you think it could diminish completely?"

"I do," David confirmed, and my heart sank. Where would we get water if the river were to disappear? "I have never seen the moisture leave so quickly. This afternoon I recorded the temperature of the soil at one hundred and thirty degrees. I placed several of your sewing needles into the dirt, Mary. I am hoping in a few days they will have obtained some rust, so we can know there is moisture somewhere."

We both nodded, acknowledging the wisdom in this. We had to know what we were up against.

But there was no way we could have known to what extent our lives would change. It seemed to shift for us all drastically. After a few more weeks, the Kolobeng river did dry up. Hyenas scavenged the area in the daytime, without fear of man, to feed off the putrid mass of fish and one unfortunate alligator stranded in the riverbed. Still, with several dozen hyena scrounging around the area, they could not finish it all, and the smell that came from these events was inescapable in any part of the town. And the smell could not be escaped by the transporting scent of the mimosa tree. During a drought, it remained closed and I felt a pang every time I walked by its bare branches.

Where the heat had been manageable before, it now became oppressive. No matter what time of day Mary and I tried to rush to the schoolroom, we would still be soaked through with perspiration by the time we arrived, the sun dying our colorful garments into a bland canvas. Enormous centipedes would come out of their safe homes, unsuspecting, and roast instantly in the scorching blaze.

We stopped washing entirely. This was almost unbearable since the hot sun made us sweat through every piece of clothing before noon. We knew we were not clean, yet we continued on, trying to make the best of it. Mary continued to restrict our water intake, trying to save every drop she could. I could feel the desperation beginning to mount inside of me. It seemed impossible that there was nowhere we could get water. But the dry, grating feel of my throat was a constant reminder that we had run out of resources.

Despite the drought, and an ever-present headache as a result of his dehydration, David held church services three times a week in the same building we held school. Sometimes when the heat was too stifling, we would all simply congregate under the shade of a tree, the women fanning themselves and their little ones. Our group generally included Mary and her children, one steady old man named Sebite, Sechele's children occasionally accompanied by their mother, and a few curious village members. All the men wore dark pants, white button-up coats with white shirts underneath, and wide brimmed hats. The women wore simple, light colored dresses, with an occasional beaded necklace or broach. Of course, Sechele attended each meeting without fail, accompanied with his massive bible and pages of notes. This night he wore a suit, boasting a jacket with a fine lapel and trousers, which may have earned the approval of even Mary's strict expectations, if it had not been made entirely of tiger's skin. On his neck he wore a cravat so beautifully tied, so blazingly white, it would have made the wealthy of London envious. Despite his attempt at majesty, however, I could not help but notice with a smile that his trousers were too short, his coat too high, and his stockings the color of the soil around. He looked over his shoulder at me and smiled.

I noticed his children were each impeccably dressed. I later came to find that Sechele took the chore of dressing his children for church upon himself, claiming that no one could do as fine a job as he.

We began all meetings in the same way. We sat ourselves down and said all together, "A re shueng," which David told me could be translated as "Let us pray." It was interesting to note that the same word the Bakwena used to denote prayer could also be used denote death. We would use "A re tsoheng" to close the meeting, meaning "Let us rise."

This night, David incorporated some of his personal experiences into his sermon. Mary translated for me.

"When I was a piecer in a Scottish factory, the fellows used to try to turn me off the path I had chosen, and always began with 'I think you ought,' till I snapped them up with a mild, 'You *think!* I can *think* and *act* for myself. I don't need anybody to think for me, I assure you.'" He spoke in a gentle, chiding way.

"I soon resolved to devote my life to the alleviation of human misery. This must, according to my experience, be the way all through. I never followed another's view in preference to my own judgment. I did a thing out of deference to another when I myself thought it wrong, but I had reason to repent of it. I don't mean to inculcate rebellion, but we must all think and act for ourselves. I recall a venerable neighbor, David Hogg, who on his deathbed had said to me, 'Now, lad, make religion the everyday business of your life, not a thing of fits and starts.' I hope we may all emulate this example. Make religion an everyday business, not an occasional occupation.

"Some of the brethren do not hesitate to tell the natives that my object is to obtain the applause of men. This bothers me, for I sometimes suspect my own motives. On the other hand, I am conscious that though there is much impurity in my motives, they are in the main for the glory of Him to whom I have dedicated my all. Pray, my dear friends. Pray to know how you can dedicate your all to Him. Pray that you may come off conqueror."

David ended the meeting with one of his simple yet poignant prayers.

"A re tsoheng," we all recited and the group disbanded.

I stood quietly holding Robert's and Agnes's hands as I watched Sechele approach his teacher and exchange a few words.

"What nice words you speak to me. You have verily come to teach me things," Sechele said to David.

The trust and brotherhood they shared was something I had never witnessed before. Sechele clapped his hand on David's shoulder and laughed as only Sechele could laugh in response to something David had said to him. Then he handed David a large container and departed with his wife and many children.

Walking home as a group, I asked David what the pitcher contained.

"Water," he answered simply.

And so the teacher supplied the student with living spiritual water, and the student supplied the teacher with literal water so that the teacher might prosper.

Since the children had been asking for water, and we had already used our supply for the day, Sechele's gift of water had come at a most ideal time. Both the children had a glass to drink before retiring to bed. Seeing the water glisten off the corners of their mouths as they smiled was extremely gratifying.

The next day being Saturday, I took some time for myself to wander around the village, seeing things I had not seen before.

Having finished my chores, I donned my bonnet and set out into the blazing sunshine.

It amazed me that so many animals came so close to the village. The scampering of little conies and the antics of the baboons on the rocks were a never-failing delight. Their soft little cries echoed around me as I walked free around the outside of the town.

"You should not walk alone." His little voice did not surprise me now. I knew, somehow, he would find me today. He was as morally opposed to impropriety as his father was.

"Well then, why don't you be my escort, Motsatsi?" I asked amiably. I continued my walk with him playing guard to my side.

I moved forward toward some low hills I had not yet explored. Their slow undulation called to me, since I had mastered our steep schoolhouse hill. I was now sure I could climb all over their shapes without becoming instantly exhausted. We were some distance from the village when I was surprised to see a significant structure in the middle of an empty field. It looked like a large V-shaped corral of some sort. It was opened wide on one end and then came to a point. It was quite a large contraption to be so far outside of the village. I wondered at its purpose. I turned to Motsatsi in question, but he was ready to explain without my asking.

"It is a way to catch a lot of animals," he said. "When the herd comes, the men urge them inside the fence and the animals are trapped inside with no way to escape."

"Ah," I said, understanding. "That must be very effective."

"Yes," he agreed. "With only a few men, we can catch seventy to eighty animals at once, depending on the season."

"Have you ever helped?" I asked him curiously.

He gave me a disparaging look.

"No," he spoke as if it were obvious. "Only men catch the animals. I have not gone through our customs to become a man."

"What, do you mean a ritual of some kind?" I was intrigued.

His chin, somehow, reached higher to the clouds. "It is not to be spoken of in front of women."

I rolled my eyes.

"Ah," Motsatsi said in surprise, "what luck! Here comes a herd now!" He was speaking of a sound he heard, but somehow I had not. He grabbed my hand and pulled me to the top of a small hill, where we could overlook the V-shaped fence.

Suddenly, I could hear what sounded like a swarm of bees, but the sound was constant enough for me to realize something big was coming. Then, suddenly, around the hill came a large herd of a spindly looking creature with long horns, and I realized the sound had been the trampling of many hooves. These were the creatures I had heard David call gnus. Several tribesmen were working on either side of the mass of animals to keep them on track toward their creation. I was amazed at the speed these men could run! They kept up with the sprinting gnus, almost without effort. And even despite the gnuses' long horns, the herd was afraid of the slight men who herded them.

Working together, the men were able to push most of the herd into the V-shaped coral. Watching the spectacle, I was suddenly confused. The fence was nowhere near large enough to house all these animals, and the men kept pushing more and more animals into the small space. To what end? I wondered. It was only in that moment that I realized that at the end of the fence, at the point of the V shape, was a large pit with long pointed stakes protruding from its depth.

Suddenly I felt sick to my stomach.

Half a second after I made this discovery, the amount of animals in the small space proved too much and the first group of unfortunates fell into the pit. I could not watch. I turned my face away, but could not escape the sound of last breaths as they fell on the sharpened stakes, their struggling bodies being crushed together as the tribesmen pushed more and more animals inside the slanting space.

What had to be the longest five minutes of my life passed and I could look up from my hiding place. A giant mound of defeated gnus covered the top of the pit. As I watched, a surviving gnu jumped over the bodies of his comrades and escaped the pit unscathed.

A sneaking suspicion had come over me as I hid my face. I turned to Motsatsi now.

"What is that fence?" I asked him. "What do you call it?"

"Hopo," he said with a shrug of his shoulders.

So my suspicion had been correct. The hopo had been the one thing the captain had warned me about.

"Are women banned from watching the hopo?" I asked, wondering if it was all the females and not just myself.

"No," Motsatsi told me nonchalantly.

So why had the captain decided to warn me against this one thing? In truth, he was right in a way. I had not desired to watch the massacre. But why, in our one chance to say goodbye, had he chosen this spectacle to shield me from? I felt guilty now for not thinking of anyone aboard the *Madras* since I came here. So engrossed was I in my new life I had not once thought of my old comrades. I wondered now if First Mate Anderson were recovering from the surgery I had assisted in.

I walked home slowly, slightly troubled by the mass killing I had witnessed and confused by the captain's warning. Motsatsi didn't understand why I walked so slowly, but stayed with me all the way to Mary's door. We were both pleasantly surprised to see Sechele walking out of the house as soon as we arrived.

"Ah, my boy and Miss Anna!" he greeted with that wide, wise smile. "You had a pleasant walk?"

"Yes, good," Motsatsi replied amiably. "The hopo was successful."

"Miss Anna, did you witness the hopo with your own eyes?" he inquired.

"I looked away," I said with a passive smile. I quickly changed the subject. "Are Mary and David home, Sechele? Did you have occasion to speak with them?"

"Yes, I spoke with Mma-Robert," he answered. "I had just come to invite your family to come dine with mine this evening."

"Oh, to be sure!" I replied enthusiastically. "I can only speak for myself, but I would be delighted."

"Yes," he said, agreeing that I would be delighted. "I will receive you all this evening then," he said with a slight bow of his head. Then without a word, he took Motsatsi softly by the shoulder and they walked forward together. I thoroughly enjoyed the fact that their way of walking was identical. No doubt from Motsatsi practicing his father's every move.

I retired into the house and removed my bonnet. I looked around the small space and saw Robert and Agnes playing with their sweet nanny in our room. Moving further in I could see David and Mary were absent. I was going to move to the lean-to to help in some way when I saw out of a back window Mary and David looking at something closely on the ground. I was perplexed until I remembered this was where David had placed Mary's sewing needles in the ground, searching for moisture to rust the small pieces of metal. As they stood and looked to each other without a word, I knew the needles must have been agonizingly clean.

Turning my head, I walked away quietly so they could not catch me witnessing their fear.

Chapter 15

I aided Agnes in dressing in her finest apparel for dinner with a chief. Robert had taken to dressing himself entirely. Mary sometimes intervened when something was backwards or inside out, but otherwise he was becoming independent. Once we were all in perfect readiness, for Sechele would be disappointed by anything less than our best clothes, we began our walk to the home of the king of the Bakwena.

The beauty of Sechele's home was not something easily forgotten. Although the massive chandelier that possessed all your senses as soon as you walked in the door took some getting used to, the rest of the house was simple and elegant, especially in contrast to the harsh world outside.

Sechele came to greet us with Motsatsi at his side. Sechele was overdressed, which was exactly as I had hoped. He sported a blue velvet coat, a white chimney pot hat, crimson velvet trousers, and withal carrying his famous brass poker for a scepter. Mary shook her head infinitesimally. Yet despite his magnificent dress, of which I was sure he had spent at least one painstaking hour, he did not seem himself. Fortunately I had something in store to please our host.

"I see you have a few new lamps, Chief!" I said excitedly. "They are fine, I must say."

The effect of my words was instant. To think that, not only had I noticed the pieces in the large room, but I also thought they were fine brought a look of satisfaction to his face.

"Thank you," he said politely. "They just arrived before you came to the door. A trader, whom I found to be nice, sold them to me for a good price."

"Who was the trader?" David asked, interested.

"That good man Andrew Bain!" he answered, and a look passed between David and Mary. "I think I shall ask him to get me a thick English rug," he said proudly. "I got the two lamps for almost nothing, because this Andrew Bain agreed to give only if I could hit a distant anthill." He gestured with his hand and squinted with his eyes so that we could know how far away the anthill had been. "He was overly confident, I think, that someone lacking experience and a mount could not accurately fire his monster gun." He laughed, mostly to himself, then leaned in our direction and lowered his voice to tell us the climax of this story. "As an extra precaution, he overloaded the barrel, but I hit the target with one shot." His laugh of triumph was enough to put us all in a merry mood.

"But enough of this, please." He gestured to his small sitting area. "Do be seated."

The sitting area was stocked with what was to be our appetizer. Mixed pickles sat in readiness in a simple white bowl and were accompanied by a large tin of sardines.

"This all looks lovely," Mary told him amiably.

Sechele smiled in response, but lifted his finger at her.

"I have told you before, Mma-Robert, I know as well as white people what is nice."

It was an inescapable fact that at least one corner of my mouth never came down while in Sechele's company.

Selemeng took that moment to enter the company. Her dress was truly something to be envied. For the first time in years I felt envious of someone else's apparel. The cut of her bright blue sleeves and the small train of her skirt so suited her figure I sat in awe of her.

"Hello, Selemeng," I greeted. "You look absolutely lovely in that dress."

She nodded in my direction and even gave me a small smile of delight. Her smile was nothing compared to Sechele's grin that was akin to a sun glare. I knew without inquiring that he had retrieved the dress for her. He did have an excellent eye for beauty.

Having finished our pickles and sardines, and actually silently thanking my mother for years of maggot-filled food so I could swallow the two foods in the same mouthful, we moved to the dining area.

The table was already set, his off-white tablecloth donned with his special white china and tall candelabras. He had liver, served from a frying pan, placed in the center of the table.

"Ah, Miss Anna," he spoke my name, remembering, "our dinner comes from you and Motsatsi's successful hopo today."

I tried to seem pleased. Motsatsi looked proud, sitting beside me, as if he had captured the animal with his bare hands.

We all pieced on the liver in amiable silence. It was served without bread or vegetable, so we all did our best to enjoy the meat, dipped in worcestershire sauce. Of course there was water on the table, but not much of it, and no one dared be the first to pour a glass. After our first course, a thick milk was brought in. It was very rich and stiff, albeit extremely sour. Sechele knew it was curdled and so supplied us with ample amounts of sugar with which to eat it. It was better with sugar, he was right, but still not very appetizing. After tasting that and being obliged to leave it, Sechele had a truly beautiful set of cups and saucers brought in, and drinking the sweet milk from these lovely cups made it thoroughly enjoyable.

I was still curious as to why the good chief had seemed so solemn upon our arrival. I tried to root out the source subtly.

"And how was your day, Chief? Pleasant?"

Sechele gave me a mocking look, with raised eyebrows, that told me instantly that my subtly had been wasted on the wise.

Before he could speak what was on his mind, there was a burst of sound at the door and several grown men came into Sechele's home.

It was incredibly impressive to me that David, Mary, Sechele, Selemeng, and, least of all, Motsatsi were all on their feet in total readiness before the door could bounce off its hinges. I sat completely stunned in my chair as their survival instincts pulled them up out of their seats.

Turning to our disruption, I recognized instantly the same Boer man whom we had encountered on the docks in Durban and who had attended Sechele's baptism. Abraham. Although both of our meetings before he had not been nearly as angry as he was now. There were two other younger men with him of a stronger build. All holstered guns in their belts, but their hands hovered dangerously above them.

I heard a gun cock from a direction I did not expect and turned to survey Sechele, who now held in his hands the largest rifle I had ever seen in reality or fiction. How had he hidden such a weapon without us perceiving it instantly? And he had it in his hands without taking a step away from his table! His rifle looked as if it could swallow all three of the other men's, now minuscule, guns. Seeing him standing there, so very calm, with such a large machine made my jaw drop open.

At least this answered the question of whether the Bakwena had guns.

"Gentlemen," he spoke low, with no threat of menace, "I thought our conversation had finished. How else may I help you?"

"You have not helped us *yet*, Chief!" spat Abraham. He was twisting and turning his head to take in every corner of the room. Was he looking for something? Coming a step closer, he could see our faces more clearly, and looking around this room, he found what he was looking for.

Me.

"There!" he bellowed. "Get her!"

Before I could gain my bearings, four massive hands were placed on my arms and I was being speedily dragged to the door. Sechele and David were on the opposite side of the table, and they could not reach me.

They had not thought to consider Motsatsi.

He had been sitting beside me, and was so small and quick they did not realize what had happened until they were crying out in surprise. Motsatsi had a small knife tucked in his trousers, and used it to expertly cut the hands of the men who held me bound. I do not believe I even saw him accomplish it, only found myself freed with him pulling my hand to keep me away from danger. The two men clutched their hands that were already covered in thick blood.

While still being towed away, David, Sechele, Mary, and, to my surprise, Selemeng had placed themselves between me and my attackers. Even in her fine dress, Selemeng looked like a force to be reckoned with. Their pursuance was immediately halted as soon as Sechele's rifle was to his shoulder two feet in front of their shocked faces.

"I tried polite, but you did not," Sechele began. I noticed that now, there was menace in his voice. "How else may I help you, before I remove you from my home?"

"You know exactly what we want!" Abraham cried in aggravated frustration. "The price for her return is enough to feed our families for weeks! The water alone would sustain them for a month!"

Horror struck me.

"I was already made aware of the price on her freedom from a less hostile messenger," Sechele replied coolly. "I will repeat what I told you before and that is that she is a member of my tribe and out of your reach."

"You ought to be grateful to us, Chief," the farmer responded bitingly. "My people shield you daily from outside threats, and you cannot give up one wandering girl who has no place among you? Who is not even liked by your tribespeople?"

I could not escape my intuition. Although the current situation was still quite dangerous, my feelings were hurt that others knew of the tribe's dislike of me.

My feelings were much different from Sechele's. The man's words had caused me hurt, but it had fanned the flame of Sechele's anger. He yelled now in a way I shall never forget, not only because his words were so poignant to me, but because there is no sound on God's green earth louder than the voice of Chief Sechele.

"You do not protect my people. You enslave them and make them your objects. You would have to rip out my insides rather than us give her up! She is my blood. As I told you before, I shall not deliver up Miss Anna, for she has become my child. She breathes the air I breathe in my lungs. I will not cough her up. We are not like you white people who have no respect for words. You put them on paper and you capture them and imprison them in the vaults of your pens. You drown them in your ink and create the magic of meaning through papers and books, but you have no respect for words. These are *my* words!"

It was impossible to be unaffected by Sechele's voice. The silence after his words was enough to make the unwelcome men inch toward the door. Abraham was the only one brave enough to speak.

"Your words mean nothing to me, Chief. Because I will always have authority over you. I have been called of God. I am a prophet, not only over my people but over yours as well. We make the people work for us, in consideration of allowing them to live in our country. That you disrespect this authority is troubling. Have you not seen the similarities between myself and Moses of old? God has visited me and made these things known to me. Denying the prophet, and the prophet's children of water is a sin. You read your Bible, but you know nothing of it."

His voice was so dark and malicious it sent chills up my spine. Sechele's chest burst out in defiance.

"You speak lies," he spat.

The men with bleeding hands had reached the door and were making their exit. Without support, Abraham found himself nervous. He lashed out at David next as he inched toward the door.

"You supply weapons to the heathen! We thought you were friend to the righteous but you are making bullets for the damned. You call yourself a missionary preacher. Nothing could be further from the truth! We shall meet at judgment for your disgrace!"

"Yes," David replied steadily. "I will meet you there, Abraham."

Soon the hostile prophet was at the door as well.

"We shall see," he said.

Having had the last word, he now felt free to go, and the tension relaxed in the room.

I realized that Motsatsi still held my hand, and what was more, had placed his other hand on mine and had his head laid on my arm. Sometimes when he was startled or afraid he could take on the appearance of such a sweet babe, no more strong or brave than a flower. I reached another hand over to hold his head and bent down to kiss his soft curly locks.

"Thank you, good sir," I whispered to him.

Suddenly, he was himself again and he nodded with a jerk and released me to take back his chair.

Everyone slowly returned to their respective places at the table and an awkwardness settled in, with only the coo of babes to break the silence.

I knew I would have to begin the conversation and yet I did not know how. Emotions warred within me. On the one hand, I was overwhelmed by the compassion of my friends. They would protect me despite danger to themselves, a show of courage I had never before seen exercised on my behalf. And yet on the other hand, I could see the desperation of the Boers. My mother was searching for me, and had offered a generous reward for my return. How could they not go searching desperately for a source of income that could mean water for their families?

Since I had no way to articulate how I felt, and because I could not form any of these things into actual questions, I simply spoke my chief's name.

He had been looking in his lap, pondering. At my saying his name, he looked up and studied my expression for a length of time. My opportunity had come to speak the truth.

"I am sorry I lied," I said to everyone. "I had hoped I was out of my mother's reach. I had hoped I could live as if she never existed." I started to shake and felt so tense I could not say more. I didn't dare look up, but I could feel their eyes on me. I took several deep breaths and then looked to Sechele again.

His gaze seemed to bore into me.

"It is unkind and a sin to bear false witness," he told me. But his eyes soon became understanding and comforting. "I forgive you," he said. I looked down and nodded with tears of gratitude in my eyes. I glanced to the rest at the table and the response seemed to be about the same. No one forced me to say more. Instead, Sechele spoke.

"The Boers sent messengers to my home after my baptism, with negotiations for the English girl I held hostage in my village." He paused. "I told them outright I held no one against their will. Today these men came and said they would split the reward with me if I could fool Miss Anna to go with them back to Durban." He shifted uncomfortably in his seat, hating that the scheme had even been brought to him. "I refused them and they became quite angry. They said there was nothing I could do to stop them, and I agreed, since Anna is a free lady."

"And yet, you mysteriously invited us all to dinner this evening," I concluded for him.

He smiled, unashamed. "I worried the men would come to David and Mary's home. A suspicion that proved to be correct. I knew the safest place for you all was right here."

Part of the story tugged at my conscience.

"How much is the reward?" I asked.

"Don't tell her," David and Mary spoke in unison.

"It does not matter," Sechele spoke firmly. "All that is important is that you be kept safe exactly where you are. Do not think these men can take you by force."

But how could I not? The only people willing to protect me sat in this very room, and the Boers by all accounts were a veritable force of men.

"Take me back yourselves and receive the reward," I urged. "I'm sure it is not a small sum. You could buy supplies for the village!" I spoke excitedly. "Things for the schoolroom, Mary! Pencils, quills, papers, books! Merchandise to help you in your work, David." I turned to confront him as well. "Clean bandages, needles, medicine," I listed them off easily, knowing he was in need of them. I was getting only obstinate stares from all of my companions so I cried out in frustration, "And water!"

"Miss Anna," Sechele began calmly, "I asked you once if you would trade the poverty in my village for the memories you have experienced."

"This is different, Sechele!" I said, pounding the table.

"We will not subject you to it," Mary protested. "It *will* rain. The Kolobeng will fill up again and we will continue on as before. We will not sacrifice your free will for money. Surely you can understand that."

"You cannot deny the plan seems wise," I begged her. David spoke up.

"The most foolish plans sometimes do," he said. "There is no use arguing with this self-sacrificing nonsense, Miss Anna. You are staying here."

Another strong silence followed. I could not argue more tonight with my loved ones. But I knew what I must do, for their sakes.

Suddenly the silence broke with Sechele piping up, smacking himself on the forehead and bolting to the kitchen, as cheerful and unaffected as he had ever been.

"Ah! Forgot my dessert!"

Dinner finished and our thanks given, we began our walk home. We had stayed later than expected and Agnes was asleep on David's shoulder. Robert looked as if he could be sleeping as well, but his four-year-old ego would not allow him to be carried. When we arrived home, I aided Mary in preparing the children for bed. All the while I was thinking how badly I would miss them when I left. For I was certain now, that if my mother was looking for me, and she was willing to give a reward for my return, it would be a source of much needed supply for this family.

So absorbed was I in my thoughts and plans of escape, that I did not realize something that was staring me directly in the face. Now, a realization hit me. Mary had kept excusing herself, again and again, from dinner. She had quickly departed from me for ten minutes at a time, then returned pale and gradually more and more withered. Now that I reflected on the issue, I knew she had not eaten a single morsel at Sechele's dinner. The last time she returned, I had asked her if she was quite well. At the time she shook her head at me, but now everything became clear. Mary wasn't sick solely because of the lack of water.

Mary was pregnant.

When David came home one evening, a few days later, she told him the news. He was shocked, to be sure, but soon gave her a very tender and warm embrace. After speaking with her quietly for a moment, he carried her effortlessly to bed. Obviously he knew, despite Mary's protests, that she was too ill to carry her typical load. In the coming days, I knew, she would need me more than ever. I couldn't leave her now.

Chapter 16

During this part of the drought, the lack of water made it necessary to choose between giving the water to your animals or to your children. Many of the people clung to hope and kept a select few of their goats, cattle, or sheep alive. Mostly, however, the animals were killed and cleaned to increase the water supply for the living. Several oxen had to be put down as well, because the lack of water was making them ill. Thus, for a time, there was meat to be had by all.

I could not watch David and Mebalwe slaughter the animals, and fortunately I was not needed in that part of the process. I hid in the home until Mary needed assistance cooking the meat.

The oxen were not the only ones to get sick. The slow, creeping infirmity of malnutrition spread among the people, producing a depressing lethargy and vulnerability to disease. My classroom became less populated because of illness. Several families began to leave the area looking for water, jobs, or survival somewhere else. No one knew if they found it or not. In just three months from Mary's announcement, sixty-six families had abandoned the tribe in search of something better. Walking through the village, the sinking feeling of absence crept through one's heart.

It was, however, the illness of my own adopted family that affected me most. Of course all our mouths were dry, the lips of the children being the most injured. Although Mary covered their little faces with a salve her mother procured, their tiny lips produced such wide cuts and sores, my heart broke at the sight of it.

Though they would not speak of it, their parents were affected as well. Mary suffered from a terrible ache in her chest. The influence of it forced her to sit outside of meal time—a habit she was not accustomed to. Their father found it difficult to go through an entire sermon without pause, his headaches being truly severe.

My desire to rescue them was so strong, sometimes it was almost physically painful to me that I could not do more. However, I could see that Mary was fading, and remembering her pregnancy always shocked me into a new wave of energy and determination, despite the ache in my throat. I urged Mary to sit as often as I saw her that day, and I took on the heavy burdens she typically carried.

Another realization came to me. Mary had taught me how to do everything that needed to be done around the house. To be sure, there were still deeds that only Mary could do. Her nurturing touch was lost when I overtook the care taking of her children, but she had taught me enough of the basics that she could sit back comfortably, knowing that I could handle what was needed.

Perhaps she had known from the beginning this could happen. Maybe she had taken me in, pushed me so hard and been unforgiving of my weakness because she knew her children would need someone capable when she was sick. Even if that were the only reason for her kindness and instruction, I could forgive her unequivocally.

When each day came to an end, I had often done nothing but cook and endlessly clean that fine layer of sand that entered our home no matter how many rags I stuffed into the window sills and door frame. David, the children, and I would sit in the main room and play delightful games while Mary slept. I had had such little time with these children as of late, since they spent so much time with young girls from the village.

One day, David entered and sat down heavily upon his favorite weathered chair.

"The world has come knocking on our door suddenly, has it not?" he posed the question, but I sensed it was not a query to be answered. He sighed heavily. "We'll have to send to Kuruman for more corn and water, as soon as Mebalwe returns."

"Where has Mebalwe been?" I asked, curious.

David chuckled humorlessly. The motion gave him a coughing fit and I waited, afraid, until he finished.

"Kuruman," he answered.

So Mebalwe was already fetching supplies from Mary's parents, or wherever else he could find it. Yet there would be more need as soon as he completed his journey.

"To add to our load, I fear I must tell you, several stock animals have been taken off in the night by lions. The tribesmen hope to assemble a hunting party to scare them away."

"Scare them away?" I repeated bewildered. "The lions?"

"We need only kill one lion," David explained. "And that is usually enough to scare the entire pride into leaving the area."

"That sounds dangerous," I hedged.

"Which is more dangerous, Anna? Seeking out one lion or allowing them to come close to our little children? I guarantee you they have been a stone's throw from this very spot."

I shivered as I watched Robert and Agnes play a game of catch. How desperate would the animals become?

I had a few days to learn a few more things from Mary in the schoolroom, before she became too ill to leave the house. I focused all of my attention on her those last couple of days, willing myself to learn Sechuana from Mary and Motsatsi in time to teach these children while she was away. I will admit I was absolutely terrified of the future, especially after Mary informed me she was typically sick for the entire duration of each pregnancy.

All too quickly for me, my first day of teaching school, without Mary to supervise, came upon me. I trudged up the hill a full hour before school was to start, dreading the moments that would come with each step I took. At least my muscles had become accustomed to the climb. There was one less thing to worry about. Because of the early hour, I was surprised to see Motsatsi waiting for me at the door, flashing me a ridiculously wide smile, despite his cracked lips.

"Motsatsi!" I exclaimed in surprise. "What are you doing here so early, good sir?" It had become my custom to call him "good sir." It pleased him tremendously.

"Father thought you would like some help this morning, with Mma-Robert becoming round," he explained logically. "Also, I am to deliver a message. Some of the mothers of the village were hesitant to send their children to be taught by an unmarried pale girl who indulges in witchcraft." He paused only to breathe as my mouth fell open. "But Father has informed them that all the same children who have been attending will attend still or their plows will be taken away."

Word got around this village faster than a team of fine horses. I shook my head.

"The chief cannot mean to take away their only means of supporting themselves on my account," I protested. "Will you please let him know his threats are quite unnecessary?"

"I will not," Motsatsi replied complacent, "because he told me I should take no message from you except your compliance. Nothing else will do."

The sun was barely up and already I was taking discipline from a child. I sighed in defeat. I suppose how Sechele threatened his villagers was up to him. He was so desperate they all learn the English way that I'm sure, to him, it was worth it. I started inside before I turned around to address him once more.

"How did you know I would be early?" I questioned him.

"Father guessed." He grinned again.

I scoffed. "Of course. Well, no time to waste then, come in and I will practice my lesson on you. I'm afraid you will need to be my translator for a good part of it."

He followed me inside and sat directly on the dirt floor with no thought to his trousers, which I suppose didn't matter, because his clothes were as dirty as the rest of us who also had no water to wash with.

In a small way, I had become excited. The children were much easier to relate to than their austere parents. Their honest little faces were not as judgmental as their mothers' and older sisters'. Still I would catch a glance of a young girl who had heard too much rumor in her home and she would eye me with fear. In response, I could do nothing but smile as genuinely as I could and continue on.

When my pupils arrived, they tried to be seated without their apparel being inspected, but I cleared my throat in such a pointed way at each that I could not be ignored. They each walked up to me, in turn, and were dismissed after their cleanliness inspection was complete. I was trying to mimic all Mary's practices in order to be taken seriously. At last, all the children were seated in front of me, and I stood in the front and began the school day in the same way that Mary had. I was determined to not let one rule slip while Mary was ill. It would not do to have Mary come back to anything less.

I continued in the Mary order by offering prayer. I had not picked up enough spiritual words to make the prayer understandable in Sechuana, so I spoke it in English. Motsatsi did not translate as I gave a simple prayer of gratitude and asked for direction.

"Amen," I concluded.

"Amen," they all mimicked me.

I looked up and smiled, and received several smiles back. Perhaps they did not know witches prayed.

I spent the day in simple review of Mary's instructions. The children and I raised our voices together singing the alphabet song and other silly rhyming songs Mary had taught them. After our songs, I instructed the children to take out their little spelling books. Mary had acquired them long ago from Cape Town on one of her many travels. Each of the books had been used, abused, and tenderly loved by so many past students that they were barely legible. Where certain letters or words were missing, the children were used to turning to their neighbor's copy to read where their copy had left off. We went through several pages of the thin little books. When there was no paper left to be written on, some wrote on corn-boxes, some on the stonewall, some on broken deal boxes or planks. All while they sat on the floor.

Our spelling segment complete, I separated the girls from the boys and began my sewing tutorials while the boys worked longer on their letters. It continued to be an absolute joy to these sweet darlings to see me stitch a beautiful flower within a matter of short minutes. I could never begin my instruction until I had made a flower or decoration. Each day I awarded the pretty little thing to a different little girl. While I made the flower, they all tried to discreetly straighten their bonnets and frocks to appear the most worthy of a pretty little decoration. They were each on their utmost polite behavior—backs were never straighter, hair was never out of place. And when I chose a recipient, her face glowed in appreciation. Motsatsi had informed me that the girl who received the flower of the day was seen as the social center for a day. Having already made thousands of different variations of flowers in an effort to impress my mother, this was in no way difficult for me. Left to myself, I would never sew a flower again, but their smiles of delight outweighed the terrors of my past.

The end of the school day came quickly, and I excused my students. Each ran to the door. As soon as they were all outside, the children began their run of joy, throwing their proper English clothing to the wind. It was a relief to me that none of them stripped down to complete nakedness. They each wore their native clothing underneath their school coverings. Softly on the afternoon breeze, their creamy white frocks floated down around them. It made my day complete to see this display. I know their white clothing on the dirty ground disconcerted Mary in a way, but it proved to me, daily, that although we taught them many useful things in school, we could not take away their spirit. We would never replace their culture.

So engrossed was I in the children's show of freedom, I had not noticed a man directly to my left. Now I noticed he was a short, middle-aged man with a large mustache and a gleaming bald head. He held his hat in his hands and looked up at me in an apologetic way. I turned to him with questions on my face. He dressed akin to David, which told me he was a missionary, hunter, or explorer of some kind.

"Hello," I tried.

"Good afternoon, Miss," he said timidly. "I was just visiting with our mutual friend Mrs. Livingstone. She sent me to you."

"Oh!" I replied in surprise. "How can I help you, sir?"

He looked down and shuffled his feet in response. It was clear he was embarrassed, although I could not fathom why.

"Mrs. Livingstone sent me here to see if," he paused and took a deep breath, "if you had an extra spelling book I could possibly purchase."

My emotions caught in my throat. I had never met a grown man who could not read. I instantly bolted into the classroom without a word and snatched up my copy of the threadbare spelling book. I returned outside to see him even more uncomfortable. Had he supposed I would refuse him?

I thrust the copy into his line of sight, which was still to the ground. He shook his head.

"I wish to purchase it," he insisted, refusing to take it and unwilling to look up.

"You may want to inspect the quality of the product, sir," I responded with a bit of a laugh.

He slowly took the manuscript from my hands and inspected it, turning the frail pages as if he were turning plates of gold.

"I know how much this is worth," he said as he handed me the book to hold. He turned on his heel and walked toward the side of the schoolhouse. I took a few steps and peeked around the corner. I knew instantly that everything he owned was in the small wagon that was parked there. It was a simple wagon bed with no covering, holding an assortment of blankets, buckets, and some oddities. The whole of it was pulled by an ancient looking mule. Now I could guess at his profession! He was a trader. Looking more closely, I could see several small items that would be of great worth in this area. Unused pots and pans, several small mirrors, and even a few little handmade dolls. He was digging through his many small belongings for what he thought would be a suitable trade for the spelling book. I was prepared for an episode of bargaining with the man, considering this is how he survived and made a living. I knew he would be proficient in getting as much as he could for as little as possible. But I had been willing to give him the book for free, so I watched with curiosity.

He returned with two large metal tins and set them at my feet. Before I could inquire what was inside, he returned to the cart again and came back with a clutch of beautiful little beads. I thought instantly how the little girls would adore such beads, but I could not utter a word before he returned to his cart a third time. This time he carried a living thing! A full-grown mother goat was lounging idly in his arms, which he deposited onto the ground and then placed the rope in my hand.

And now I could not speak. One would have thought, with my experiences thus far, that I would have understood the value of things that used to be inconsequential to me. This booklet would not be exchanged for a farthing in London, but here it was of such great worth that it could be traded for all the precious ware now laying at my feet. How could I barter with him now? I could not try to convince him that these thin pages in my hands were not valuable enough for what he offered. To him, knowledge was the most valuable item of all.

Too stunned to speak, I simply handed him the book. He received it with both hands, and looked up at my face as if I had just handed him a king's ransom.

"Thank you," he spoke softly and sincerely. Then with nothing further he returned to his cart.

I admit I struggled to return home with the precious load I had received. Luckily, the goat was calm and obedient. She would simply follow wherever the rope pulled. However, the two metal tins were heavy enough to make my arms ache by the time I reached the bottom of the hill. I wondered if there was any way I could lighten the load, and I was also curious as to its contents. Stooping down, I removed the lid from each tin in turn and discovered they were full of milk, the top three inches, at least, being thick cream. I guessed this was his store of milk from the goat he had just given away. Looking at the thick liquid, I fell to my knees, sobs jerking my chest up and down.

I was thinking of Robert and Agnes's thirst the last few nights, the desperate plea in their tiny little voices asking for moisture. I was grateful beyond expression that I could be the means by which they would receive a glass of milk. The weight of it sank me down to the ground,, and I stared at the life giving moisture in awe for several long minutes. When I could finally regain my composure I carried the tins home. I did not care that my arms were screaming for relief.

David saw me coming from afar off, returning from his work with the men of the tribe, and trotted over to me to help with my load. It was embarrassing how easily he handled the two tins after I had struggled so much. I thanked him profusely, but he stopped me.

"Are these milk?" he asked in wonder. I nodded. This gave him pause. Slowly he turned to face me, his eyes so full of suspicion and dread that he suddenly had my full attention as to what he was thinking.

"Did you steal these?"

Even worn as I was, his question made me laugh until my sides hurt. He watched me for a moment and then laughed too. However, he kept that fearful look until I told him all that had happened. He was not as amazed as I. He told me in the past Mary had been obligated to hide the spelling books because the adults would come in the night to study and learn from the scrap pieces of paper.

"So you believe I got a good price for the book?" I asked, now hoping I had not sold something that ought not to be sold.

"Yes," he answered. "It would appear you met an honest trader, something that is not as common as you would hope."

Taking the milk inside and hearing the children's squeals of excitement healed my burning arms instantly. Mary still lay in bed, but when I brought in a tall glass of goat's milk, her face brightened. We all gathered around Mary's bed and drank our glasses of milk together. It was clear from the first sip that the milk was quite sour. This did not keep us from finishing our portions in quiet contentment. Already seeing a marked difference in Mary and the children, David proclaimed, "Another glass, I think!" and the children clapped and cheered. I thought my cheekbones would break from all the smiling I did in just one hour.

The children instantly took to our new goat and affectionately started calling her Banana, the reasons of which, are still unclear to me. We tied Banana to a post on the shady side of the house, and Robert and Agnes found it great fun to find dried grass (for there was no other type of grass to be had) for her to eat. She looked well nourished, as if she had had plenty of water to drink with her last owner. I worried about her future condition with little to no water to drink. By the look on David's face, he had the same worry.

The bulk of my days in Kolobeng passed by in this manner. In my mother's house in the glorious land of England, I began my days by receiving callers, immaculate in dress, to speak of frivolous topics of the day. Now in the life I had chosen, deep in the heart of Africa, I began every day, for a full six months, by milking a goat while dressed in soiled rags. Sometimes I amused myself with imaging their reactions if they were to see me now, sitting in the dirt before the sun rose, milking a mother goat with my bare hands. David said I should learn, and perhaps learning how to milk a goat would be easier on my tiny hands than a full-grown cow. Although, even with our combined efforts, we could not even fill a quart. Still, we were grateful for every drop we could obtain.

David and I brought the milk together after we were finished. He was done with his ten cows before I was done with my one goat, but he waited for me patiently. We strained the milk through a thin cloth into a small container while David disclosed to me some news.

"There have been many animals that have gone missing during the nights these past few weeks. I've been in villages where women and children who went out at night alone were also picked up by lions. I told you how we suspected lions, but we could not be sure until this morning. Sechele himself saw their pride only a mile away from his home. There can be no doubt now that the lions are picking off our cows, goats, and sheep. We won't let it go on so long that we start losing tribesmen."

"What has changed to make them unafraid to come around man?" I asked him. "I thought lions were supposed to fear hunters."

"Lions do fear hunters," he confirmed, "but with the drought being what it is, they are as desperate as we are. They have nowhere else to go for food."

I considered that.

"So what do we do about it?" I questioned.

"We wait," he replied. "Wait and see if the situation becomes truly perilous, and then if need be, we will do some hunting."

Hunting frightened me, so I excused myself.

◇◇◇

None can tell what a precious thing water is but those who have been deprived of it. After that night's evening sermon, the family and I sat in stillness—unwilling to move. The dry ache of my throat seemed to resonate to my ears and dry out my eyes. I held Agnes, her thin cheek resting against my collarbone. Though she did not move, I knew she did not sleep, her eyes wide open against the heat. My eyes blinked and I had difficulty opening them again, the dry air attempting to seal them shut. There was no moisture to spare, even to assist my sticky lids.

Mary did supply refreshment for the group, but now instead of water, bread, or jams, the only option was fried locusts. My eyes were as wide as they could be as I watched everyone politely take their handful of locusts. When it was my turn, I nodded politely to Mary and then took one locust. I closed my weary eyes and took a crunchy bite. It tasted like vegetable and was not altogether unsatisfying. It was the closest thing we had to meat in weeks and weeks.

At the house, I set Agnes on her bed and began to remove her shoes and day clothing. I mechanically moved to her trunk to retrieve a nightgown, forcing my arms to move. Mary came into the room, with Robert clinging to her leg. I looked up in question as Mary forcefully removed Robert. If there was any water left in his miserable little body, it would have been coming out his eyes. Where there was no tears to be had. He simply heaved and choked in his misery. He asked Mary for some water again and in response she simply shook her head. This brought on an all new level of emotion from Robert. He threw himself to the ground and beat his fists against the unfeeling floor.

I remember seeing a scene similar to this once in shop in London—it had been Whiteleys. A little girl had been denied a second pair of gloves and had thrown herself to the ground just as Robert did. I watched, unable to assist in my water-deprived stupor, as my mind compared the two scenarios.

The little London girl had shrilled her demands and easily articulated her distress, whereas Robert was so desperately dry, his cries came out rattled and incomprehensible. The girl had rained fresh tears and had soiled her pretty dress with them. Robert's eyes gave forth nothing but bright red splotches and an insatiable itch that haunted us all. When the hysterics were over, the little girl daintily wiped her eyes with her perfect cream colored gloves. Robert rubbed his eyes viciously with dirty fingers, not to clean them or make them tidy, but to try and conjure some kind of moisture out of them. There was none to be had, and the light red color that surrounded his eyes now turned dark and welted.

The girl had received her gloves that day. But this boy received no water.

Mary snatched his hands to halt his attack on his eyes and restricted his arms across his chest. She moved him over to the children's bed and held him on her lap as his thrashing and screaming slowed. She had no choice. If we drank water now, there would be none to be had in the heat of the day tomorrow. That kind of distress could kill a person. My mind knew this to be true, but my heart ached to help my little friend.

"Mary," I said, my voice weak but pleading. "Let him have my water."

"Hush!" Mary lashed out at me. "Stay silent, Anna. If anyone is going to give up their water for these children it will be me. *You* do not take that away from me. I have much experience in water deprivation and the children are not yet destitute. Let them be. They are mine."

I turned from her, her reprimand hurting me deep inside. My chest constricted—not in physical pain—but emotional pain. Would Robert ever get his cool glass of water? Or would his body reject the heat and expire? Would we all?

I finished my assistance to Agnes and kissed her forehead with my cracked lips. Her eyes remained open. I moved to my bed and did not bother to undress. I simply laid atop my blankets and closed my parched eyes. Mary finally got Robert to sleep and laid him down gently. She then snuffed out our candle and retired to her bedroom in the dark.

The howling of a strong African wind rocked our small house. Amidst the sound, I thought I heard the cry of a tortured soul. The rise and fall of sound was almost identical to the pitch of the wind. I turned my ear in an attempt to discern the noise, but as soon as I thought I heard a distinct, mournful cry, it halted and blended into the breeze. All that remained was the deafening tone of silent bodies, unwilling to move until water, or morning, came.

No water came, but somehow morning did.

And it came with drums and guns.

Chapter 17

I bolted upright in bed to the sound of guns being fired. For a moment I panicked and knew not what to do. But soon enough I slipped my shoes on and stepped out the front door. David and Mary were already there. It seemed to me as if they had been there a long while.

"Did I hear shooting?" I asked, doubting myself.

"Yes, you did," Mary answered. David did not speak. Then the drums began.

"What is this?" I was irritated I had to ask, they were so quiet.

"It's the beginning of a funeral," Mary said as she stood. "Let's get the children up."

I wondered if children should attend funerals, but I had learned my lesson last night to not question Mary's parenting. I wanted to ask who had passed away, but they seemed to be purposefully avoiding the subject. My throat closed off at the thought and I suddenly dared not ask even if they had been willing.

"Here." Mary handed me a large square piece of cloth. "Your head needs to be covered."

I nodded mutely. I did not question her today.

With both the children up and dressed and given their meager sip of daily water, we headed toward the center of town. There were drummers everywhere. Men, women, and children sat in large circles beating on the drums in complicated rhythms. Mary answered my question without my having to ask.

"It is with the hope that the sound will put *barimo,* or spirits, to sleep."

I nodded, understanding but a little. The melody was rather calming. As if hearing my thoughts, however, the drumming suddenly stopped and the wailing began. The sound of their cries was more piercing and heart-wrenching than I had ever heard. They threw themselves on the ground in agonized appeals to an absent being. Most were covered in dirt and sweat. Their eyes red and swollen from the heartache and lack of moisture. My chest was quite tight and I had trouble breathing.

"Mary," I began to address her to ask the question I didn't want to know the answer to, but I never got the chance. We had arrived at the kotla. A little girl was ready for burial, dressed neatly lying on a high bench for everyone to see. Her family surrounded her, with her mother in a special place right next to her, the mother's head covered in blue, her face covered in grief.

The tears sprung to my eyes the moment I saw the little one. I could not remember her name, but she had been in my class. The flower I had stitched for her was clutched in her hand.

I couldn't breathe. I couldn't think. I had to escape. I turned toward home but was met by a small woman with wild eyes, red from crying. I had seen her with the little girl before. She had taken her to the schoolroom once or twice. I felt the heat of her anger pressing on me.

"Baloi," she hissed, quietly at first. She advanced toward me and I took a step back. Before I knew he was even present, Motsatsi stood in front of me. I tried to push him to the side, but he was adamant. There was a lot of yelling, mostly from the woman. She was soon joined by at least thirty mourners who rallied behind her.

"Baloi, baloi, baloi," was the only word I knew. It was the word for "witch." I needed no translator for the rest. They thought my coming had brought the drought and killed this precious girl. They held me responsible. I had been warned they were superstitious. Maybe they were right. My gut hurt from lack of water and lack of human sympathy. David suddenly came to my side and began to plead with the people in his fluent Sechuana, but it did not seem to be going well.

The woman, who I assumed was the mother, went to the body and roughly snatched the stitched flower from her dead hand, flinging it at my face. I picked it up from the hot dirt with an involuntary sob.

Then I did what I do best.

I ran away.

Back at the house I tried to cry, but with no tears inside me, it seemed almost pointless. I soon felt silly and tried to busy myself with washing dishes and dusting—there was forever dusting to be done. But the heartache physically pressed on my chest and I found myself having to sit often. When my family returned, they tried to convince me that after the passion of the funeral was over, things would go back to normal. Especially when it rained. Whenever it rained. *If* it rained.

I did try to work as hard as I could, for the sake of my loved ones. I did as Mary told me in the unending heat, but I excused myself to bed early that day. I slept and dreamt of my mother for the first time in months.

I was broken out of a deep sleep by the claw of desperation. Even in the dim light before sunrise, I could see Robert's and Agnes's cracked lips and their little eyes surrounded by red rings. All I could do was stare at them. All of this over something as simple as water, something I had never thought to be grateful for. Perhaps if I could make my way back to the coast, they could use my water for the children. Despite Mary's angry reaction to my offer last night, I still could not help but feel a burden to this family. A portion of their water was being used by a guest. If anyone kept water from these little ones, I felt sure I would turn violent. The sink in my gut told me that it was *me* who kept water from them.

Despite my determination, I knew that any attempt to return myself to the coast would kill me. So many from the village had tried to reach the city, but only had to turn back around when they knew their water supply would not last. And these natives had much more experience surviving in the heat than I did. There was no possibility of surviving the trip.

There must be another option! I stood upon my cracked heels and dressed in near silence.

Stepping out of my small home, I thought the crisp air of the morning would revive my senses and give my mind clarity enough to find water. However, stepping out into the dark morning gave me no pleasure. The air was so lacking in moisture it instantly made my head ache and my chest to burn. The breathing in of air gave the sensation of inhaling hot sand again and again.

Still, the thought of Robert waking up to no water urged me forward. I wasn't sure I could survive another one of his miserable fits.

I put one foot in front of the other and headed toward the hills behind the house. As I walked, I realized I had not seen any animals in several days. The thought occurred to me that they must be looking for water as well. The idea pushed me toward the short climb to the top. From there I could see a small cluster of trees below. Though they looked fairly dry and worn, there must be some moisture to keep them standing.

I pushed a large branch aside to enter the small forest this bunch of trees created. They were so close together they created, at least the sensation, of shade. My parched eyes opened and beheld the captain.

Somehow he was well hydrated and standing erect. His eyes were clear, his lips unchapped, his hair swept to the side. Had he always been this handsome? No mark of water deprivation tarnished him.

"How are you here?" I asked in a raspy voice. No thoughts could make sense in my mind. I could not fathom how he had come to be standing before me.

He did not smile, but came to me and put his wide calloused hands on either side of my face. I drew in a surprised breath as he brought his face just inches from mine. Slowly, he moved his thumb across the cracked and bleeding lines of my lips. He let out a long sigh and held his forehead to mine.

"You are stronger than you know," he said. He pulled back and his piercing blue eyes willed me to believe what he said.

I blinked. He was gone.

I stood still for quite some time. It must have been a hallucination. My thirst was affecting my mind, making it weak. That much I knew. The question I could not answer was why I had dreamt of the captain. If given the choice, with a sound mind, I would have instantly chosen to see my father.

Wouldn't I?

Unable to find water, and afraid of the illusions my own mind could conjure up, I began my return home without water.

Having milked the goat, prepared and cleaned breakfast, kneaded some bread dough to put in our makeshift oven after school, administered to Mary, and left the children with their beloved Abeo, I began my trek to the schoolroom. I could not help feeling a little excitement. I had prepared a special lesson for the day, in the form of a story.

Soon, I sat down on the children's level and began the tale. Motsatsi was right there with me, translating where I left off. It was a story of a king who enjoyed his bath so much he refused to be evacuated from it. His subjects came in groups with unique strategies on how to coax his corpulence out of the tub, but none were successful. Their amusing anecdotes so entertained the children that I believe I heard a few unsuppressed giggles. In the end, a simple servant girl pulls the plug and lets the water drain away—proving, once again, that children are often more clever than adults.

I looked up in the children's faces expecting to see more smiles and giggles, but instead their faces were horror-stricken. I was struck back from my happiness.

"Children, what happened?" I pleaded. Motsatsi spoke for them.

"What happened to the water?" Motsatsi asked simply.

I paused. Then stuttered, "I-I don't know. It is the palace of a king." I attempted a stale explanation. I thought the story of an abundance of water would be comforting.

"So the water is used to clean the servants?" Motsatsi tried to root out the answer from me.

"Well," I tried again. Their faces were so desperately hurt at the thought of water running, barely used, down dark pipes. I could not swallow for the knot in my throat.

"Children," I began, trying to explain, "there are a lot of places in the world that do not need water as desperately as we do." I waited as Motsatsi translated. "In those places, water is sometimes used only once and then discarded."

"Ah! I see!" Motsatsi acted as if he understood. "The water must go to their gardens of corn!"

All eyes instantly shifted from him to me.

He rendered me speechless. How could I tell these poor darlings that some people were so rich they did not have to grow their own food? How could I break it to them that some were so wealthy they sometimes let water pour out without even using it once? I decided it was not for me to tell.

"Yes," I lied, "that is how it works in a rich king's mansion. The water from the tubs go straight to his fields of corn."

The tension in the room instantly vanished. The hurt on their faces immediately lessened and we could all breathe again.

Several children spoke at once and I looked to Motsatsi for translation.

"They say they like the story," he told me, "especially how fat the king is. He must be a very good chief indeed. He must grow lots of food."

I laughed. "Yes, he must indeed. And how lovely to think of having such a long glorious bath like that. I find that thought alone refreshing."

Motsatsi laughed at what I said. I looked at him, wondering, as he translated, but as soon as the other children heard my words through his tongue, they all laughed as well.

I cocked my head at Motsatsi. "Good sir, what is it that amuses you? Should you not like a long glorious bath?"

"We would not have a bath like that," Motsatsi explained, smiling. "That is only for white men."

Shock filled me from the chest up. "Only for white men?" I asked incredulous. "What can you possibly mean?"

He rolled his eyes at me as if I were missing something obvious, then he explained it to me very slowly, like one would speak to an infant.

"God made black men first, and did not love us as he did the white men. He made you beautiful, and gave you clothing, guns, horses, and wagons and many other things about which we know nothing. But toward us He has no heart. He gave us nothing except the assegai spears and cattle and rain making and he did not give us hearts like yours. God has given us one little thing which you know nothing of. He has given us the knowledge of certain medicines by which we can make rain. We do not despise those things which you possess, though we are ignorant of them. We don't understand your book, yet we don't despise it. You ought not to despise our little knowledge, though you are ignorant of it."

It was the most tragic speech I had ever heard. And it appeared I was the only one in the room who was not in agreement with it. They all felt this way. It hurt me.

I struggled to compose myself. When I did, I tried to continue on with the class as if I hadn't heard the most truly sad thing that had ever been subjected to my ears.

Finishing my lessons early, I decided we could all use some fresh air. I conducted a miniature nature class only a minute away from our school hill. I did not want to wander far. I had the children follow me in a single file line through the sparse brush to a large anthill. I showed them how the ants worked through the heat and still managed to carry such loads as were astonished in comparison to their size. I had brought a corner of Mary's bread in my pocket, and keeping the children's attention, I placed the square on the ground. The ants quickly worked together to lift the manna that was extremely heavy to them. We speculated on their resilience and what we could learn from them.

I stepped slightly away from them and sat on a large rock in the shade. The children stood a short distance from me, observing the ants, as I took a moment to relax and ponder. How could Motsatsi think of God in this way? I agree that my knowledge of deity was scarce. The only exposure I had to an organized religion was the one Mother had forced me to. A natural side of me wanted to turn away from any God my mother had worshiped. Her forcing me to Sunday meetings had instilled in me only one thing: contempt for polite society. But since my experiences here, I knew a God who was much more personal and loving than the one she claimed to know. This God I felt in my heart would not abandon Motsatsi. Why else would people like David, Mary, and Sechele exist, if not to bless and gift those around them? There had to be a God, and He had to love Motsatsi! Because Motsatsi was so selfless and wonderful, surely it was because there was some godliness in him. And yet, how to convince him of it?

David would be proud of me, I thought, I just had my first missionary desire. Perhaps I would tell him of it.

I was watching Motsatsi, considering the eternities, when he and I heard a strange sound. For some reason that is still unknown to me, I continued to watch Motsatsi instead of turning my face to the noise. I wanted to see his reaction. Perhaps it was my carnal instincts, determined to protect my children. I watched Motsatsi as he saw what was coming. He heard the sound and looked confused. He turned his face to better hear, and the sun lit up the side of his little features. He squinted as he tried to discern the commotion. As soon as he understood, his eyes widened, his brows lifted, and he was absolutely still.

Thus far, he and I were the only ones to hear the sound. The other children soon noticed, however, that Motsatsi was not his usual riotous self. They all turned to observe him, then mirrored his expressions as they squinted to see, then froze.

I stood and turned, squinting my eyes as well. The first thing I saw was the men of our village. They were sprinting toward us, hollering and waving their spears. They were somewhat far away, too far to understand their words, but close enough to see desperation filled their features, and several appeared to be close to tears. Hopelessness. Grief. Loss. I had seen that look many times before. But had someone already died? Was someone hurt?

I knew the answer immediately.

No, but we were about to be.

Because between me and the men of my tribe, a majestic lion loped directly toward me. The beast had several assegai protruding out from his sides. It appeared their hunt had begun early, without the consent of their chief or missionary. Despite the wounds, the beast still had strength to run at an amazing speed. I could see spittle dripping from his large teeth. He was tired, but not too tired to hurt someone before he fell. I am happy to say my instincts came alive.

"Motsatsi!" I called in a loud voice. "You will hide now! Take them all with you!"

He nodded in such an energetic way, in any other situation I would have smiled at his youthful enthusiasm. He rounded up the other children as their capable leader, and they ran away from me. Seeing them run away made me realize the true danger. And for a moment, I became desperately sad. I almost wanted to call to the children and hug them close to me as I died, protecting them physically with my body. To die knowing they were safe could be enough for me, but I also wanted their company as I went from this life to the next. I was desperate for my loved ones.

The moment passed, and suddenly, I was back to facing a king. I positioned myself firmly between him and my children. He was obviously just looking for an escape from the hunters, but we were directly in his way. I considered my options. I could run with the children, but that might only lead the lion closer to their defenseless little bodies. I doubted, in his distressed state, he would differentiate between adult and child. For the same reason, I could not run to either side of where I stood in this precise moment. I had to stand in front of the threat, in case he did want to take someone before he died. It would have to be me. I had no weapon. No assegai. So in my options of where to run or what to do, in an infinitesimal amount of time I realized my only course of acceptable action.

I smiled, in spite of the lion, and ran directly for him.

In desperation, I lunged to the ground and grabbed a handful of earth seconds before the lion reached me. I threw the dirt in its face. This halted him only half a second, where I got to observe that he was by far the largest lion I had ever seen. I knew this to be true, despite my shock. If both of us stood erect, his eyes would be level with mine. Large gashes covered his sides, and I could see inside of him, his lungs working hard to stay alive. The lion would die. The pack would leave our animals alone, but this one would live for a few moments more.

I realized I was screaming. The volumes I produced hurt my ears—the fear of death made me loud. I flapped my arms and bore my teeth in the most menacing fashion I could.

His eyes quickly recovered from my toss of dirt, and his attention locked on me.

His eyes were yellow, coordinating with his tawny fur. His snout scrunched in his growling, creating layers upon layers of skin above his nose. He had two miniature rows of small teeth in front, with two horribly long teeth at the sides. These peculiar details ran through my mind as the lion crouched and jumped at me to sink his mouth onto my shoulder, my collarbone resting on his long teeth.

A sort of odd feeling consumed me as I saw my feet reach eye level, then drop to the ground as the lion threw my body to the dry floor like a rag doll. I could feel nothing. Even the impact of my head to the ground made no noise or pain. My mind was clear, my heart strong. I felt no pain for long peaceful moments. This state of dreaminess left me free to dwell on my happy memories.

Though I had not allowed myself before, now in the face of certain death, I could allow myself to think about her. The little girl. The one I first saw swaddled in her mother's arms inside a dank forest cabin. Her name was Anna.

As she grew, I remembered playing simple games with her as Father and her mother, Maria, looked on. Infinitesimal snatches of time were stolen away from the heartless world as we sat content in that small cottage. It was there I came to realize, I didn't need any material thing. I looked around us at only the bare needs of life and found myself happy! With only the bare necessities I was the happiest I had ever been. Mother had been wrong. Joy was not where she found it. When I sat very still, I could find gladness in a moment, without anything in my hands.

It was the little girl's name I took as my own as I started out on this adventure. I wanted her to live so badly, I felt in this way she could live again in some small way. Anna was exactly the type of strong, yet sweet, being I wanted to become. I was Catherine no longer. Catherine was my mother's daughter. So I took on the name of the lost. The name of a starved child: Anna. My Anna.

The lion released me, my mangled shoulder dropping to the ground in a sickening thud. The numbness continued to fill my body and leave me in my happy, dreary state. I turned my head in an effort to check on the children. I could see no sign of them. They were so good at hiding, and for this I was supremely glad. I felt they would be safe. I had saved them. They could grow strong and tall. I wished for a long, cool bath for each and every one of them. The lion placed his paw on my chest in an authoritative way, his claws digging through my dress and into my skin.

I knew he was standing over me. I knew soon he would bite me again. The tribesmen were getting closer, but not close enough.

The lion lifted his giant paw and set it down on me again, only to rake it down my front. He stopped at my abdomen, then sank his teeth into my shoulder again and pulled with all the strength he had left. He was trying to take a bite out of me. I felt several pieces inside me snap and tear. Yet still, I continued to feel no pain, the shock to my body and my adrenaline keeping me, for now, safe from those feelings. Now, I was able to act more as a spectator to the hunt than an actual participant.

Yet in some recessed corner of my mind, I knew the pain would come eventually, and panic began to set in. I started to hyperventilate, looking at this giant animal directly on top of me. I began to claw at his fur.

Through the haze of the heat, I saw a figure standing stationary, the only being holding still in this sudden world of movement and chaos. He was tall, strong, capable. While the world crashed with uncertainty around him, he stood still and immovable.

I stopped thrashing about. I couldn't make out his features, I couldn't discern by logic who the man was, but in my heart I knew for certain.

Father.

I stared at his figure as the tribesmen rushed toward me still. I hoped they would pass me by and search for the children to make sure they were safe. I hoped they would allow the lion to consume me, if it would save the children. As they rushed, I would not take my eyes off of the man who stood still.

I heard a shot and felt the lion jerk and shift.

All of my sensory feelings came back to me like a flash of lightning. Instantly I could feel searing pain through the entire left side of my body. Jolts of panic thrashed through me as I strained under the paw. I felt bones cracking under the strain.

My eyes were still set on Father, willing him to take me away from all of this, begging him in my mind to take me away to heaven. Was that not why he was here?

"Please remove me, Father!" I whispered under the weight of the beast. "Please!"

Suddenly Father began to move.

He was running toward me!

"No!" I cried out, miserable. He was supposed to be my angel. He was supposed to stay there. And I was supposed to come to *him* in spirit and walk together into eternity. Why was he moving?

He got much closer, and I could begin to see his face more clearly. In the midst of all the pain, the heat, the blood, and the agony I discovered it was not Father.

It was the captain.

Chapter 18

The Captain

I had visited with Sechele and he had sent me in the direction of the school. Of course I knew where it was located. As I walked across the African ground, hot even through my thick boots, I wondered what I was expecting to find.

I had taken the *Madras* back to London where I was given the opportunity to dock her for up to three months for a holiday. I had been on the sea for years now, with only occasional snatches of time to wander lands here and abroad. In truth, I had come to miss London. Certainly not her people, for no one held my interest there. But the familiarity of the country roads, the feel of hard earth under my feet, the smell of foods not meant to last months in a dirty sailor's kitchen. Something in my subconsciousness pulled at me to stay and set up a new life.

And yet there was a pull I could not reason away. I tried to dismiss this as a simple guilt of conscience. I had allowed a young girl, barely out of schoolroom braids, to wander about the interior of Africa with no prior experience of living off the land or taking care of herself. I knew the Livingstones to be reliable people with more salt in their character than the whole of London. Still, it might have been wrong to allow her to wander away, even with such good care.

I told myself that was why I pulled up anchor. I told myself it was a matter of duty. I could not allow such a frail thing to be killed in such a harsh atmosphere, even if every conversation I had with her left me seething.

My misguided justifications were suddenly interrupted. For in the distance, before I had time to reach the school, there sat on a rock a striking young woman. Unless there were other proper English girls wandering about the interior, this had to be her. This had to be Catherine Kensington.

My footsteps sped as I squinted against the blazing sun. It could not possibly be her! The woman I saw in the distance was just that—a woman. In Durban so many months ago, I had dropped off a dangerously thin young girl with skin so white and ill it sometimes appeared clear, even seeming to show her haughty cheekbones. This lady I beheld, possibly a quarter mile away, was stunning in the kind of way only a being of triumph can be.

She sat on a rock with a few books and papers in her hands, lightly clasping them as she watched her small band of children. Her hair was pulled up into a loose bun atop her head, thick pieces of which fell down to the sides of her face. Her skin had darkened with its exposure to the harsh climate, but it did not make her appear gruff or unapproachable—it added to her appearance. The hunch of her shoulders was gone, now replaced by a back ramrod straight. But it was not only that her posture had somehow corrected itself, but that she carried with her a purpose, a sense of being, a direction! One would know simply looking upon this woman once that she was a sower of seeds and a worker of fields. It made her beautiful, if I was being honest with myself. She had integrity and a sort of quiet dignity, earned through many long days of hard work.

Although I still had not the faintest idea what I wanted to say or what my purpose was in Kolobeng, I marched forward, determined to see my expedition to the end.

I had been approaching Catherine from her right, her profile distinct under the shade of one dry, solitary tree, her school children playing directly in front of her. Among the children I recognized Motsatsi, Sechele's boy. I had been in the home when he was born. He had grown tall since my absence. I was watching when I saw him straighten and look behind him as if he heard something. I followed his line of sight and felt adrenaline barrel through me as if it wanted to burst through my fingertips.

All that followed happened in only a matter of seconds, though the agonizing length of the scene would threaten to steal my sanity.

Sechele had warned me that the lions had become a problem. I had volunteered to be a part of the hunting party. I had not thought my participation would come so swiftly. Instinctively I ran for the soon-to-be victims. The lion was headed right for them. A rock in my stomach told me I was too far away, but I silenced the doubt and sprinted anyway.

"Motsatsi!" I heard her shout. "You will hide now! Take them all with you!"

Even her voice sounded stronger than it had been.

The children grouped together under Motsatsi's direction. They started to run in the opposite direction of the lion, their small legs moving quickly as only children can run. My attention instantly turned to her, hoping she was following the children.

Of course she wasn't. I was aggravated, although not surprised.

Running as fast as my legs could carry me was not quick enough to reach her before I witnessed her reckless courage. My legs became heavy against the psychological strain of not being fast enough to make a difference.

She had watched the children for a moment, her hair drifting across her now strong jawline, with an odd smile on her face. I was still a good distance away, my feet painfully slow. Her face turned toward the lion. I knew what she intended to do and the thought of it made me so angry I growled under my breath.

No!

She would not have listened to reason even if I were close enough for her to hear. She would not survive. She ran at the beast, taking handfuls of hot dirt in her hands. It would only save her for a few extra seconds. I was right, although being right held no victory now. When the lion recovered from the sting to its eyes, it crouched and then sprung at her. Knowing full well I would now never make it to her before she was mauled, and feeling absolutely helpless, I stopped like an imbecile in my tracks and could not tear my eyes away from the carnage in front of me.

The animal grabbed her on the shoulder and threw her to the ground in one swift motion, almost instantly followed by placing its paw down the front of her. Her eyes closed shut. He bit her again.

How is it that she made no sound? How could she have possibly trained herself to be silent while being eaten by a lion? She had yelled before in an attempt to scare the animal, but now remained quiet. I wanted her to cry out so I might know if she was still alive, yet I knew she was for now. As this thought passed through my mind, her eyes flashed open and looked directly at me.

Realizing she could see me, and possessing this evidence that she was alive, I stood as perfectly still as adrenaline would allow, then took my pistol out of my belt and fired. I struck him. The cloud of fragrant white smoke obstructed my view and I started to run again, to get closer to her and to get away from the haze. The giant animal placed a paw to the side of her face, crushing her under its weight. She did not seem to notice.

Suddenly I doubted my reason, for I had left Sechele's home only moments ago, but there he was only a few strides from her! I could not even tell which direction he came from, but there he stood with all the majesty of kings before him. Was this Sechele? He seemed different than the Kgosi I had known for years. He wore an English coat, like always, which was now button-less and altogether ruined after what must have been an amazing run to this spot. The man I knew was a chief and a disciple—but the man who now placed his hands on the lion was an alarming predator. Suddenly I felt a pang of sympathy—for the lion, not the man.

With both hands gnarled in rough fur, the chief shoved the animal off of Catherine. Mebalwe suddenly stood next to him, assegai pointed and prepared. Either my sanity was leaving me, or these men's hunting skills rivaled this lion to such a terrifying degree that there really was no hope for the animal. Quick as summer lightning, the chief had the animal on its back and Mebalwe flipped his assegai downward and plunged the weapon straight into the animal's heart.

After what seemed an excruciating lapse of time, I reached her.

Sechele and Mebalwe were there with me, speaking in their native language so quickly I could only understand two things: she was breathing, and she was a fighter.

I began to assess her wounds. The openings in her shoulder were grotesque to say the least. The wounds resembled gun shots. I felt certain her collar bone and several ribs were broken. Why is it, then, that the wounds that disturbed me the most were the gashes across her face?

The tribesmen who started the hunt finally arrived. Sechele had not been angry as he had fought the lion. Now the rage started in his jaw and moved up.

"Where is the doctor?" I interjected. I hoped to prolong the time before their discipline so I could get Catherine to safety.

"He is attending the sick in the south part of the village," came the reply.

"Go and fetch him! And quickly," I commanded. "Have him meet us at his own house."

"As you say, Captain," A man, whose name I vaguely remembered being Akanni, agreed and ran in the direction I hoped would be quickest to find Livingstone. That left three of the miserable men left to stand and wait their condemnation from the livid Sechele. I refer to them as men, although they were closer to children. Before I left, these same four had not even completed their male initiation into the tribe. It was possible they had gone to hunt the lions to prove their own worth. The thought made me shake with rage.

"She has been staying with the missionary family then?" I questioned again.

"Yes," Dakarai gave me the answer I needed while the other young man, Gahiji, stood with a gaping mouth and horrified eyes. As gently as I could, I hefted her into my arms, trying as I might to avoid her shoulder wounds. Sechele and Mebalwe looked on with stone-cold faces. I could feel her heart beat ferociously everywhere I touched her broken body, and it was a comfort to me because it meant she was fighting hard to stay alive. And in the same instance, it frustrated me because she did not make a sound and I did not know why she worked so hard to stay alive. I cannot say that if I were wounded thus I would battle against death so well.

I started toward the home of the doctor's family. I knew it well. Sechele and Mebalwe flanked either side of me, with the guilty party of men trailing miserably behind us.

My step was suddenly halted by a sharp drop on the top of my head. I was aware of the severe drought that had plagued the village, and so I slowed, as did my comrades.

Had I imagined rain? Was the heat beginning to affect my mind? Sechele and Mebalwe had relaxed their hunter's stances, if only slightly. Nothing immediately followed and after a moment we continued.

Approaching from the same direction I had come, Dr. Living-stone, Mary, and Selemeng came sprinting toward Catherine and me They reached us at last and the doctor assessed her with furrowed brow, calculating the chance of her survival. Exhaustion drained all their features, exemplifying their emotions. The expression that caught me off guard, however, was Selemeng. From the look on her face, I suddenly felt as if I were holding the dead body of one of her children. Her mouth wrinkled and her eyes closed as she shook her head and ran clumsily toward us. I felt she did not want to see what was in my hands. The evidence of Catherine injured. They must have become great friends.

A barrage of questions came at me as soon as they arrived.

"How did this happen?"

"What can we do?"

Before we could answer any of these, it happened again.

All sound stopped.

"Did you feel that?" I asked every soul surrounding me. Their eyes were wide and hopeful, and a few of them nodded their heads. Sechele jerked his hands out in front of him, palms up, and looked to the skies.

I heard a strangled sob and looked back into the face of Kgosi.

"Please," Chief Sechele whispered to the heavens. "Please."

I was torn between wanting to move Catherine and waiting for the rain. Soon I did not have to choose.

The rain came down in torrents.

Chapter 19

ANNA

I do not remember much besides the writhing of my shredded body. My body thought it needful to move constantly in an attempt to move away from the pain. I was told, after the fact, that my chief, Mebalwe, and the captain had rescued me. Then the captain lifted me and carried me back to my house. He was yelling a great amount. I wondered why he was so angry.

Back at the house, the writhing would not stop. I heard a woman's voice asking me questions in broken English—I did not know what she was saying and I did not want to answer. I wanted David to attend to me. What could be keeping him? I looked around me in desperation to find a friendly face. All I saw was the face of the captain in the corner of my bedroom, scowling as always. I closed my eyes again.

I felt a coolness on my burning wounds and heard David's voice trying to break through my many layers of trauma and pain, but I could not answer him. All too quickly there was a disturbing tugging focused on my shoulder, and on several other places along my legs, arms, and face. Something was being poured in my mouth. It tasted absolutely vile! I hoped that meant it would lessen the pain. I was right. After a relentless amount of time I slept.

I was not strong physically, but I was stronger in mind than I had ever been. I forced my consciousness to imagine a peaceful setting.

I sat up in the thickest, most comfortable, and by far the ugliest chair in Father's library. The back of it towered so far above my head, it made me feel like a little child again. It was my dream, after all, so of course Father was there. He sat in a chair facing the door so I could take in his profile. He still had the strongest chin of any man I had ever encountered. Strength was his way and knowledge his beacon. How was he so perfect with such terrible surroundings? I wanted to ask him, but I was becoming so very tired of sound. This place could be quiet a little longer.

My eyes rolled open again as the pain returned. I groaned despite my best efforts to remain quiet. Someone jumped to their feet and came to my side. I didn't care who it was, I just wanted the pain gone again. My body felt tighter, like I was wrapped in some kind of tourniquet. It made it hard to breathe.

"Too tight," was all I could breathe out of my strangled body.

Rough hands jerked my head upright and gave me more putrid liquid to drink. I was grateful. My head laid back down on my pillow and I waited for the pain to leave. My eyes opened and found themselves, once again, locked with the captain's. How did that happen so often? I fell to sleep.

This time, in my mind's eye, Father and I were walking up the path behind the house. I held Father's arm. The path was more defined than I remembered. All the trees remained stationary, but the sun was brighter, the air was warmer, and the ground was softer. Everything around me was better than it had been before.

I looked up into Father's face. He was smiling, enjoying himself in this place. Again, we did not speak. Only moved forward gracefully, not going anywhere.

I felt I didn't have enough time to dream, the pain always returned so quickly. Didn't they have anything stronger? I awoke again. This time the liquid was ready as soon as I awoke. The same hands lifted my head and bade me drink. I willed my eyes to open to prove what I already knew. It was the captain. He looked so angry. Why did he have to look so angry? What had happened to him? I could not ask. I was too tired.

I continued on the path with Father. The sun was bright and I enjoyed the constant warmth it gave to my bare arms. Father spoke this time.

"Where are Anna and her mother?" my dream-father asked me suddenly.

I jerked and then breathed in and out slowly, panic threatening me. "What do you mean?" I asked, not knowing what else to say.

"I mean, this is the place where their cottage used to be," he continued. "Why is Anna not here? You used to love playing with her."

"There is too much pain, Father." I slowed. "I cannot have them near without feeling tremendous guilt."

"Did you not do your best to save them?" he questioned me.

"I did everything in my power, although the flesh was weak," I declared.

"Then what is the need for guilt?"

"I don't know, Father, please do not ask me," I begged.

"My darling girl, you cannot go on forever not speaking of this and keeping the memories out. You have to remember them!"

Sobs came instantly to me. Why would he bring this up now? Wasn't being attacked by a wild carnivore enough punishment for now? It hurt my chest to think of them.

Somewhere a hand touched my forehead and I was brought to reality again.

"Miss Anna," came a voice. A voice I had come to know well. I tried to come up closer to the surface. I tried to wake.

"Miss Anna," he tried again, but all I could do was sob. I couldn't endure the physical or the emotional pain. Even Sechele could not soothe me now. He waited a moment before he said.

"Thank you for saving my children." I felt the emotion coming through his voice.

That made me force my eyes to look at him. He was squatting next to my bed with his head in his hands. He looked so hurt, so broken. Surely there was nothing so precious to Sechele than his children. I wanted to comfort him, but I was unable. I fell to sleep again.

I was sitting on a tree stump, not attempting any further to reign in the sobs that overtook me. Father had broken my heart wide open again. He knelt down next to me, his broad knees breaking branches as he came to the earth.

"You weren't there, Father!" I choked out, "Why weren't you there every second for me? Couldn't you see how I needed you?" I cried desperately now. "Why weren't you my Beowulf?"

He was crying as well. Large tears ran down his weathered cheek.

"It was not you alone that she hurt, Anna. I had to spread myself thin to try and protect everyone she took a disliking to," he tried to explain. "I spent hours appealing to your grandparents, uncle,s and aunts. Anyone who would listen! I begged them to understand what a monster she had become. Everyone believed her charm over my truth. And I could not divorce her or leave her in any way without the law taking you away from me. The magistrates were good friends of your mother's."

"Then why didn't we run away sooner?" I wondered. "Why couldn't you take me away from her?"

"And leave the rest behind?" He tried to make me look at him but I could not. "There were so many to protect!"

"But I was the most important!" I yelled angrily. "She hurt me the most, Father! Why could you not protect me first?"

He grabbed my chin and forced me to look into his eyes. "You were always first, but I was a single man against the world."

I woke again. And once again, my sobs were met with drink. I wanted to open my eyes again to see Sechele, to comfort him if I could. But once again only the captain was present. His eyes bored into mine.

I dropped into sleep and into Father's arms. He rocked me as I cried away years of hurt. Softly, quietly, tiny feet approached us. I looked up into the eyes of my Anna.

She had grown! She had to be almost five years old now! Her hair had lengthened into beautiful, natural curls that glowed in the golden sunlight. Behind her, her mother stood perfectly healthy and blissful. They both remembered me. I could see it in their faces.

I righted myself to see them, still remaining on Father's lap. I cried in joy now at seeing her. She had been in my mind every day since she had died, I had missed her so terribly. She continued to walk timidly to me as I continued to cry. I doubted I could ever stop now.

"Hello," she spoke sweetly. I wiped my eyes roughly with my hands to see her more clearly.

"Hello," I answered. She smiled at me. I continued the conversation. "Are you well?"

She giggled. "Of course!" she said, shaking her head. I smiled at that.

"And your mother? Is she all right as well?" I asked. Her mother took a few steps forward in response. I looked into her face. It was as if she had never seen hardship.

"We are well," she answered.

"I cannot tell you how happy that makes me," I said, tears still covering my face.

They both smiled and I tucked myself into Father's chest and breathed in the relief.

A small hand touched my face. Then reality returned.

My eyes came open easier this time. It was Motsatsi, his hand on my wet cheek. I turned my face and gave his hand a quick kiss. That made him smile. The rough hands held my head again to give me drink.

"Just a moment," I whispered. The hands froze, but one remained under my head. "Hello Motsatsi," I said.

"Hello," he responded. He had been crying as well.

I responded to his grief. "Are you quite well?" I asked him.

"Of course!" he responded, almost mad. "You saved us."

"All the children?" I asked further. "Everyone is safe?"

He nodded miserably. My battered hand reached up to wipe away a tear. It was amazing the pain the simple move produced. I flinched in surprise, and the captain forced me to drink again. In that space between reality and dreaming I smiled at Motsatsi and whispered again.

"I am well too. I am healing," I whispered, and I was asleep again.

I still sat wrapped in Father's arms. Anna and her mother surrounded me. Somehow I was done crying and sat happily as they all created a circle of healing around me. An eternity in bliss passed by me.

"There is one more you need to allow into this circle, my dear," Father spoke into my ear. I jerked my head up, racking my brain for anyone else in the world I wanted here.

"Who?" I asked him.

I looked into my father's face. He was so familiar to me. His eyes were deep set and his nose was broad. His forehead was tall and held inside wisdom I had not even begun to understand.

"It is someone you must come to understand," he told me.

"No!" I begged him, "Please don't send me back. I want to stay, I don't want to work anymore,"

"The work left to do will bring you joy," he promised me. That halted my pleadings. And I simply stared into his face—willing my mind to remember it forever.

I opened my eyes for a fraction of a second.

The captain had been with me through it all. I peered deep into his eyes and for a long moment we said nothing, we just enjoyed a moment of clarity and understanding.

At last, I slept without dreaming.

◇◇◇

I was back to reality now, and this time I felt it was permanent. In the midst of my body healing itself, my mind had begun to heal itself as well. I was now more whole, more me. I could take a breath without the thought of little Anna's limp body wracking my chest. My mind was clear and focused. I had won.

I was silent, but I looked around the room.

It was a bright, still, and familiar atmosphere. My mind and body had quieted at last. The thick, thatched roof over my head, supported by whitewashed walls, painted by David so long ago. All that I possessed sat at the foot of my bed. Not much survived of the overflowing chest I had brought with me to Kolobeng.

I turned my head to view my caretaker. He sat in a chair that looked unstable and most uncomfortable. His head rested precariously on one shoulder, his coat turned backward to cover his arms and chest. It took me some time to recognize the man I thought I knew. This man had sat by my side for what must have been days, at least. Now I looked on him as First Mate Anderson must have so long ago. He was akin to an innocent little boy when he slept.

The captain awoke, startled to see my eyes open and gazing at him. He threw off his coat and stumbled to my side to feel my forehead with his rough hands. I kept my eyes on him. As soon as he woke, the rough lines around his mouth and forehead instantly appeared. As soon as he was satisfied with my temperature, he sat back on his heels and let out a deep sigh.

"It's about time," he said sharply.

In my pathetic, frail state all I could do was furrow my own brow, wondering what exactly he meant. Before I could even contemplate a response, Mary entered the room. Having heard the captain's exclamation, she rushed in and also put her hands on my forehead in assessment. As if purposefully mimicking the captain, she sighed in relief.

"My sentiments mirror yours, sir," she told him.

The sight of Mary startled me, her now much larger belly being a symbol of how long I had been unconscious.

"Mary," I said warily. "How long has it been?" I almost did not want to know the answer, because it would represent how torn up my body truly had been.

She took a moment to look at the captain and they exchanged a quick, silent conversation. Why was Mary consulting with the captain?

"Four weeks," she answered.

The amount of time I had laid completely useless made my heart ache. That Mary had to do so many chores, while she was obviously still sick, was devastating. Robert and Agnes must have been traumatized by my still form in their room for so long, unable to play as they liked. But it was the loss of water that was the hardest to consider. I realized that Mary would have used a larger portion of our daily rations to help me heal. The evidence was in my fully hydrated throat. To deprive a pregnant woman and her two small children of water that was already scarce was absolutely deplorable, no matter the circumstances. I suddenly wished I had died the instant the lion sank his teeth into me.

I started to cry. The tears rolled down my cheeks, proving that I had sufficient water inside me. It made me cry all the more.

Seeing it, the captain and Mary jumped and started evaluating me. Mary pulled back bandages on my shoulder, trying to find the reason for my tears.

Robert and Agnes took this moment to run at their top speed into the room.

"Miss Anna is awake!" Robert cried, ecstatic. He came to my side and I turned my head away from him to hide my tears. After he spoke my name several times, I began to feel a fresh wave of guilt that I was ignoring him. I turned my head to survey the damage I remembered: the cracked lips, the sunken eyes, and that awful look of general loss of fluid.

To my bewilderment, his lips were pink, healthy, and entirely missing of cracks. His eyes were wide, bright, and shining blue. No sign of dehydration touched his face. Next I considered Agnes who toddled behind. She never looked so healthy, so well fed. Had she gained weight while I slept? Her little dimples were deeper.

I jerked my head back to Mary, who knew what I was going to ask.

"It rained," she spoke reverently. "And also, the people of the tribe . . ." she started to explain but then was suddenly unable to speak.

I was amazed. Mary? Emotional? Begging for an explanation with my eyes, I turned to the captain.

"The people of the tribe have been supplying us with daily water from their personal supplies," he explained more fully. "It has been all we could do to keep this room clear of people wanting to give you their rain water."

Chills began at the peak of my head, resonated in my legs, and reached my toes. Not only had it rained while I slept, but the people had wanted to share their portion of blessings with me. They forgave the witch who took care of her little ones.

And so, I did the only rational thing a capable, well-educated woman can do in such a moment.

I cried some more.

I received several more visitors that day, despite Mary's and the captain's protests that I should rest. Motsatsi was absolutely unstoppable. He brought me a lovely shining apple.

"Motsatsi, where did you get this?" I asked in perplexity.

"Never you mind," he spoke dismissively. "You will eat it and become well again."

It felt like years since I had held fresh fruit. I could not bear to eat it, so I set it aside.

"I want you to tell me what happened, Motsatsi," I implored.

He shrugged his small, yet strong, shoulders.

"There is not much to say. Some of our men were out hunting and a few lions began making their way toward town. They took it upon themselves to kill the leader to try and save the village, but the big one, he got away and bit you," he would not look at me as he spoke. I knew it had been a traumatic experience for him.

"And no one else was hurt?" I asked him quietly.

He shook his head and I could not help but notice his eyes were brimming with tears. My little soldier was sad he could not save me. It made my eyes brim over as well.

Though it caused me great discomfort, I reached out and took his hand. He still looked down, the picture of tragic self-loathing.

"I feel so very grateful that I could save you, Motsatsi," I told him. "Even if I take years to recover, I would do it again." He still would not look at me. I paused. "Do you know that?"

He nodded his head and tears ran off his cheeks and onto the floor.

There was water everywhere today.

At that moment, I heard a commotion outside. The sound worked its way farther and farther into my head until the noise became almost uncomfortable. A strong, capable voice spoke from the door of our home. The voice was speaking in Sechuana, but it was not David. Another tribesman perhaps.

Soon the sound came inside the house, and I watched in amazement as the room filled to capacity with members of the village. A month ago if these same tribes people had filled this room, I would have assumed it would be to end my pesky existence. I felt silly laying there so still, unable to move, while they all peered down at me. However, from this perspective I could quietly take in their expressions, and there was no hostility.

Last to enter the room was my chief. Sweat was pouring off his temples, because despite the blazing heat, he was dressed in a wide, orange straw hat, a Mackintosh overcoat, and possibly the largest water boots I had ever beheld, with added tassels and a buckle.

Oh, how I had missed him.

Despite his unconventional appearance, he spoke with authority.

"Miss Anna," he addressed me formally. "You saved our lives by wounding yourself. Henceforth, our hearts are yours."

To my dismay, he removed his hat, placed it over his chest, and bent his head to a slight degree.

I was about to tell him, embarrassed, that there was no need. My plea was silenced by the quiet respect of every other person in the room. Their dark, uncovered heads lowered before me in a wave. I knew very well how beloved their children were to them. It was not only that I had faced the threatening animal, but that I had placed myself between him and their children. Would I not also bow at the feet of anyone that rescued my Robert or Agnes?

I squeezed Motsatsi's hand tighter for support, before I whispered, "As your hearts are mine, so does mine belong to you. Thank you."

Motsatsi spoke up and translated my words. A few faces looked up at me with guilt on their faces. They knew they had been wrong about me. Although I had wished they could have come to this realization on their own, I found that I did not want them to feel guilty for how they had treated me. How could I be upset with them when I had provided a perfect avenue for them to vent their frustrations at the lack of water. I would have wanted someone to blame as well. But I secretly wished their forgiveness could have come without such great pain.

Selemeng took the opportunity to step forward now and kneel by my bedside. She gave me a long and warm hug, the tears dripping off her cheeks just like her son's. As she pulled away, the gratitude on her face was clear.

"May we move forward now?" I asked tentatively. "As friends?"

"As friends," Selemeng agreed, and I was awarded by a room full of sincere smiles.

The captain jumped in at this moment, I had not realized he had been standing at the door this entire time. It was not that he jumped into this conversation that startled me, it was that he rattled off in perfect, clear, and fluent Sechuana. His words were so fast I did not catch a single word from his speech, but quickly it was over and it had a great impact on the people, who all stood, gave me tender little smiles, and exited my room without another word. Even Motsatsi let go of my hand and headed to the door as if the captain pulled him physically. Did he have authority with them?

I was left to observe my caretaker. I had so many questions for him. He spoke as if it had been easy for him, when I still could not say more than a few words myself, after months of living among these people. It appeared as if the Bakwena knew him, or at least were comfortable with him. Was it possible he had lived here before me? I knew he had been missing for some time after his wife's death. I had assumed he was sailing on his ship around the world, but perhaps not.

And there was another point of question. Where was his ship? Docked in Durban? Had he returned to London and then right back to our port? That seemed especially peculiar. Had the Missionary Society sent more supplies? I almost literally jumped at the possibility of fresh linens, cool water, and new school supplies. Had he come here to deliver them? I disliked my lack of information.

He was preparing my sleeping drink on the washstand, and as soon as he finished, came toward me with the putrid stuff. I shook my head, wanting to delay the sleeping for just a moment longer.

"It sounds as if you have many stories to tell me," I probed. "It is a fortunate coincidence since I have nowhere to go."

He did not find me amusing. He spoke with a straight face. "How are you feeling?"

His question reminded me. "It is difficult to move, I confess. And I cannot feel my fingers."

"I would almost say you deserved it, for standing in front of a charging lion." His words were harsh, but his tone was somehow sympathetic. I cocked my head, confused, as he continued. "The doctor wondered if that would be the case."

I assumed he meant David.

"Where is he?" I asked. I wanted David to examine me and see if I was healing properly.

"Gone," he said bluntly. There was obvious irritation in his voice.

"Where did he go?"

He sighed. Looking at the floor, he warred within himself. His hesitation told me something was wrong. He was not one to treat my feelings delicately.

"What happened?" I asked, afraid of the answer.

He squared his shoulders and, with a deep breath, turned to face me.

"Doctor Livingstone and Mebalwe are on a peace crusade, of sorts," he said.

"A peace crusade to whom?" I asked, although the dread in my gut suspected the answer.

"The Boers," he informed me. "They have declared war on Sechele and his people."

Chapter 20

Despite my friends' arguments, I could not help but feel that I was the cause of the sudden and forceful hostilities of the Boers. Our neighbors were still desperate for water and supplies, and the money my mother promised was still too tempting to resist. I was so surrounded by good people, however, that any attempts to give myself over to the Boers would have been easily thwarted, not to mention my inability to walk or take care of myself.

My caretaking fell to the captain. I could not be sure if this was because of obligation or genuine concern. Whatever the reason, he was proficient in the calling. His years as the captain and doctor of his ship had lent him experience, this I knew. However, as he attended to me, a gleam of suspicion and fear would occasionally cloud his features. He would look upon me in such a peculiar way that I finally spoke my mind.

"You look at me as if you expect me to scream and run about the room," I said.

My words seemed to physically affect him. As if I had stood and shoved his chest with both hands. He appraised me with a startled expression.

I could not think of how to react, so I simply said, "I won't."

He kept staring at me, his eyes wide. After a few moments, he relaxed.

"I know," he whispered.

My mind went to Marianne, his wife and my friend. I knew she had been sick near the end, and I had to ask . . .

"Did you care for Marianne in her illness?"

He looked pained again and became rigid. Nevertheless, he answered. "I did. I could not be sure she was not contagious, and I was the only one left that had been exposed to her."

"The only one left?" I wanted clarification, but I dreaded where this conversation was going.

He nodded.

"My parents could not tolerate the illness in their age."

My heart sunk. His parents had died because of Marianne's infection. They had all passed away at the same time, leaving the captain an orphan and widower in the same instance.

I suddenly felt I was a modern day Narcissus. So obsessed had I been with my own story, my own sorrows, my own path that I had never learned to comfort others in their grief. If I had any hope of becoming like Mary, I had to learn. I allowed myself to feel the desire to comfort him and allowed my instincts to take control. With all the uncertainty in the world, I reached out and clasped his arm with my good hand.

When first I touched him, we both tensed and were still. I regretted my hastiness and thought of retreat. My grasp twitched. Soon, however, we became calm and his expression turned gentle and sorrowful.

So slow I wasn't sure what he was doing until it was done, his other hand raised and came down on top of mine. I felt comforted, enclosed in his touch.

I smiled meekly at him. He smiled back, though it looked like it took some great effort.

I felt extremely grateful for his help and told him so.

"I have only done what was necessary," he retorted.

"Thank you," I repeated, persistent.

He looked up at my face with a most peculiar expression.

"I am only glad to see you yourself again," he said in a gruff voice. "I was sure you had been killed."

I was amazed that he cared this much. My hand began to feel hot in his grasp.

All I could say was "thank you" again. He nodded and released me, turning his back to me.

◇◇◇

David, Mebalwe, Sechele, and Selemeng gathered in my room that night to discuss the peace attempts. Before we could begin, however, a knock came at the door. Mary opened the door to a man and a woman whose skin was as fair as her own. She recognized the couple instantly and beckoned them inside. The man put his weathered hand on the small of his wife's back and ushered her inside. I wondered at their situation while David perceived my questions.

"Family," he addressed us all, "this is Johannes and Roosa Pretorius. They have been our friends for some time. They accompanied us from the Boer encampment."

This told me one thing for certain: they were Boers themselves. I tensed at the implications and my eyes flew to David. To my astonishment, he was already looking at me, guessing my reaction. He shook his head and gave me a disparaging glance before he continued.

"They have much to add to our report," he said, defending them. I noticed sheepishly that no one else in the room had tensed in fear as I had done. Sechele and Selemeng seemed as comfortable in their presence as if they had been in their own home. I was suddenly acutely aware of my prejudice against an entire race of people. Was I judging all Boers based on a select few? This would explain the disparaging look David had just given me. He had already suspected me. I cringed and resolved to do better in the same moment.

"And so, Ngaka," Sechele asked, "what have they said?"

David paused. He had a difficult time revealing the news to his chief. His friend, Johannes, interjected for him.

"They are determined to attack," he spoke as if he had no connection with them, although his thick Dutch accent betrayed him. "This group of men are a dangerous breed. They believe themselves to be peacemakers, and yet we have watched as they destroyed their enemies and made slaves of their friends. There were no words to persuade them to forgo their strike, not even from the revered David Livingstone."

"So what is their reasoning for attack?" I asked, baffled and confused. "Have they been attacked by any of our people?"

The captain answered my question.

"They have never been attacked by us. It is like Johannes said," he echoed, "they believe themselves to be peacemakers. The Bakwena people pose a threat to peace because Abraham believes Sechele to be like Dingane, the chief who killed his friends. Wide knowledge of Sechele's armory does not help his case."

I remembered Sechele's exceptionally large rifle the night of our unfortunate dinner. I suppose I should have guessed there was more.

"What's more is they find David and any other man in Sechele's village a threat because they are all rumored to have been supplying Sechele with weapons."

I could not handle the mystery any longer.

"How do you know all of this?" I asked.

The captain looked on me candidly.

"Because I have heard the rumors," he answered simply. There was a long pause after his short explanation and I noticed Selemeng had one eyebrow cocked. Pressured by the silence, he added with a smirk, "And also, I have been the one supplying the Bakwena with guns."

Sechele returned the grin tenfold, adding excitedly, "I have a cannon!"

The simple Boer couple were taken aback. Obviously they had not heard of this. I hoped this changed the outlook of the battle.

"Perhaps if the other Boers knew of the extent of your weaponry, Sechele, they would not be so aggressive," I suggested hopefully.

"The Boers have weapons of their own," David countered. "No amount of bullets would keep them from protecting a land they claim to be theirs."

Sechele scoffed in an odd agreement that I didn't understand. Luckily, David expounded, possibly for my benefit alone.

"The European way of staking a claim to a piece of land is to obtain a preliminary certificate of ownership. The land is then inspected by a commission, and if no one protests, the land becomes the property of the applicant. The farm boundary would be half an hour's walk in each direction from the homestead.

"In a system so haphazard as this, native rights were often overlooked. When the whites presented the chiefs with an agreement on paper, and the chiefs made their mark on it, the two parties to the agreement were starting from quite different premises. The whites thought they had obtained the land, free and clear, whereas the chiefs, to whom individual tenure of land was a thing unknown, believed that they had merely granted a tenancy. The gift from the white man that usually sealed the bargain was almost a token of vassalage in their eyes.

"Thus, many of these European squatters, having occupied some attractive looking piece of land, would refuse to move, and the Native would find himself declared a trespasser on a farm that his family had used for generations. It is easy to see how bitter misunderstandings might arise, the white man accusing the chief of bad faith, while to the chief the white tenant, by asserting proprietary rights, seemed to be a landgrabber subverting the ancient laws."

"By that reasoning then, whose land are they occupying now?" I asked, trying to understand.

"Mine," Sechele responded, suddenly forlorn after listening to David's explanation.

"What is your assessment then, David," Mary spoke up, directing us back to the point, "of how the Bakwena would fare in a battle against these men?"

It was the one question I had been too afraid to ask.

The silence was deafening.

After an immeasurable amount of time, David finally answered with the truth. "I don't know. There are too many factors that are not yet decided. We know not how many guns and ammunition they possess, when they will attack, if others will come to our aid, or if we will receive more rain before that," he trailed off, almost listless.

"Are there other tribes that would help us?" I asked, my eyes widening.

"I feel certain of some of my friends," Sechele replied. "The Bangwaketse, Bakgatla bagaMmanaana and Bakaa," he named off, which I supposed was a few other tribes nearby.

"Although a good number of them may be coming to you for protection instead of support," the captain clarified.

"Nevertheless," Sechele said, "they shall be protected."

"Is there any guess, then, of when the attack will happen?" Mary asked.

"Boers fight on horseback," Johannes answered. "To avoid the dreaded horse-sickness, they send their horses during the rains into a district that is free from the disease. We can also be sure they won't attack on Sunday. They are devout Sabbath worshipers." He paused in some obvious chagrin. "The month of May is when we may expect them."

Two months away.

David and Mary exchanged a glance that could have been spoken aloud, so easily it was understood by all the occupants of the room. That was the very month Mary would deliver her child.

"If taken by surprise, my men and I will rush with our guns and assegais to this mission house to protect David and his family," Sechele spoke bravely. "The old loyalty between the doctor and his people will be rekindled."

◇◇◇

It is a peculiar life awaiting and preparing for an imminent fight. For days it was all we could discuss. We speculated on their motives, their methods, and their madness. Preparation was well thought out, especially focused around Mary's baby. It was finally decided that Mary and the children should accompany David to Kuruman to stay with Mary's parents who ran the mission there. The drought was not so severe there, and Mary and the children would be well taken care of.

In their preparation for departure, Mary appeared to either be much improved or becoming a better actress. She bustled around the home as if nothing ailed her. Especially when she was around me, she appeared completely serene, and yet I would have been curious to see how she acted when she was alone.

David visibly dreaded the upcoming fight, and it affected him physically in the form of more serious headaches. Not only was there a violent threat to a people he held so dear, but in the many years of his missionary work, Sechele was his only convert. He was leaving his home unhappy with the results of his labor. In addition, no man is pleased when forced to run to his father-in-law for assistance—at least I knew David was not.

There was one obstacle, however, that kept them from departing immediately: me. Despite my vehement protests, they were convinced if they left my bedside with the much needed medicines, I could become infected again and have no hope of recovery. They could leave medicines for me, but could not know how much would be needed and did not want to waste any. All were adamant that I not be moved, and despite my horror at my frail state, I could not help but agree. The smallest movements threatened to reopen the giant circular wounds left by the claws of the lion. Even the smallest obligations left me so weak I could sometimes not even lift a spoon to feed myself. Traveling in any capacity would have been incredibly difficult.

The decision was made. The Livingstones would stay with me for another month so that David could closely watch my progress and administer medicines when needed without being wasteful. Mary insisted it did not make much difference if she traveled now or in one month. She would still be just as sick and just as uncomfortable as she was now. It was sound reason that they would trust Mary's strength, and word of strength, more than mine. She had—and would continue to—survived much more than I had ever seen.

Then there was the unavoidable fact that I would be in the house as the battle commenced, unable to fight. Not only would I be of no use to the people who I had come to love so dearly, but I would also be a burden. I would be protected by Bakwena men who should be standing on the lines with Sechele facing their enemy instead of protecting a young wounded girl. And yet, once again, nothing I could say would convince them that this was folly. And so I attempted to live amiably in my containment. If I were to be a burden, I would not be a bitter and irritating burden.

Mary and David had readied their belongings to depart in an instant if need be. All preparations had been made to be ready for the attack. Despite Mary becoming more active and capable, she also had more to do, so the captain continued to be my primary caregiver. Mary took care of my personal, and sometimes quite embarrassing, needs. Occasionally, women from the tribe would come to sit with me while the captain ran his mysterious errands. But the majority of my time was spent alone with this man.

At first, when I was permitted to be conscious throughout most of the day, having him so close and alone was supremely uncomfortable. There was very little I could do to ease my discomfort. Every motion disturbed a wound or a healing broken bone, of which there were many.

The only thing I had control over was my eyes, and I came to know the details of my ceiling well. In my mind, I repeatedly commended David on his fine craftsmanship. The captain must have sensed my uneasiness, but he dismissed it forcefully when it got in the way of his nursing responsibilities. I could keep my eyes focused on anywhere but his person for hours, but when it was time for a meal, medicine, or changing my bandages, he would brusquely proceed despite my chagrin.

The Captain did not urge me to speak or make polite conversation. He took special attention to my needs, mixing medication, giving me water, and even baking bread without any assistance from Mary. In those times when all my needs were met, he would write letters or read David's books quietly. Never once did he question me about anything unrelated to my condition.

Gradually, I will admit, I began to watch the captain more than the ceiling. He was often close enough for me to take in several details about him at once. I had thought his hair an unkempt raven black, graying at the temples, but it was actually a dark brown. He was neat, precise, and in an odd way, graceful. He made no movement without a purpose. He was not one of these men to fidget about unnecessarily. He did not tap his feet, nor shift uncomfortably. He was always perfectly at rest and ease, knowing his duty and performing it admirably. And he was admirable.

It was while contemplating these features that I was caught looking at his face. He had lifted my shoulders gently off the hard bed with one arm to carefully feed me a thin soup Mary had prepared. In the days since his arrival, this had become a daily occurrence for us, and yet something about this encounter was different. He checked my face, as he often did to check for signs of pain. Finding none he returned his gaze to the soup for a fraction of a second before slowly moving his striking eyes back to mine.

And how shall I describe the moment when I realized the magnitude of my foolishness? How shall I tell you that in that moment, I realized I had loved him since the days I saw him standing resolutely in the corners of those warm ballrooms? Yet, oh, I was still so acutely humiliated by my past treatment at his hands. My thoughts warred within me, and I wished I could walk away from here, that I could leap from this bed and shove my way through the door. But I could not, and still the thoughts came.

In those days, in my mind, I had begged him to come out from the shadows and save me from my life of empty echoes. When he had not I had shut him out as harshly as I had everyone else excepting my dear father. Since his marriage, I had looked for faults in him to lessen the pain I had felt at having my hopes thwarted.

And yet, on the other hand, how could I have trusted him? I was taught nothing of love. My mother beat and abused behind doors and became a sweet actress in public. The only feeling I had in that life past was survival. There had been no room for passion, no room for tenderness. I had not known my own mind. Like so many things, Mother had taken that away from me.

And now, finally, I understood the ballads, the poems, the stories. All tales of love and devotion had been opaque, so incapable was I of understanding that side of human emotion. Now I understood. Love between man and woman is crowned with loving service. The relationships devoid of money or gain could be the most tender and genuine. I had not understood, even though it had been told to me hundreds of times. But in that moment, my mind caught hold of that fact, and knew it now.

I had little experience with these matters, but I looked into his eyes unashamed, searching for requited feelings.

At first I could not understand what I saw in his hard, dark eyes, but the longer we sat there unmoving, the more the feelings magnified and became more apparent. Eventually I could tell what the emotion was that encompassed his features.

Hope.

But hope of what? The tender feelings that had welled inside me were suddenly beaten back by dread. I wanted to stay in that moment with him, staring into his eyes, but I could not deny that he had been married. What fault had he found with her, with Marianne? She was in every way superior to myself. Tall, handsome, articulate, excellent in the handling of people's feelings. He'd had a reputation of denying advance after advance of scores of young females, but he had been swept off his feet by her, and picked her instantly out of the crowd of now crushed hopefuls.

A crowd that had held me.

He had passed me by, a girl the same age as his future wife, and had pursued Marianne openly. If he cared for me now, what was it that had changed his mind? He had come to know me better, but in the meantime had scolded me, corrected me.

Was he grooming me to be like his lost Marianne?

I turned from his gaze and presence so forcefully that the soup fell from his hands and made a mess on the floor.

I pretended to sleep while he cleaned it up.

Chapter 21

I took time every day to sit up in my bed, attempting to be careful and delicate with my one mangled shoulder, while avoiding eye contact with the captain. This allowed me a view outside the one small window, and the prospect was still incredibly dry and empty. Although I was told some rain had fallen while I slept, you would not know it from looking at the sparse trees in the distance. I was sure Motsatsi could push them over if given the inclination.

I suddenly craved conversation.

"Has there ever been a drought like this one?" I asked the captain.

His head snapped up from a letter he had been engrossed in. Seeing me look in his direction and speaking to him directly shocked him for a few seconds.

"Not that I am aware of," he replied slowly, treading around me softly as he would an injured animal.

I nodded, taking that information in.

"Do you think it is because of Sechele's baptism that it does not rain?" I asked candidly.

He shook his head.

"I have never claimed to be religious, but what I do know of God, he would not punish someone for wanting to be better. The drought has to be a coincidence. And such a powerful coincidence," I added. "How can the people stay with him if they believe God is punishing him?"

He thought for a moment before giving his opinion.

"I believe the Bakwena are an excellent example of trying to do the right thing, even when faced with unfair circumstances."

That was an apt description of these people. Despite the anger they felt with their chief and with us, they never attempted to hurt me or run me off. Neither did they attempt to replace Sechele as King. Sechele's father had not been so fortunate.

"And how is it that you know so much of the Bakwena?" I asked him at last. The question came out more harshly than I had intended.

A corner of his mouth lifted slightly in slight amusement.

"I found myself in the interior of Africa, much like you. The Bakwena became my hosts for several months."

"You came alone?" I questioned.

"No, I traveled with the Livingstones," he clarified. "Although they had no children back then."

"So our adventures have been similar," I remarked, with an almost bitter tone.

"Quite," he answered simply.

"Where is the *Madras*? Is she docked in Durban?"

"She is docked in Durban. The crew will stay with her until I return. First Mate Anderson has everything well under control without me."

"Anderson," I breathed in relief. "He is alive, then."

"Yes, alive and as strong as ever. Infection did not set into the sloppy surgery we administered."

"I'm glad," I said.

He gave me a tender smile. Unfortunately, it did not help his case. Resentments from the other day and my conclusions crept up on me.

"Why are you here?" I demanded to know. "Why did you come so far into the interior?"

He gave me the most peculiar expression. I could not place the composition of his features. Was he irritated?

"I don't know," he finally replied.

I grunted in a way not suited to a lady.

◇◇◇

220

Four weeks after I awoke, I was allowed to stand on my own. My shoulder, face, and hands were still so battered that my companions struggled to allow me any movement at all. David, however, came to my rescue in saying I would do good with some fresh air, and I was permitted to take short walks around the village. My arm was so tightly strapped to my chest and my shoulder so covered in fresh bandages I felt a regular spectacle.

I was not permitted to take these walks alone, however. The captain trailed either slightly behind or directly to my side at all times. His presence chaffed my good mood. I realized that what I was experiencing was rejection, past rejection, that felt fresh now that I'd allowed myself to feel it. I also realized I was not handling it well. However naive I felt, I still could not forget the fact that he had walked right past me into the arms of Marianne, and that fact nettled me into a constant feeling of hostility.

Walking through the village was a different experience now. Since I had given up my arm for their children, I could not walk ten paces without being stopped and thanked for my sacrifice. The captain would step in to translate when I didn't respond immediately to their rushed Sechuana. I should have been thankful, but I resented that he knew the language better than me when I had been here more recently. After his second attempt to translate I stared at him frankly, my mouth a hard, straight line. He evaluated my expression, rolled his eyes, then did not interrupt my disjointed conversations anymore.

In preparation for imminent battle, the walls of the city had been reinforced with new layers of mud and sand, the holes in the walls made smaller to allow less space for incoming fire. Sechele's home had become a veritable fortress. Rifles and pistols hung from window pots that, when last seen, had held flowers. Sturdy boards had been nailed to windows and the front door, fortified from both sides. Although it was widely known that Sechele would be at the front line of battle with his people, his home was being reinforced to hold women and children. At least the mimosa flowers were back to remind me of more pleasant things.

Outside of the chief's home, the kotla floor was being covered in threadbare blankets. It seemed they were preparing for a gathering. Sechele chose this moment to step out of his home.

"Ah! Miss Anna!" he hollered and threw out his arms to me. "You walk!"

"Yes I do, Chief," I confirmed. "It has been a delight to see the village once again."

"Not just *the* village anymore, Miss Anna." He shook his finger at me. "It is now *your* village."

I looked to the ground and grinned.

"And you have company!" He turned his attention to the captain. "Accompanied by an arms dealer. That is exceptional."

They began a long discussion on the specifics of a certain gun, which I had no interest in. Seeing that my interest wavered, they reverted into quick Sechuana. David was opposed to carrying a firearm himself, but the captain and Sechele had no such qualms and were armed every moment of every day. The men of the tribe who stood guard over the house were also equipped with guns, the size of which sometimes shocked me to see in their thin arms.

As I wandered away, I soon noticed Selemeng was one of the villagers laying thin blankets on the floor of our meeting place. I came to her side and she surprised me by wrapping her thick arms around my shoulders. The embrace tortured my injuries, but I dared not say anything against this rare affection.

"How are you today?" she asked as she held me close.

"I am well enough," I lied against her warm arm.

"Good," she released me suddenly and gave me a meek smile. A lion bite seemed worth all of this acceptance and love I was receiving.

"Are we having a meeting?" I asked her as I gestured to the coverings.

"Telling stories," she said. "Sechele will tell, and then we will dance!"

"Stories and dancing," I said, trying to imagine the scene. "Sounds fun!"

"We give cheer," she smiled at me sincerely. I could get used to this side of her. She humbly continued laying out blankets, and I helped where I could with one hand.

Mary walked past with a large basket of things to give away to the side of the village we had visited so many times. What did she have to give away? I beckoned her over and told her the plans of stories and dance.

"Oh wonderful," was her response. "I do enjoy Sechele's stories."

"So you've heard them before," I said unsurprised. "What of the dancing?"

She chuckled as she patted her ever-growing belly.

"The good chief begins with a foreign cultural dance and then they revert to their own traditional dances."

"Oh," I began, confused. "What is the foreign cultural dance?"

"The waltz," she said, smiling. "And if I were to have my guess, I would say he has two experienced dancers in his midst that he will somehow coerce into performing for the rest of the tribe." Her eyes were full of suggestion.

"No," I moaned in dread, understanding her implications perfectly. I looked around for an exit. If Sechele asked me, I knew I would be hard pressed to reject his enthusiasm. Without stepping on Selemeng's work I had very few options of escape. I took the path that would take me directly opposite of Sechele's front door. I walked as quickly as I could without breaking into a jog. The thought occurred to me to sprint, but I quickly dismissed it as painful and possibly unnecessary. The heat was beginning to make me sweat as I came closer to a small cluster of trees. I could go behind them and then change my course in case Mary sent them after me. Only two steps away now.

"Miss Anna!" called a deep African accent.

His voice startled me and I stopped in my tracks. I was disheartened at my lack of proper expletives. Ever so slowly I turned on my heel to face the chief. He was as cheerful and jovial as ever—completely oblivious to my attempted escape. I could see the others behind him. Mary had her basket on her hip, thoroughly enjoying the fact that she was not the subject of his excited pursuit. Selemeng

seemed to be aware of something amiss but she could not understand what. Seeing me looking upon her, she broke out into a smile
instantly. And finally, there was the captain, his back to us, his
expression hidden from me.

"I have the best idea," he began. I need not repeat his designs. I
could not deny this man his delight or my submission.

Suffice it to say, the conversation was swift. I would be dancing
with the captain later that night.

I began my slow trod back home. David had been far and wide
on this continent and he assured me there was no other like our chief.
How was it possible that I had become a citizen of the one village in
all of Africa with a chief who was fascinated by a culture that now
repulsed me? I had been glad to be accepted so easily by him, but was
now regretting the connection. Because, to please my dear leader,
there could only be one dance partner for me. The captain. We had
both been raised in the social, dancing circles of London, and Sechele could not resist the pleasure of seeing the spectacle exactly as it
should be performed.

I sighed.

The truth was, I had wanted to dance with the captain back
when I knew him as Mr. Ashmore. I had looked upon him as a naïve
youth and longed for him to cross the crowded ballroom to beg my
companionship. In my daydreams, I would deny him, of course, but
he would insist and then I would graciously accept at long last.

And it was for this very reason that I so disliked him now. He
had never crossed the room for me. In fact, I had seen him cross the
room for Marianne once, and then again after they were married to
scold her in front of me. She had not filled his expectations exactly
and was therefore a disappointment. When you marry the perfect
woman and find her disagreeable, the reasonable thing to do was to
discard her and find another to mold into a suitable companion.

The thought physically hurt my chest.

But then the optimist in the back of my mind spoke up. He may
not have crossed a ballroom for me, but he had crossed an ocean. He
had left me in Africa, but then returned to where he knew I would
be. He stayed with me without complaining. There was sure to be

more adventurous and interesting things to be doing for an independent man in the interior of Africa. And yet, he had stayed.

But why? He could have asked me to stay on the dock in Durban when we first landed. He could have told me how he felt then, if he did truly care for me. Why now? What had changed?

I looked behind me. Of course he was there. Protecting me.

Irritating me.

Chapter 22

I have several memories of climbing small trees with Robert and Agnes in the evenings, prior to the lion attack. As we played, the sun would drearily sink, taking its time to descend as we finished a hard day with simple joy. And now, on the night I had to face the captain in an intimate dance, that same sun betrayed me by plummeting faster than a boulder down a dark pit.

Because I dreaded its descent, it fell faster still.

The entire village was converging on the kotla, eager for some sort of celebration in the face of imminent battle. Sechele was right. We needed this. But I dreaded it.

I had come behind the Livingstones. Several of my dear students came and wrapped themselves around my legs, nearly toppling me over. A few adults came to my rescue, extricating their children with grins on their dark faces. I beamed during and after the event. This simple experience had left a firm message on my heart.

I belonged here.

I thought of what Sechele had declared the night Abraham and his men had tried to arrest me. I remembered his words perfectly.

You would have to rip out my insides rather than us give her up. She is my blood.

And now I understood how he felt. These were my people. You would have to rip out my insides rather than me give them up. They were my blood.

Perhaps physical blood relations can never be changed. Perhaps there would always be a physical tie from my mother to myself. But I claimed the Bakwena as much as my blood as any relation in the history of man.

I halted my musings and sat quickly and quietly, for Sechele was urging those present to quiet their chatter and listen to his storytelling. Motsatsi planted himself next to me with all the grace a boy can muster on a dirty blanket. To my surprise, he had become even more protective of me. Every time someone came to close to me, his hand would slowly clasp his spear and his eyes would slide in their direction, suspicious. I sighed and shook my head. When he shrugged his shoulders at my angst, I smiled.

"I'm not made of lace, good sir," I told him.

His droll little face looked up at me. "I am not interested in lace," he answered.

I looked to Mary and we shared a silent laugh.

Mary translated Sechele's story for me.

"There once was a warrior who was born in this very village," Sechele said through translation. He turned to Selemeng and spoke under his breath, "Although, he was not as handsome as me." Mary translated while rolling her eyes. Motsatsi nodded his agreement.

"This man was raised from the beginning to fight and to make war. He learned how to protect the people by fighting large animals. I saw once, as a boy, this man fight and kill an elephant all alone. He was ten years old."

The crowd gasped.

"As the moon and sun changed position again and again, the man became more ferocious in nature. He ran faster, he hit harder, and at last he accomplished his goal to fight a lion, and he defeated it."

My mouth dropped open.

"Much like our Miss Anna!" Sechele said to my surprise. Everyone looked to me and smiled and nodded. I felt a little annoyed. I hadn't killed a lion. He had mangled me and then died on top of me. Motsatsi was holding his assegai tight.

"But the warrior was unhappy. He felt empty inside his heart. He only knew to fight. He knew nothing about friends or love. He decided to leave the village and go exploring. Along a river bank, he was gathering water and hoping to find some fish to eat, when he saw a little girl with black hair weeping. He could only stare at her. He did not know how to make her happy. The Great God spoke into the man's ear. 'Here is one who needs a friend also.' The man would know better how to slay a dragon than talk to a little girl!"

Everyone chuckled.

"But still, he followed the voice of the Great Creator and sat next to the weeping little girl. 'Why are you crying?' he asked her. 'Because I am saddened,' the girl replied. 'That is no reason to cry,' he replied simply. 'What shall I do instead of cry?' the girl asked. 'You shall run,' the man said. For several weeks, the man got to know the little girl better. He met her parents and broke bread with them and started to become part of the family. He taught the girl to run as fast as a cheetah and to make herself useful in the world."

I whispered to Mary, "You've said something like it to me." I smiled. Mary smiled too, but she looked as if her mind was elsewhere.

"The man was sitting on the river bank with the girl one day when bad men came to that spot. They began to cross the river with their large knives and guns, wanting to hurt the little girl."

Motsatsi stiffened.

"The warrior jumped in front of the men and started to combat them, but one man was able to move behind him and he grabbed the little girl by the arm and lifted her high into the air, shouting. The warrior stopped his fighting as his heart filled and swelled with his love for the small girl. She had tears of fear in her eyes, though he saw she was trying to hold them back. That fact made the warrior crazed with fury and he beat all the men, then the man that had the little girl, he attacked him so viciously, his arm was separate from the body."

I cringed. Motsatsi nodded.

"From that time on, the man could not be separated from the girl. He became a permanent protector. He stayed with her and watched her grow as he grew old. He was with her when she got married. He was with her for the birth of both her children."

A feeling came over me, as if I knew the end to this story.

"He became the protector of the entire family. Although he could not stay with all of them when they have to be separated, he stays with the family who needs protection the most. And so the protector learned about love from the Livingstone family. Our warrior is our friend, Mebalwe."

Chills ran from the peak of my head down to the heels of my feet. I turned my head all around searching for Mebalwe and finally found him in the shade of a nearby tree, the smallest smile on his face. Had he been standing there the entire time? I then turned my attention to Mary who had a content smile on her face. Mebalwe was not their employee or even just a friend, he was their protector. I turned back to Mebalwe who did not smile, but when he caught the eye of Mary, he bowed his head and closed his eyes in reverence of the story.

"And now!" Sechele said, but I didn't need a translator for the rest. The time had come. I was now expected to dance. And after the exhilaration of such a story!

It shames me to admit that I considered using my shoulder as an excuse to not participate. If I could get across to the people that my wounds were paining me, I felt sure there would be a band of protesters on Chief Sechele's door. What was the Sechuana word for "mutiny"?

Before I could recall it, I was being pushed to the empty space in the center of the kotla. My one arm strapped to my chest, I fidgeted nervously with the other hand, picking at a stray string on a seam of my dress. The captain was nowhere to be seen. Eyes were darting every which way, trying to find the man, with no success. I looked to Sechele to know what to do. His consternation was comical. Searching through the throng of people, his features crumpled at the thought of not being given this one opportunity to see a proper English dance. His plans were being thwarted.

All at once, Sechele's face relaxed into his easy smile, and he nodded at the space over my head. I turned to see.

The captain was crossing the kotla for me.

Pessimism told me he had been commanded to do so. Optimism told me he could have simply been absent if he had wanted to be.

He shrugged past the group until they began to make a wide opening for him. He did not look happy for the attention he was receiving. His eyes stared at nothing as he made his way to the center. At last, he looked up, and I could relate his feelings. We did not want to be here on display, but our love for this chief kept us here.

He came to stand directly in front of me. A sigh escaped him. He did not look me in the face.

The chief was well prepared. With a broad drum as accompaniment, a young lady from the tribe sang a sweet African melody with perfect three-fourths time.

Without the use of my left arm, this dance was doomed to be disjointed. I held out my one good hand and waited for the captain to reciprocate.

He stared at my hand for a moment before placing my hand in his. He then slowly and gracefully moved his right hand onto the back of my left elbow. As we began, he cradled my injuries with his broad palm. With each step and each movement, my left side was protected by the watchful eye of my partner. He, more than anyone, knew the extent of my injuries and was not willing to have them relapse. At one point, I slipped in the warm, thin layer of dirt and instantly his arm was there to catch me in a way that would never hurt the wounds. He had thought ahead to the possibility of my falling and had planned accordingly.

The slip was what made me look into his eyes. He looked into mine to judge if he had hurt me, despite his efforts. But I looked into his simply because I wanted to.

He seemed to realize this after a moment and his expression softened. Our dancing became more fluid then. He moved back slightly to make room for my shifting feet, but his hand remained on my elbow and occasionally my waist.

I don't remember the words of the song, nor the eyes of the crowd or the heat of the setting sun. I don't remember the steps I took nor the way he dressed nor the fear of an upcoming war.

I only remember how he felt.

The warmth of his presence made me feel as if I had been cold and had not even realized it. All of a sudden, I was handed a thick, warm blanket and I wrapped myself in it now, berating myself for not knowing before that I was freezing.

I did not look away for the rest of the dance, and neither did he. All too soon the melodic notes ended, the beat ceased, and the group erupted in whoops of approval.

As quick as summer lightning, he softly put his forehead to mine and we took a deep breath together.

We broke the connection and turned to thank the swarms of Africans coming upon us to thank us for such a beautiful performance. Some of them had confused looks on their faces. The waltz was completely other to them, but I was the new tribal favorite and so they approved of everything I accomplished.

I attempted to make eye contact with the captain again across the mob of my people, but he would not look my way and soon dismissed himself and strode off into the darkening sky, his hands in his pockets.

◇◇◇

All too soon, the time came for me to say farewell to my family. Robert and Agnes came and gave me sweet little hugs, each saying goodbye in their small voices. I would have cried freely but I was afraid of scaring them, so I kept up an easy flow of comforting optimistic language. I would see them soon, I was sure of it. Mary looked on with a straight face, even more stern than usual. All morning she had seemed not quite herself, more cross than I had ever seen her. I assumed she was angry having to leave her home because of threat of war and lack of rain.

David walked briskly into the room and announced they were prepared to leave. Mary gave a short nod and turned to depart, but David caught her arm and turned her around to face him. To my astonishment, she squirmed from his grasp and would not look into his face. This was unusual behavior indeed! I had never seen Mary upset with David.

"Mary?" he asked, a suspicion growing in his tone that I did not understand. She shook her head, but he grabbed her face with one hand, a little too harshly, I thought. At last she had nowhere else to look but his eyes, and I could see tears suddenly gush from her eyes down her dry cheeks.

The sight of it made me gasp out loud. Never had I seen Mary cry, and I felt I had seen her endure much. Something was wrong, and I did not know what it was.

David knew.

"Oh Mary," he said consolingly and pulled her to his chest for a sweet moment before releasing her and jumping into action.

"Mebalwe!" he cried out of the open door. "Go and fetch Selemeng! Mma-Robert is laboring."

It took my mind a moment to realize what was happening. Perhaps because I had never been in a situation like this before.

Mary was having her baby right this moment.

She dismissed herself and began making slow laps around the house as Mebalwe went to retrieve Selemeng, whom I assumed was being summoned because of her experience. David made preparations in their bedrooms for the coming excitement. I could hear him muttering under his breath, reminding himself of everything that was needed.

The captain and I were put in charge of supervising the little children. We sang songs, played simple games, and did our best to distract their attention while ours was riveted on the goings-on in the house. Selemeng had arrived with her commanding voice and took charge. I could hear she had brought several other women from the tribe, and they chattered on in excitement with a dash of worry. Since the situation had turned to an emergency, and because they didn't need to worry about my understanding them, they reverted to Sechuana and I occasionally looked to the captain for translation of their quick speech.

The captain would speak in hushed undertones so as not to alarm the children in any way.

"She started labor last night but said nothing, hoping she could make it to her mother's house today. She is now too far along in the process to travel."

I felt that somehow I should instinctively know more about childbirth. After all, I was a woman! I should understand in some part what Mary was going through and how to offer comfort. But I knew nothing of this. I had heard, of course, that laboring was absolutely painful, hence the tears running down Mary's face, but that was the extent of my knowledge on the subject.

I saw through my window Selemeng and Mary occasionally passing by together, conversing in quiet tones while they slowly trod around the house. Selemeng appeared as if there was nothing amiss. Mary's eyes often closed as she tried to remain calm and collected through the pain.

In spite of my embarrassment, I inquired of the captain.

"What's going to happen?" he looked at me with a slightly perplexed look. "I don't know anything of this."

He nodded, understanding the culture we had both come from and how this was not something we ever spoke of, let alone see it and sit in the adjoining room.

"Mrs. Livingstone is having labor pains, meaning that her body is slowly pushing the child out. The pressure will build and increase in strength until she is ready to push."

"How do we know if things are going well? How do we know if they are both healthy?"

"We won't know the health of the baby until it is born, but Mary they will monitor closely by checking her temperature, her pulse, and other signs. Selemeng has done this hundreds of times. She has been responsible for the birth of most of the children and teenagers in this village. If there are any problems, she would be the one to know the answer."

"Are there often problems?" I asked, truly nervous.

"I have known of many, yes," he told me truthfully. "There is a reason they call childbirth a miracle. It can be a precarious business."

I appreciated that the captain never treated me as if I were weak. It would be so simple for him to dismiss my worries and questions and tell me everything would be fine. That he told me the truth on how he felt and what he had seen told me that he respected me. He treated me as if I were strong.

After a couple hours, Mary came back into the house. I caught only one glance, her head down, eyes shut, and both hands on the underside of her belly. She took long, controlled breaths, which I assumed was difficult for her. In the face of so much pain, I admit I typically held my breath. It seemed Mary was not so unreasonable.

Selemeng and David accompanied her into her room. We heard much more Sechuana mingled with Mary's controlled breathing.

After a few moments, David came into our space, his head held low, his features fallen. The children were asleep for a midday nap, and for this I was glad, because David looked truly broken. I could not take my eyes from him. It was quite difficult to see someone whom I had always known to be strong, so crushed by circumstances. He did not speak, I imagined he did not have the desire. But I could not bear not knowing how my friend was coping. So I asked.

"Is she in a lot of pain?"

David looked up in slight surprise, as if he was shocked I was still in the same location I was in. He did not answer right away.

"It must be a lot of pain for Mary to cry," I clarified.

Slowly, he shook his head. "She cries because she fears for the child." He paused and then told us the news.

"The child is breeched." The captain stiffened, but I did not understand. David, seeing my confused expression, continued. "It means the baby has flipped, and its head is up where it should be down. Its feet are trying to come out first, which is dangerous for the mother and child. Selemeng is attempting to turn it."

"And how does one turn a baby inside the womb?" I asked.

"Not easily," David responded. "The hands are placed on top of the belly and the child can be massaged into the correct position. As you can imagine, however, this can be excruciating for the mother."

His voice caught at the word *mother* and I bit my lip to keep myself from crying on his behalf. Still, I could not be silent. I had to know the extent of the news.

"What happens if the baby cannot be turned?"

His head was down when I asked the question and remained down for several aching moments after I was silent. I knew the captain watched to see how I would manage as the possibilities sunk in. I could not tear my eyes from David.

"We shall see," David finally responded. It seemed he feared dreadfully the death of his wife and child, but spoke these words as proof of hope. We would not know until the labor progressed.

I could not bear to think of it, and yet, I could think of nothing else. How could we possibly cope without Mary? It seemed impossible to me. She was the root of the family, the stability we all needed to function. She was the glue, the mortar that shaped us all! How critical the role of the mother was, I had never known. Now, sitting here helpless, as she lay dying in the next room, I could see how this family centered around her.

My mind jumped from possibility to possibility, wracking my brain to the point of physical pain. I thought of the consequences of her death. What would become of these little ones? What kind of a man would David be without Mary? What kind of person would I be?

Then I moved to courses of action. How could I help them? What could I do? Although I put my best mental facilities to the task, I came up short. There was nothing I could do to help.

An idea struck me suddenly. There was something I could do to help Mary and David.

Pray. David had taught me in his sermons that sometimes all we can do is not enough. Sometimes we needed to beg for divine assistance.

I looked to David and his head was still downcast, but now his eyes were closed. He was praying already.

If I had not been more healed, I may have hurt myself with how forcefully I jerked my head downward and began my plea for the lives of those within these walls.

To that God who rescued me from my mother's house, and who now holds my father as companion, I pray for the family you have given me in the desert. Please save them.

Please save us.

I did not err in my choice of words. I begged God to save them *all*, because without Mary, we would all be lost.

Selemeng continued into the evening, attempting to turn the child. Robert and Agnes woke from their naps and asked me where their mother was. David stepped in.

"Mama is having the baby," he told them excitedly. "Selemeng is with Mama now trying to get the baby out, but it wants to stay inside Mama because it is cozy and warm."

To fulfill his description, he picked both children up into his arms and placed them on either knee. He hugged them close on the use of the word *warm*.

"Papa," Robert began in his serious voice. "I have decided, if the baby is a boy, his name will be Thomas."

I gasped. That was my father's name. But he didn't know that, so how . . . ?

"Is that so?" David inquired. "Well, that decision will be left up to Mama. Since she does the work, she has the greatest say in the matter. Selemeng says we should call the child 'Tlhogo e thata'!"

The children laughed, understanding the reference, and I cocked my head in question.

"Pig-headed," David translated for me. I half smiled.

"I want the baby to be a girl!" Agnes cried.

"We shall see, sweet girl." David kissed her head. "We shall see."

I tucked my head away from their sight and made my way to the lean-to to make some dinner. I had barely made it to the sink before the sobbing began. I could not seem to help myself. I wanted so badly to see Mary and help her in any way that I could but I was little better than a cripple and absolutely ignorant of all things medicinal. The woman I admired most in the world was in terrible pain and there was nothing I coulddo.

I felt weak and I was never so angry as when I felt weak. My fingernails grated against the wooden counter in frustration.

The captain came to stand beside me. And I knew that he would. I tried to keep my crying as quiet as I could. He didn't seem to mind it. In a motion as slow as the passing time, he reached for my hand and smoothed out my fingers against the grain.

I looked to him with tear-filled eyes. I was afraid for Mary.

He knew that. He kept his hand on mine.

Sechele arrived in a blue velvet suit coat accompanied with long white tails that were beginning to stain and wear on the bottom edge. He did not pause to let us admire his garb as he typically did.

"Mma-Robert?" he asked simply.

"The baby is breech. We are waiting," I stated.

He looked to me with an understanding in his eyes. He put his hand on my good shoulder and squeezed me gently.

"Children have an instinct of survival," he told me. "If they do not survive with Selemeng in the room, it is because there were no other options."

I was not sure if this made me feel any better. At the moment I only cared about Mary's situation, but I thanked the chief and allowed myself to be escorted to a chair.

Suddenly I heard a triumphant yell from Mary's bedroom. David leapt out of his chair so quickly it toppled to the ground behind him as he sped away. The silence in the air hung heavy. Even Robert and Agnes remained perfectly still, mimicking the adults who listened for a single sound of hope.

David returned and announced.

"The baby has turned! We will now try for a normal delivery."

Sechele actually whooped in celebration, making me jump and then laugh at the process. I put my hand to my heart. One obstacle down.

During the next hour, I gave my small family a thin soup from the day before and each a half glass of milk from our friend Banana. We ate in silence as the adults listened to the steady and even breathing of our matron. I could not imagine what Mary had experienced, but then, forty-two minutes into the hour, I heard a sound I had never before experienced.

The cry of a newborn child.

David rushed to his wife's bedside. What relief that sound could create! I felt the stress wash away from temple to toe. The child had arrived, and its crying must surely be a sign of healthy lungs, for what a loud sound it was!

"They are checking the baby now," the captain explained. "First appearance shows he is healthy."

"He?" I asked elated. "It's a boy? And Mary is well?"

"Yes," the captain replied, then paused for a moment as we both listened.

Quietly, almost too low for us to hear, we heard Mary's exhausted and elated voice whisper the child's name.

"Thomas."

Tears sprang to my eyes.

Silently, I prayed. *Thank you for saving us.*

Chapter 23

Such joyful events are often followed by tragic ones. I had almost never heard of a birth without the news of a death in the same month. And so it was with us. Sechele's baptism came with the drought. My personal success at the school came with the lion attack. Now Thomas's birth came with battle.

I got to see the babe only once before the calamity began, the morning after his birth. Sechele and Selemeng had returned home, exhausted by the stress. Mary was sleeping away the effects of childbirth, and David was walking around the small house with his new son. He came wandering into the children's and my room with his arms full, seeming as if he did not see anyone other than his child. His eyes were full of wonder and reverence, and his arms were immovable under the bundle he carried. His attention was soon diverted, however, by his two other children. They tugged at his pant legs and attempted to grab at the blanket that held their little brother captive.

Without a single word, he crouched down to the floor and presented to the children a person they would spend the rest of their lives with. The baby's eyes were closed, softly sleeping. Robert and Agnes looked at him with the same eyes full of wonder that their father wore. Robert softly moved his hand to caress Thomas's downy hair. Agnes reached out, unconventionally silent, to clasp the baby's hand in hers. David took his time to look upon each of his children individually, his emotions clear on his face.

There never was, nor ever shall be again, a father's love greater than that of David Livingstone.

David stood and brought Thomas to the captain and me in polite introduction. He offered Thomas to me, but I felt obligated to refuse, since I was not confident in my shoulder's ability to hold even this six-pound infant. My qualms were dismissed in this instance, however, and the sweet bundle was set upon my right arm. What a wise forehead he had! And what a knowledgeable chin. I had never held a child so small before, but even if I had, I felt certain little Thomas would still be my favorite.

The captain then took a moment to hold the boy. He spoke not a word but the corners of his mouth slanted up in admiration. Robert and Agnes surrounded him to get a closer look while the child was down on their level.

It was in this precious moment that Motsatsi came barreling through the door, shouting in Sechuana. His words put David and the captain in an instant state of alarm and readiness. And for this I did not need a translator.

The Boers were coming.

David bounded to Mary's bedside, leaving Thomas with the captain. I heard him speaking quickly, comforting his dear wife and answering her questions. He then took two giant steps and was back in the room with us, retrieving Thomas from the captain.

"She is not well enough to move. The delivery was too harsh on her body," he spoke quickly and articulately. "We are staying."

"No," I moaned in the same instant the captain spoke.

"Let me take the children and ride as far away as I can," he offered.

"It seems counterproductive at this point," David said. "The Boers may not even come here, but if they do, I want as many men surrounding this house as possible. If you take the children, you would be an island surrounded by many. Here we can create a fortress."

"Motsatsi," I addressed him. "Did you come by way of your father?"

"Yes Miss Anna. He is sending some men to surround this house."

Despite the assurance of a small army to stand guard in front of Mary and the children, I still felt a sudden surge of panic and fear. David noticed.

"You need not worry," David said comforting me. "The Bakwena have been fending for themselves for centuries. If many are hurt, it will be in the protection of their families and loved ones. You cannot take responsibility for a land dispute. It will pass, and we shall escape unharmed."

I nodded, unable to speak further for the knot in my throat, the cannon on my chest, and the pressure on my lungs.

Sechele arrived with ten strong men who were to be our bodyguards. Sechele came only to assign the men and give them specific instructions as to my protection. He only spoke a few words in passing, and I admit I was too stunned for further conversation. Not only because I was so terrified of the coming events, but because he wore his traditional dress, and it was absolutely impeccable. A gray cat-skin caross was draped around his one shoulder, dropping all the way to the floor. Brass rings covered his arms and legs and four red feathers adorned his hair. His chest was bare and puffed out in defiance of attack. The glint in his eye told me there was no possibility of failure.

The men were positioned in several locations around the house. It was a comfort to see tribesmen willingly working to aid my family. The missionaries and the people of Sechele, so at odds over the baptism, were now bound together by a common peril. Sechele departed to lead his small army. According to Motsatsi and other scouts of the tribe, the Boers would attack by nightfall.

The men worked to prepare us. I was well aware they sought to prepare us for the worst. Reason demanded it. However, their preparations did nothing to belay my worries. They rearranged the room for optimal protection. We, the children and I, moved to Mary's bedroom. I held Robert and Agnes's tiny hands as we moved to the back wall of the home and sat on the floor next to the bed where Mary and Thomas lay. I watched silently as the men gathered all the food, medicine, and water we would need to spend the night in this small temporary fortification. They scavenged several long boards from around the house and used them to bar the one window in Mary's chamber, nails keeping it secure to the inside walls. The men would protect the front door.

Having gathered all the provision we would need and conversing quickly with all the men standing guard outside, we settled down in our cramped corner to spend the hot afternoon.

I watched the captain, as was my habit as of late. He was serious, but not frantic or afraid. As for me, I couldn't help but think about the danger coming to my people. Given the opportunity, I would have happily stood at the front lines and battled to protect them. I would give much to protect these people, especially the children. However, with the added stress and strain from Thomas's birth and the coming fight, my wounds were becoming sore, several cracking and sloughing infection with the fidgeting of my nervous body. The captain looked at the broken wounds with disapproval. He reapplied my bandages and then encouraged me to sleep, as the babes now did on my lap. I shook my head fervently. How could I possibly relax in the face of bloodshed?

He stared at me thoughtfully, his face strained with sincere concern. Without warning, he reached his hand up and stroked my face from temple to chin.

"No one is going to hurt you," he told me. His broad, rough hand moved to my hair, which had grown substantially since our time together on the *Madras*—almost to my shoulders. "Your only concern and worry should be to heal."

I looked on him tenderly. "Thank you."

He nodded gruffly, then moved to the front of the house with the other men.

I sighed, content to have some resolution between us before the chaos began. Suddenly, I felt myself watched and I turned to see Mary was awake and had seen the entire spectacle. She was laying on her side, her face toward me, while tiny Thomas was curled up next to her.

She smiled at me.

"I have always liked the captain," she told me.

"I haven't," I responded.

We both laughed. I feel the stress of the moment made us laugh much more than the comment demanded, but it was nice to see Mary smile.

Darkness came too quickly. Motsatsi ran back and forth from the site of the battle to us, to give us updated news. The Boers had indeed arrived on horseback, but not alone. David warned us that fraud was as natural to the Boers as paying one's own way was natural for everyone else. Now I saw what he meant. The Boers had abducted natives from other tribes. They used the natives to stand in the front line of the battle, then they would simply shoot over them and allow the captives to die first. I was horrified by the news, whereas the captain did not seem surprised. After this, Motsatsi stayed with us in our corner. The battle had begun in the distance.

I did try to appear calm and confident in the face of such carnage, not for myself but for Motsatsi, Robert, and Agnes. They was still so young, so unaccustomed with so many horrors the world held. I knew that Motsatsi acted prideful and confident in his abilities, and in truth, his skills were many! Enough to put to shame any young girl or lad or London. And still, watching his thin frame sitting silently on the hard floor holding a large assegai, I felt all his confidence was a simple act to mirror his father. In that moment, he was just a small, inexperienced child holding a very large spear.

Nothing could have possibly prepared me for the events to come. We all sat silently, waiting for any correspondence from the others, when we heard the unmistakable sound of hooves approaching on the dry African ground.

All our heads perked and turned at the sound. The captain ducked his head inside to report.

"A small group of Boers, maybe thirty, are on their way from the east." he spoke quickly.

Mary needed not even a second after his announcement.

"Robert. Agnes. To me," she spoke calmly but direct, as was her way.

They both climbed into the bed of their mother, ever watching to make sure they did not tread on Thomas, who was next to Mary on the bed. Mary moved the children so their heads were just under her blanket. It was a small effort in safety, but perhaps if the Boers did break through the door, the simple fact that the children could not be seen would make the difference.

Motsatsi and I took our positions in front of Mary's bed. The Boers would have to make it through the group of thirteen men outside and then through us to get to the children.

This small faction of Boers must be using the battle as a distraction so they could come to attack the missionary's home. And there could only be one true reason they would expend so much effort to do so. They still desired to take me hostage. They still wanted the reward my mother had posted.

My heart began to beat at triple its usual speed. The enemy was coming to capture me, and so many that I cared about stood between me and them.

"Please," I begged Motsatsi. "Please can't we just let them take me? I feel certain they would leave all of you safe if they could just have me. Please."

"Stop it!" Motsatsi barked. "Even if we were all heartless cowards, willing to give a young girl up as ransom, you would not survive any type of travel." He looked at me directly, angry. "If you try to take any type of trip, even on a nice horse, it will kill you."

"I could not possibly care less, if it would save you!" I yelled.

"You will make this considerably harder for us if you are determined to make a ninny of yourself," he growled. "Think of how Mary would act and behave accordingly."

I wailed, completely miserable at the prospect of what was about to happen.

The captain, as if able to hear our entire conversation, stepped inside the door again, making my heart leap up into my throat.

"Do not let her sacrifice herself," he said to Motsatsi, then returned to the front steps.

The two small stairs I had jumped up so many hundreds of times had now become the site of war.

A struggle began almost as soon as the captain stepped outside. It was incredible the decibels a fight could reach by simple hitting of swords, the throwing of spears, and the occasional firing of pistols. Several blows hit their mark as I heard the last cries of men I did not know. What was more, I could not be sure if the cries of pain came from our men or theirs. There was no torture as acutely painful as this, waiting to see who came through the door. My brave protector stood in readiness beside me with his large assegai in his hands. His eyebrows came down in serious concentration, making him look more like his father than I had ever seen him.

Suddenly, a man burst through the window, breaking the boards quickly with a small hatchet. He must have thought us defenseless, and had climbed into the room without a look for defenders. But Motsatsi met him head on. The man raised his hatchet, but it was quickly batted away by Motsatsi's weapon. The man did not hesitate for a moment without his weapon and grabbed at the end of Motsatsi's stick. He pulled my boy closer to him and hit him hard across the face.

"Motsatsi! No!" I cried.

Motsatsi did not hesitate either, coming back at the man with kicks, while keeping a firm grasp on his assegai. At least one of the kicks met its mark, and the man was obligated to hunch over in pain as Motsatsi tore the spear from his hands, slashing the man's hand deeply. The nine-year-old took one step back before running to the man and ramming the spear into the man's chest. Mary did not cry out, but hid the faces of the children.

I was reminded of my first day in Kolobeng, when the men of the town had stabbed the unfortunate ox. This man bellowed and moaned in like manner, swatting at the boy without a hope of reaching him. I have never been so grateful for a man's death, a fact that I would feel guilt for later. For the moment, though, my Motsatsi had defeated our foe and stood triumphant and safe.

Too quickly, however, two more men climbed through the window. Seeing their companion lying in his own blood on our hard floor did nothing to soften their features. They attacked Motsatsi viciously, and this time there was nothing he could do to protect himself. I bolted to one of the men in an effort to at least distract them. But the man instantly took hold of my bad shoulder and dug his fingers into my wounds before throwing me to the ground. The instant, overwhelming pain amazed me. The room spun and the floor tilted as I tried to keep my eyes on Motsatsi. One man took away Motsatsi's assegai and the other took hold of Motsatsi himself, tearing the two apart. The boy kicked and screamed and attempted to tear at their faces and arms, but the men took this little boy, raised him higher into the air, and threw him to the ground as if he were a ball.

The crack of his small body against the unforgivable ground is forever burned into my mind. The harsh sound woke Thomas and his newborn cries filled the air. These two grown men then used massive fists to hit Motsatsi's face and stomach again and again.

"Stop it! No! Halt!" I screamed from the ground. "Can't you see he is a child? He's not a man! He's a child!"

They did not hear my cries, so busy were they in the beating, their anger swelling in revenge for their fellow soldier. Motsatsi had given up his struggle and took the abuse, his face becoming bloody and mangled in the process.

I jumped up, despite the pain I felt and barreled toward the same man I had tried to attack before, his back to me, still assaulting Motsatsi. I dug into his back with what strength my fingers and fingernails could conjure. I pounded on his arms as hard as I had ever hit any closed door or solid wall in my childhood. But my strength was not sufficient to affect him at all. I felt as if I were in a nightmare, unable to run, unable to hurt, only able to watch and scream in aggravating paralysis.

Seeing now my attempts at violence were going unheeded, I threw my useless body on top of Motsatsi, my mangled shoulder covering his bruised face, protecting him. A moment later, I heard the unmistakable roar of a gunshot. I looked up to see a bloodied hole in the chest of Motsatsi's attacker, the revolver resting in Mary's hands.

Despite the death of his comrade, I was being lifted off of my precious child and thrown over the shoulder of the second man. I did not struggle. From this height, I could see Motsatsi's broken features on the ground, his face almost unrecognizable, but I felt relief in being taken. Now this man would carry the danger away and this small room of tender people would be safe.

He carried me toward the window in which he had entered, but he did not reach it. Motsatsi had managed to get up off the ground and had speared the man in the leg. The man bellowed and dropped me to the ground, I landed on my back, and pain shot up my spine. The man then turned and took hold of Motsatsi's arm.

Our men burst through the front door in this moment. Seeing real danger coming toward him, the Boer ran for his only escape, the window, still holding onto Motsatsi.

The boy started suddenly, realizing now that he was being taken captive. His eyes desperately searched the room looking for help, but all his eyes beheld was me, on my back on the hard floor.

His expression changed. His countenance altered. Now perceiving that he was unable to protect himself, the faux confidence he always wore vanished. His face turned as innocent and afraid as a babe. His mouth opened and he let out a sob of terror and heartache as the Boer man pulled him toward the window.

"No!" I screamed furiously. "They're taking Motsatsi! Captain! David! Mebalwe! Go!"

My soldiers raced up the stairs to retrieve Motsatsi. But they were too late. The man had taken Motsatsi and shoved him through the window. The captain tried to climb through the window and Mebalwe ran out the front door to capture him from the other direction, but the man had a horse ready. He threw Motsatsi's sobbing body over the neck of the animal, kicked the beast into a full out gallop, and sped away from his pursuers.

We had no horses of our own. There was no catching them.

Motsatsi could not be saved.

Chapter 24

There was no reason to rush now. Mebalwe and the other men went to reorganize with the rest of the tribe, suspecting they would not send a second attempt for the broken English girl.

The tribesmen were right. The Boers did not try again. They had been too confident in their first attempt. The captain stayed with me, however. After ensuring that Mary and the children were safe, he helped me dress my injuries in my own room, and as he finished my shoulder, I clasped his hand and would not let him go. I looked into his face, bewildering misery threatening to overtake me. His eyes echoed my sadness.

There was nothing left to do for Motsatsi. We sat silently, unable to run to him, unable to rescue him. So helpless we felt! So desperately weak.

I could not remember moving over to lay my head against his chest, but somehow I ended up in his arms. I had simply been drawn to him naturally. There was no thought of wanting his arms around me as I wept. They simply were.

Long moments passed as I cried and sniffled softly. Finally he surprised me by speaking.

"Why would you subject yourself to this place?" he asked slowly. "And once you got here, why would you continue to live here?"

I had mistrusted him in the beginning as I mistrusted every other soul associated with the polite society I had left. Now as I felt his heart beat beneath my ear, my feelings somehow changed.

My story broke from my lips before I had consciously chosen to speak it out loud.

"My first memory is of my mother separating my twin brother and me. My days as a young child were wholesome and good, until one day she would not let me see my brother, or her. We had never been separated before, not even in the womb. As a child, I thought the world had suddenly been taken away from me. I cried myself to sleep until I thought that was a natural thing to do. I had no other soul around me. Not even my twin or my mother. I was convinced this had happened because I was bad."

I knew he had been waiting for me to trust him. Now he even slowed his breath in case it was too loud to hear a word.

"My father seemed to enter my life like a beacon. I remember seeing him like I had never seen him before. He entered my room and walked toward me slowly with hands in front of him, a physical sign of peace. I remember he said 'Catherine, I'm your father.' He brought food. He would play games with me. We became friends in an instant and were inseparable soon thereafter.

"From then on, I thought my childhood was typical, even though I was usually kept within the confines of my bedroom. On most days, Father would come and eat meals with me, play with me, and tuck me into bed. Those days were full and happy. I would get a glimpse of joy being with him, then he would be away for days at a time. When he was gone, Mother would beat me and starve me without mercy. Then she would give my brother the superior food, clothes, and respect. She wanted it imprinted in my mind that my brother was superior to me."

My voice became rough, not out of grief, but now out of anger. "Once, I repeated the things that mother said to me and Father was so angry. He confronted her and she denied it profusely. The next time Father left, I paid dearly. That was my first broken bone and the last time I confided in him about her dealings with me.

"Once I came of age, Mother began to dress me up in beautiful gowns and jewelry. I relished the new clothes. To me, they represented how she had always secretly cared about me. I thought she was using them to apologize for everything she had done."

Speaking became more difficult as the memories grew more fresh and painful.

"After I had a proper coming into society, Mother would find ways to . . . get me alone with eligible men." I paused, then added, "I . . . don't want to talk about that."

The captain's chest sunk as he held his breath in shock. Somehow I knew he was angry and was trying to control that anger. The thought softened my heart. He loosened his arms around me slightly and touched his forehead to my temple, my warm and gentle captain. I dared, in my mind, to call him Benjamin. I continued.

"Father thought I was slipping into Mother's world. My mother is a supreme actress, and I could have inherited it. He wanted to save me from being greedy, spiteful, and useless like her. And since I wouldn't talk to him about what was happening, he thought I would do well to work in the service of others."

I paused for a moment to collect myself. The tears started again. I couldn't hold them back. I began to choke words out, hoping he would understand them.

"He took me to the cottage of a woman who had recently lost her husband. It was a young lady, now a widow, and her little baby girl, maybe six months old. They were starving, living in a hole of an existence. Father took them to a bigger cottage where he and I supplied them with food and water for almost a year while Father tried to find them a better situation. Finally, he found a large house in Ireland in need of a governess, with a family who would look after her sufficiently. Father needed time to travel and set the way for them to follow him. He was going to be gone two weeks. I wanted to beg him to stay so that Mother couldn't subject me to any more abuse. But I knew that Maria and Anna's futures depended on finding a permanent home, so I did not ask him to stay. He left and I kept visiting the two with food and supplies. Mother had no idea that we were helping them. We kept it a secret from her because we knew she wouldn't approve of us spending money."

I needed another moment to breathe. The captain still seemed to be intermittently holding his breath.

"She found out. Somehow she found out about them. On my way out to their cottage one morning, she grabbed me by the arm and locked me in my room with no way out. She had one of her loyal footman stand as security guard over me, and another over Maria's cottage."

I could barely choke out this story. It was too real, too painful.

"Mother gave me one meal a day. Enough to survive. She didn't do the same for Maria and Anna. She left them with nothing. She—" I choked on my words, but forced them out. "She . . . discarded them, as one would a litter of rabid field mice."

I had tried so desperately to convince myself that it hadn't happened, or at least that it wasn't my fault. I turned slightly to look at the captain's reaction to my horror-filled life. His jaw was set and his eyes were stone-cold, set straight ahead.

"Did they die?" he asked through set teeth.

I nodded miserably.

"I screamed at her to feed them, to care for them. I told her they had nowhere else to go. I begged her to make sure they were safe. I screamed in my room until I was sick. My arms and hands bled from pounding on the door. I had no idea she had locked them into their own home to starve. I survived the two weeks it took for Father to come home. They didn't."

A long quiet moment passed. Tears ran down my face. "I remember the look on my father's face as he burst through my bedroom door and saw my bleeding arms. When he had gotten the story from me he had rushed to Maria's cabin to check on them, with me tight on his heels. He nearly killed Mother's guard, he hit him so forcefully. Finally we made it to them. But we were too late. They had died in each other's arms."

The tears fell freely now. "I had watched the baby learn and grow. She had come to almost recognize me when I came in the door." The captain held me tighter as I lost control of my words. "She must have died so slowly. How could my mother do that to a child?"

The captain held me as I sobbed. I cried out so many months of hating myself, because I had survived her and they hadn't. Hating my mother for giving me a meal a day to survive. Hating myself for eating it. And now hating myself for watching as Motsatsi was taken away from me as well.

"My father, he went after Mother in a fierce way. I listened to the muffled sound of his booming threats. Mother defended herself by accusing him of spending their fortune on widows and bastards.

"After a few days, Father took me into the library and told me of his plan to move to America. He cut my hair. He gave me boy's clothes so that I could be discreet and so that the voyage would not be as hard in my heavy skirts. We were set to leave the next morning. But my mother must have known about the plans, because by morning he had been poisoned, and lay dead in his bed. I sat with him, soaked in grief. Mother was there too, slowly slipping the rings from off his fingers."

I had stopped crying. Our breathing coincided and comforted me.

"How did you come aboard the *Madras*?" he asked quietly.

"While my father lay dead in his bed, and I lay next to him weeping, Mother informed me there would be a funeral, wherein I would have the responsibility of placing roses atop his casket. She then told me as soon as the funeral was over, she had arranged my marriage to the cruel and heartless Duke of Solven.

"After the funeral, I stood tearless in my room. I could not sleep. I couldn't cry any longer. I simply stood still. I knew that soon my engagement to the Duke of Solven would be announced and that would give Mother more opportunities to leave us alone together. He was a truly perverse and malicious man. I was terrified of my future. And yet, I stood perfectly still. I felt trapped in my own body. There was nothing I could do to save myself.

"Then a voice came." I smiled, remembering the moment my life changed, and spoke in hushed tones, more to myself in that moment than to him. "A voice as clear and brilliant as the sound of a church bell. It was Father's voice. 'Run, Anna. Oh please, run.'"

"I knew I could not have imagined it, pure and clear in that way. I knew it was Father. I knew that he knew of my situation. And I knew that only a kind and loving God could have allowed one of his angels to direct me. He used the name Anna, the baby's name, to encourage me to take a new name. And what better name to take than the name of the precious dead?

"I knew a hiding place where Mother kept a large amount of money, to be hid from Father. I took every pound she had hidden and walked out the front door. I moved forward, completely confident, from that moment on."

I felt as though literal bricks had been balancing on my heart, moving and causing frictions every time I moved too quickly. Now they were removed. They had been picked up and removed by this patient man. Finally, I could breathe. He sensed my relief and mirrored my breaths. We sat still for several moments.

After a while, he chose to tell his own story, his breath warming my hair

"I was lucky enough to be raised in a happy home. My mother almost died while giving birth to me. I was destined to be an only child. My mother, my father, and I spent most of every day together. They were true, honest, loving people. I never knew we were different than any other family. I was proud to be an Ashmore."

"When I came of age, I noticed that girls would flaunt and boast in front of me. I asked my father why they would suddenly act this way, when they had mostly ignored me until this point. He said, frankly, it was because their mothers told them to impress me because of our money," he said with disdain. "That was the first time I realized we were wealthy."

"The older I got, the worse it became. They would pretend their horse had gone lame or that they themselves had sprained an ankle just to attract my attention. Soon, I spent the majority of my time rescuing damsels from make-believe catastrophes. I felt absolutely ridiculous. I was useless except to perform random acts of fake gallantry."

"Soon, however, I came of age and my mother and father approached me about the real possibility of my getting married. They said I should watch for those who would only want me for my estate that I was promised. They said to find someone with an honest disposition.

"I searched for her. All I saw were fluttering eyelashes and lying mouths. I disliked them all so thoroughly for their materialism. If I couldn't spend an hour with any of them, how would I spend a lifetime with one?

"You approached me, that night, with most unfortunate timing," he ducked down and pecked me on the cheek, sending a thrill through me. "I had spent an entire day saving these defenseless females. I thought you were coming to ask me to fetch punch, or to aid you in the rescue of a lost dog. I could not handle another rescue."

I nodded, understanding.

"Then Marianne Steele came in with a flourish. Everyone was impressed with her. Everyone said how genuine and kind she was. I wasn't excited to meet her, however. I had heard so many good things about mindless, insipid girls before that I could barely trust anyone's word."

I wondered if his jaw would ever relax, or if his gaze would ever break from the opposite wall. His words seethed with bitterness. He continued.

"When I met her, I thought somehow she didn't know I was wealthy. It surprised me. She did not pretend at anything. She got her own drinks. She had no inheritance to speak of, yet she refused suitors she did not admire. I could not help but be drawn to her. Because I could not have her, I wanted her all the more."

"After a lengthy courtship, and three proposals from me, she finally accepted my offer. We were married quickly. I thought my happiness was complete, but within a day she had revealed her true character to me. To this day I curse my own blindness. She was expertly manipulative, drastically emotional, and corrupt to her very core. For months I wondered what I could do to get my Marianne back, while she spent my father's money like a queen.

"When we went out into the polite world, and it was often, I could count on her acting badly somehow. She refused to be seen with my parents whom she declared to be monstrously dull, and whom she spread vicious rumors about. She would take flight with small groups of people she did not know, and usually end up in a gaming house, or other functions that no lady of integrity would find herself. Time after time I would search for her and find her disheveled and unconscious on the floor of another filthy establishment. Her own circle of friends knew nothing of her true behavior and habits."

I listened in shocked disbelief. So that was why they had fought that day. I never could have guessed Marianne's true character.

The captain continued. "So quickly I could hardly believe it was happening, Father approached me to say she had spent not only what was my allotted amount per month, but also theirs. She was out of control. I approached her again and again. She would simply laugh and say she would slow her purchases. But she didn't slow them. Instead, they doubled. We gathered as a family and tried to speak reason to her. She would not heed.

"One day, my mother went into Whiteleys to purchase a day dress. The store clerk refused to fit her for it, because our debt had not yet been paid. We had not realized that Marianne had been intercepting the largest bills and hiding them.

"We held another family meeting. While Mother sobbed, my father brought up the idea of us removing to the country for the season to try and regain what had been so recklessly spent. The calm persona Marianne normally portrayed broke loose. She screamed and kicked, proclaiming she was being stifled and she would never be taken from her friends and belongings. My perspective became clear in a moment. In my view, my mother sat to one side crying soft tears, Father was directly in front of me—he looked ten years older—and my new bride on the other side screaming about being treated badly. I looked at them all, and finally saw what Marianne had wrought. I knew what had to be done. The time had come for me to become a tyrannical husband.

"I placed the both of us in a carriage destined for our country home. I did not wait for luggage to be packed, or friends to be notified. She cried and screamed for days, and I did not think there would be an end. I started the rumor that I had taken her to the country because she was ill. My parents followed us even though I begged them to stay in town. They would not let me go through the ordeal alone."

He stopped thoughtfully.

"Marianne contracted a fever from an unknown source not two weeks after our arrival in the country. Only hours after, my parents were ill as well."

He paused.

"It was scarlet fever."

I gasped.

"I caught the fever, but it left me quickly," he said, bitterly. "It did not affect me the way it did them in their old age, or her, in her heightened state of stress. My parents died within a week of each other."

He did not elaborate. I knew he must have been by their sides to the end. I knew he must have watched the light go out in their eyes. I knew he must have dug their graves with his own hands. Yet he could not admit those things.

"My bride held on for three long weeks. She would not let me comfort her, nor would she let me hold her hand as she suffered. I brought flowers into her room and she got out of bed only to pick them up and throw them against the wall. In her anger, she would yell for hours how I had brought this on her and how much she hated me."

This explained why he was so wary of me when he first began to care for me after my injury.

"Near the end, she said she would bring shame to me as her revenge. She said she refused to be a good wife, or to treat me well. She said she refused to be my puppet any longer. She swore if she lived she would only work to make me miserable. As her final act, she used crude scissors to cut her hair to stubs. She died with mutilated hair and an angry expression." He paused, looking down on me. "You may understand now why I was upset when you cut your hair."

I nodded, understanding at last, as he continued speaking.

"She had not left us completely destitute. I had the Ashmore estate left, which I could not bear to sell, and a small amount that I could have lived comfortably on for the rest of my days. However, I could not stay in the place where my parents had died, or where my wife cursed me for marrying her. My parents had come there to support me in my trial. If they had stayed away, Marianne would have passed away alone in her misery. I had brought her into our happy family. I felt responsible for their deaths because of my ignorance. I could not move to town either. I would, no doubt, be invaded by the social atmosphere."

"I used a large portion of my inheritance and bought the *Madras*. I changed my name from Ashmore to Dunna so I would not raise gossip from that group of stupid girls I had come to avoid.

"I began a new life as a ship's captain. I knew very little when we started out, but I learned many new things every day. I divulged my past to my first mate, Anderson. He instructed me on everything, down to the fine details of ship life. He became my mentor, my steward, my father. I had almost achieved a mental tranquility with the help of the sea. I was finally beginning to heal, when suddenly a girl trounced aboard who seemed to me, at the time, the epitome of social prowess.

"She walked around as prideful and lofty as the best of them. She came unbalanced up the gangway to the ship, and I had to help her step down. The memories of other young ladies in need of help flooded my mind and clouded my vision. I knew her mother and others like her. I thought the mother was crafty enough to send the girl after me, seeking my fortune again. She may not have known that my fortune was diminished, but still, this seemed another performance of a damsel in distress."

He broke his stare at the wall and turned to look into my face.

"I did not know you, Anna," he said gruffly. "I was so wary of all social women that I shunned you as best I could."

"I am glad to understand," I said finally.

He gently placed both hands on the sides of my face. I took in a sharp breath.

"I love you," he confessed suddenly, sweetly. "I used to watch you in social settings, but I did not trust myself. I knew you to be honest, straightforward, and quite possibly in trouble. Yet you asked for no help. I would have helped you. I watched you around your mother and I knew you were afraid of her but I did not know the extent. I did not know how to help you, and I had come to distrust my own judgment."

My heart raced.

"Please say that you forgive me. I saw you in pain, yet I did not assist."

My right hand began to move without consulting me. It moved slowly up to cup his left cheekbone. I expected a hard, rough face and found it tender and warm instead. He closed his eyes. I moved to his hair and put my hands deep inside of it. He looked up again and we looked into each other's eyes.

"Of course I forgive you," I told him, smiling.

He bowed his head, laboring under all the new information he had received, the information he had given, and the confession he had made. How peculiar that I had ever considered him prideful! His story helped me see that there was a distinction between his pride and strength.

His hands still on my cheekbones, he turned my jaw up slightly as he gently brought his mouth to mine. Kissing was different than I had anticipated. I had not realized a simple touch to my lips would make my whole soul rejoice. Perhaps it was because we seemed to completely understand one another. No matter the reason, as his lips moved against mine I was sure I had found the man I would stay with forever. Even as I tried to kiss him more deeply, he only indulged me slightly, keeping the wounds on my back from opening. The realization that he was protecting me, afraid to hurt me, made me smile, and my smiling made him grin as well.

He kissed me once more on the mouth, then slowly moved from my chin to temple, absorbing me, it seemed.

Somehow I made a coherent thought in the midst of heaven. Motsatsi's kidnapping came back to hit me like a rock. It was not fair for me to have so much joy while Motsatsi and his family were facing a harsh future. How dare I submit to heaven while he was confined to hell? Who knows what he would be subjected to? I froze still and my demeanor gave the captain pause.

"You need rest," he said softly as he began to stand. "I think we should reconvene in Sechele's home. We can protect you all better there and I believe—"

"No," I said resolutely, a realization hitting me. "I can't rest. I know what we need to save Motsatsi! We need money—and a lot of it! And I know where to get it."

He was understandably confused as he helped me to my feet. "Where do you need to go?"

I looked his face over again, savoring the sweet moment we had shared. Then I pushed it aside, locked up my heart, and answered his question.

"I am going to my mother's house."

Epilogue

The dining room was uncommonly cold for Easter Sunday. Mother had ordered the fire extinguished so as not to spend what we need not. She was always logical with funds. She was also logical with cleanliness, and required me to wash my face again since I had appeared at the breakfast table with, what seemed to her, still too much proof of sunlight on my face. I returned straightaway to my water basin to scrub with rough lyme soap. Each basin of water pained my heart—remembering the drought and the thirst from not too long ago.

After finishing our dainty portions in silence we came here, to the sitting room, to await our morning callers.

There were sure to be many.

Since my return from my missionary experiences in Africa—which my mother claimed to have helped me execute and keep secret, so as not to parade our goodness about—I had many callers as I sat in the comfort of a crisp, clean sitting room. And I intended to catch them all.

The streets of London were buzzing with talk of Catherine Kensington who had gone for a cultural experience to Africa, and had landed upon a fortune, which she had added to the one she already had. She had transformed into even more of an heiress than when she left. She had even brought home an African man to be a free servant in her home.

Or at least, that's what they were saying.

And it was all true, just not in the way they supposed. I had landed upon the fortune of freedom and connection. That added to the worthless monetary inheritance I would possibly receive, if I survived. And I had brought home a man from Africa, but Mebalwe was no free servant.

He was my bodyguard.

Mother's economic mind had allowed him to stay under the impression that he would never need to be paid, but she could tell everyone that she compensated him handsomely.

One of Mother's friends had arrived, and the two were conversing on my many prospects while I sat mute, my eyes always on Mother.

"I cannot understand why Mr. Ashmore still persists in his visits," Mama spoke softly. "He has merit to be sure, and looks—why I feel sure I've never seen a more handsome gentleman, but he spent all his family's earnings from trade on that boat of his. One cannot think to squander all their fortune and still be worthy of courting my angel." She gave me a sweet, quaint glance.

"I agree, Mother. I can't understand it at all."

"Yes, well, he makes for lively conversation and he did escort you from Africa himself. He is also a marvelous dancer and does dote on me in an extremely fine way. We shall add him to the guest list, shall we?"

"If we must, Mama."

"And how is your son?" Mother's friend inquired. "May we not see him at the ball this evening?"

"I am afraid he is too ill to dance about like other boys his age, but only the best of care has been permitted to surround him, and I feel confident he will be up and dancing soon enough."

I twitched involuntarily every time she mentioned Allan. I had not seen his face since I arrived home three weeks ago. Where could he be?

Morning callers included the Duke of Salisbury, the Duke of Coventry, the Earl of Chiswick, and Mr. Ashmore.

I smiled when they entered. I laughed when they meant to be funny. I respected my mother. And I did not fall to the captain's feet and beg him to take me away from here.

I played my part perfectly. We all did. For Motsatsi.

Author's Note

David Livingstone (1813–1873) was a Scottish-born Christian missionary and pioneer doctor turned African explorer. He created maps, kept thorough journals, taught people Christianity, stopped disputes, put a serious hitch in the slave trade and saved lives. His direct quotes are used as often as possible throughout the text so as to preserve his unique personality and the legacy he left behind. Modernly, he is ambitiously criticized for his supposed neglect of his family—a notion that the author finds wildly displaced, false, and counterproductive. To his sweet wife these words in a letter speak the loudest: "You may read the letters over again that I wrote at Mabotsa, the sweet time you know. As I told you before, I tell you again, they are true, true; there is not a bit of hypocrisy in them. I never show all my feelings; but I can say truly, my dearest, that I loved you when I married you, and the longer I lived with you, I loved you the better". Hats off to Dr. Livingstone and his love of his family and the African people.

Mary Moffat Livingstone (1821–1862) is also fashioned after the original article. She was the daughter of Robert and Mary Moffat and wife of David Livingstone. Although she left no journals, there are glimpses of her through the journals of her husband and her sister Bessie Price. Some quotations from Bessie's journals were used as a firm possibility on how Mary would have experienced this lifestyle. Mary

was born and raised in Africa and crossed the Kalahari desert with her husband and children. Despite modern scrutiny of her marital relationship, there is no evidence that she resented the hardships that came with her native home.

Chief Sechele I of the Bakwena (1812–1892) ruled with dignity in what is now modern-day Botswana. He was converted to Christiantiy by David Livingstone then served as a missionary among his own people. By all accounts, Kgosi Sechle was eager to learn most things and especially interested in all things weaponry, English and Christian. The author has tried to stay as true to his original nature as possible through the writings of those surrounding him. Many of his words in the novel come from firsthand accounts of those who spent time with him. He really did love Isaiah, his house really did look that way and, yes, he really did dress that way.

Acknowledgments

First and always to my Higher Power who cares about what I care about. To my sweet husband who loves David, Mary, and Sechele as much as I do, who has been my most avid supporter even through his own heartache, and who encourages me to spread my wings. I love you. To my babies—you inspire your momma daily, and your elk are breathtaking. To Barolong Seboni who believes in first-time writers and who spreads mountains of love and understanding. To Arthur E. Nifong for having endless patience for book requests, late returns, and incessant questions. That quiet support does not go unnoticed. To my friend, Erin Collins, for believing in me without reading the book and for being my cohort in espionage. To my enthusiastic beta readers—your support is immeasurable. To my editor, Erin Tanner. The force is strong with her. Thank you for such an attentive edit! To the staff at Cedar Fort—I'll be calling you guys, instead, when Gotham needs help. To my goodly parents who give and give and give. To my parents-in-law for raising such stellar children and for their constant state of support. And to Stephanie Hibbert for keeping me sane (or something like it) through it all. Love you all. My heartfelt gratitude is yours.

About the Author

Photo credit: Alyssia Baird Photography

Scarlette Pike writes like she thinks and has been writing and thinking for some time. Her love of writing came from her adoration of Georgette Heyer and her regency romantic comedies. Scarlette is Utah born and raised and remains there with the love of her life and three minions. Pike is also massively interested in emotional empowerment, as a means to combat trauma, and is the founder of the "She Likes Her for Her" campaign and retreat program.

Scan to Visit

scarlettepike.com